CANDLELIGHT REGENCY SPECIAL

CANDLELIGHT REGENCIES

257 THE CHEVALIER'S LADY, *Betty Hale Hyatt*
263 MOONLIGHT MIST, *Laura London*
501 THE SCANDALOUS SEASON, *Nina Pykare*
505 THE BARTERED BRIDE, *Anne Hillary*
512 BRIDE OF TORQUAY, *Lucy Phillips Stewart*
515 MANNER OF A LADY, *Cilla Whitmore*
521 LOVE'S CAPTIVE, *Samantha Lester*
527 KITTY, *Jennie Tremaine*
530 BRIDE OF A STRANGER, *Lucy Phillips Stewart*
537 HIS LORDSHIP'S LANDLADY, *Cilla Whitmore*
542 DAISY, *Jennie Tremaine*
543 THE SLEEPING HEIRESS, *Phyllis Taylor Pianka*
548 LOVE IN DISGUISE, *Nina Pykare*
549 THE RUNAWAY HEIRESS, *Lillian Cheatham*
554 A MAN OF HER CHOOSING, *Nina Pykare*
555 PASSING FANCY, *Mary Linn Roby*
562 LUCY, *Jennie Tremaine*
563 PIPPA, *Megan O'Connor*
570 THOMASINA, *Joan Vincent*
571 SENSIBLE CECILY, *Margaret Summerville*
572 DOUBLE FOLLY, *Marnie Ellingson*
573 POLLY, *Jennie Tremaine*
578 THE MISMATCHED LOVERS, *Anne Hillary*
579 UNWILLING BRIDE, *Marnie Ellingson*
580 INFAMOUS ISABELLE, *Margaret Summerville*
581 THE DAZZLED HEART, *Nina Pykare*
586 THE EDUCATION OF JOANNE, *Joan Vincent*
587 MOLLY, *Jennie Tremaine*
588 JESSICA WINDOM, *Marnie Ellingson*
589 THE ARDENT SUITOR, *Marian Lorraine*
593 THE RAKE'S COMPANION, *Regina Towers*
594 LADY INCOGNITA, *Nina Pykare*
595 A BOND OF HONOUR, *Joan Vincent*
596 GINNY, *Jennie Tremaine*
597 THE MARRIAGE CONTRACT, *Margaret MacWilliams*
602 A COMPANION IN JOY, *Dorothy Mack*
603 MIDNIGHT SURRENDER, *Margaret Major Cleaves*
604 A SCHEME FOR LOVE, *Joan Vincent*
605 THE DANGER IN LOVING, *Helen Nuelle*
610 LOVE'S FOLLY, *Nina Pykare*
611 A WORTHY CHARADE, *Vivian Harris*
612 THE DUKE'S WARD, *Samantha Lester*
613 MANSION FOR A LADY, *Cilla Whitmore*

THE TWICE BOUGHT BRIDE

ELINOR LARKIN

A CANDLELIGHT REGENCY SPECIAL

Published by
Dell Publishing Co., Inc.
1 Dag Hammarskjold Plaza
New York, New York 10017

ISBN: 0-440-18607-2

Printed in the United States of America
First printing—November 1980

With love to Lanning and Marilyn
and wishes for the happiest of marriages

CHAPTER ONE

"Dear, dear jug!" exclaimed a curious figure, scampering to the top of a rocky ridge with a natural grace that even her dingy and mended petticoats could not hide. "Without the jug of porter, how insupportable my life would be!" And pushing aside the boughs of a mountain myrtle, this strange and seemingly shameless personage clutched the much-praised jug to her heaving bosom and stared out at the vista before her with gleaming eyes.

Had a passing stranger overheard the girl's remarks, he would have sadly misjudged young Caroline Bramwell. But no strangers ever traveled by the dreary three miles that wound up through the cleft of the mountain, leading from the town of Merthyr Tydfil to Pemberton Hall, and so her indiscreet exclamation was carried off harmlessly by the wind.

She reclined a moment against a convenient outcropping of stone and gazed at the valley below. "He *will* come back. He *will*," she whispered fervently, twisting a myrtle leaf in a tiny, but red and calloused hand.

A faraway look stole over the green eyes which, in their almond shape, gave Caroline's lovely face a somewhat exotic cast. In fact, had a passerby looked once into the depths of those green pools, and seen the gentle flush spreading over the high cheekbones, turning Caroline's milky white face to the soft pink of sunrise, he would have been cautious before judging her to be a drunken cook-maid praying for an assignation with some country swain. Her face proclaimed for Caroline a position which her ill-used hands and rude dress belied.

"Roderick!" she whispered, then shivered perhaps from the condensing mists which set her thick black hair to curling gently, or perhaps from the thought of the man whose name she repeated in her low and tender voice.

"Onward to the alehouse," she ordered herself abruptly, breaking out of a sweet revery.

Caroline tripped on down the rocky path, ignoring the pebbles that found their way into her torn slippers. The town of Merthyr Tydfil disappeared now from view, and the bleak way she pursued held no natural distractions to slow her progress. It was more than likely, however, that even the sight of a crystal cataract of rushing water would not have drawn Caroline's attention at this moment, for her mind was full of the image of a tall young man, hair black as her own, falling over his forehead in curly locks. His gray eyes were laughing, his voice gentle, and his hands were firm and warm.

At last the great stone arch of the New Bridge appeared before her like a rainbow, and there was the town on the other side of the river Taff. Instinctively, Caroline felt in her apron for the book she had borrowed, felt its shape beneath her hand, and practically ran the last stretch of ground to the bridge. It was good to be in town again!

Merthyr Tydfil was not the prettiest town in Wales, nor even in the county of Glamorgan, but to Caroline, to come into town was close to a visit to paradise. And her only opportunity to walk the streets of this heaven came when her uncle desired strong drink and sent her to town to fetch it.

No one so much as glanced at her as she picked her way through the winding streets, sometimes finding her way blocked where workmen were using the narrow thoroughfares to pile bars of pig iron. In this unlikely paradise, the music of the angels playing on their harps was replaced by the incessant clamor of hammers, rolling mills, and the forges that had made Caroline's uncle one of the wealthiest men in Wales.

Most of the town's ten thousand inhabitants relied on Caroline's uncle, Lord Asbury, for their livelihood, but he was generally held to be more insane than poor King George. No one had visited Pemberton Hall in years, but the wondering townspeople knew the appearance of the building was as desolate as the landscape around it.

Its bleak appearance was in part due to the owner himself. When he took possession, Lord Asbury had ordered that all the trees surrounding the house be cut down. His next step was to board up all the windows which looked out over the cultivated dale below, so that the only view afforded from the Hall was of the unfrequented wilds behind the estate.

The one improvement this old eccentric brought with him from Yorkshire was an old-fashioned rook-rattle which he hung by a loose chain over the roof. One would have thought the old madman would have been pleased to have rooks perched by his chimney, screaming their raucous cries, but the rattle gave them notice that not even they were welcome. The constant crash and clatter of the rattle against the roof was still another disagreeable aspect of life at Pemberton Hall.

To make matters worse the stately residence had fallen into almost total disrepair. Occasionally, Lord Asbury would close off another wing or another suite of decaying rooms, but aside from that he seemed to take no note of the problems he could easily afford to solve. For his conduct in business was in sharp contrast to his behavior in his personal life. Lord Asbury could tell with a glance whether a plot of land contained valuable ores. Those townspeople who weren't content to call him insane sometimes whispered that his uncanny sense must come from consorting with witches.

As for servants, they had all either died or been sent away, till Asbury relied totally on Caroline to see to his needs. Almost since her arrival at Pemberton, in her thirteenth year, Caroline had been told to sleep in the kitchen and was left with the responsibility of cooking and cleaning. If Lord Asbury had not shot his horses one night in a fit of anger at their noise, Caroline would surely have been made to act as stableboy as well.

Her duties were lightened only by the fact that her uncle was not overly fond of changing his clothing. He wore the same clothes day after day and Caroline did his washing only once every two months. She washed all of her own cambric and muslins every sennight. These garments had been simple yet elegant and well-fitted, four years earlier. But years of constant use and mending and exposure to coal dust had rendered them shabby. Besides, they no longer fit Caroline's body which had become that of a woman. Another young lady would have been vain and proud of such round firm breasts. To Caroline, these newly formed orbs had only made her life more difficult. Since Asbury had no intention of providing clothing or pin money to the "beggared chit," Caroline had cut up a few old frocks and used the material to refashion the bodices of her other dresses. It was extra work for a child already overburdened with responsibilities.

Caroline's first stop in town was not to the alehouse, but rather to the back door of one of Merthyr Tydfil's book societies. The usual clerk received the volume she returned and smiled to see her eyes light up upon receipt of a book of lyrical ballads written by William Wordsworth.

Yes, Roderick would surely return, for the book in Caroline's hands was proof enough that there were good people in the world and that Providence had not forsaken the seventeen-year-old girl of Pemberton. Caroline had passed by the Society at least six times, and stared longingly at the door she dared not enter, before one surprising afternoon when the clerk had directed her around to the back. A gentleman who wished to remain anonymous had paid her fees so that she might enjoy what literature the small club could offer. Since then, Caroline always had a small volume about her person, and even when confined to the dark world of Pemberton, she could manage an occasional escape into the magical world of books.

Out on High Street, the new book snuggled in her pocket, Caroline was met by still another surprise.

"Mary! No!" cried a woman's frantic voice, and then a child, black with soot, threw herself at Caroline's feet and grabbed tight hold of her legs. The tears that fell down the inky visage melted away the dark mask, leaving tracks of pink on the dusky countenance. "Oh, Miss, Miss, please don't let them send me again to the mines!"

"Mary!" The woman who grabbed the child away

had a big red face over her heaving body. "Can't you see the young Miss 'as troubles of 'er own?"

"Mary Williams is me name," cried the girl as her mother bore her away. "Tell yer uncle I can cook an' sew and would gladly work at Pemberton though others say it be haunted. Please Miss . . ."

Caroline's gentle heart was moved by the girl's plea, but what could she possibly do to help? Indeed, when she thought of the horrors of work in the mines, she had to feel her own wretched plight at Pemberton was not so bad after all.

By the time she was waiting outside the alehouse door for Edmund Griffin to fill the jug, although young Mary's plaint was not completely forgotten, Caroline was thinking again of her own situation.

"I just hope he gets jug-stung enough to be early asleep," Caroline wished to herself. When Asbury drank to excess, he was sometimes subject to fits of violent temper and it was Caroline who bore his wrath. Other times the spirits rendered him quickly unconscious, and this was for Caroline the greatest blessing.

She started her way back to Pemberton without the gaiety she had shown when traveling in the opposite direction. This was in part because heading home was no bright prospect, but also because she dared not spill so much as a drop from the old jug.

She paused only briefly on the outjutting prominence of the ridge. She placed the jug securely on the ledge and opened the book of verse at random.

Five years have passed, five summers, with
the length
Of five long winters and again I hear
These waters rolling from their Mountain springs,
With a soft inland murmur . . .

The girl heaved a sigh because the words brought to her mind a very different image from the one intended by the poet. "Three summers, with the length of three long winters . . ." Caroline rewrote the poem to suit herself. ". . . since Roderick Montgomery did find his way across our bleak and wasted land."

She closed the book and thrust it back into her apron.

"Three years. It's only been three years," she reminded herself. Then lifting the jug, she hurried on, for the sun threatened to sink behind the hills and leave her in darkness with Pemberton still some distance away.

Caroline's father was a Yorkshire country squire with a great love of life and of his family. One spring day, after hearing the gabblemongers talk of English defeats in the Egyptian campaign, he kissed his wife and Caroline good-bye, saddled his grey, and headed for London. He had some well-placed connections there and hoped they could help him gain news of his son's regiment.

Caroline watched him ride off in his double-breasted riding coat, the tails flying out behind him. He turned once to wave to her with a flourish of his tall, curly-brimmed hat. Caroline remembered the bulky bow of the white linen stock around his throat, and how she clapped her hands gleefully in response to his wave. Her father had seemed the bravest, dearest man in the world, and the only member of the male sex to outshine her brother Perceval, off with his regiment in Egypt. A thrush broke into song. As Caroline waved back, she had no idea that she would never see her father again.

For London proved too much for the Yorkshire country gentleman. His first night in town, an acquaintance took him to White's, where the entire fortune of

Caroline's family was lost on the green-baize gaming tables. Sometime in the early hours just before dawn, the wretched loser drew his pistol and took his own life.

The widow cried for days, while Caroline, unable to understand the tragedy that had overtaken them, chided her mother for being such a watering pot. At last they packed and said good-bye to the fine old house, to the fields where Percy had taught Caroline to ride, and to the garden where the children had recited their lessons on sunny days.

While Mama clutched her smelling-salts and lay sprawled back against the plump squabs of the carriage, Caroline looked out the window, still trying to pick out a last view of her favorite yew trees, standing in their mysterious row. She'd seen them from her bedroom window every morning for as long as she could remember, and Percy had made her shriek with terror and laugh with excitement when he told stories of the ghosts who stood silently among the yews at midnight.

A farewell tear rolled down her plump and pretty cheek, but Caroline had no idea that she was saying good-bye not just to home, but to childhood itself.

It was a long, sad journey to Pemberton.

Once there, Caroline found she could talk her mother out of her tears, but not out of her decline. Within a month of their establishment at Pemberton Hall, Caroline was an orphan and at the mercy of the madman who could ship two hundred tons of iron to Cardiff each week, yet chose to live in a dark, dank ruin. His workers had no choice—they crawled through tunnels in the bowels of the earth in order to earn their wages. The Lord of Bedlam, as the rich man was sometimes called behind his back, lived immersed in dirt as a matter of preference.

The town learned of Caroline from the stories

brought back by the men who delivered provisions to the mad Lord. She was an object of general pity, yet no one dared do anything to ease her distress; her uncle was too powerful a man to cross.

Down in the kitchen, Caroline roasted her uncle's fowls and joints and ate his leavings. In the summer, she suffered with the heat from the brick oven, but in the winter, the extra warmth helped to keep her alive. One bitter night, she even opened the iron door to the oven and crawled inside to sleep among the ashes that still held some gentle heat.

It was Caroline, who had never even seen the kitchen or the butter churn in her Yorkshire home, who poured the milk into large pans and scalded it over a copper. It was Caroline who then skimmed the milk and put the golden cream into the churn. Making butter left her hands so calloused that she was no longer troubled with blisters from the hot cooking pots.

The first time her uncle beat her was when she asked for sun raisins to use in a plum pudding for Christmas.

"Plum pudding, my beggared chit?" he cried in a rage. "You should be living on oatmeal bread and miserable cheese!" And he had lashed out at her with the riding crop which was all that remained to show he had once owned a stable full of horses.

When she could escape from the house and run off to read a book, or sit in the shade of one of the magnificent oak groves that covered the other side of the hills, Caroline could almost forget the ill treatment she received, for her disposition was so naturally cheerful that a moment's happiness tended to put unpleasant thoughts from her mind. It was at times like these that she would think of her brother and tell herself that Percy would soon come home and find her and take her away.

One January afternoon in 1808, even that hope was

taken from her, but a new hope grew in its place. That was the day that Captain Roderick Montgomery galloped up to the door, astride a high-spirited black stallion. His appearance was like a miracle, as snow had been falling for days. The rutted path to Pemberton was not only virtually impassible, but the risk of mortal accident would have discouraged all but the bravest and most determined—or most foolhardy—of horsemen from attempting the ascent.

And it was a veritable miracle for a dashing man to break in upon the habitual gloom of Pemberton Hall. The Captain's lean and handsome face was bronzed from the sun of Egypt and Constantinople; he was a strange and wonderful sight to appear, like a dream, out of the whirling clouds of snow. Still more miraculous, and much to the amusement of the old madman, Roderick Montgomery wanted to speak with Caroline.

She had stepped forward blushing, her head hung low, while his keen gray eyes took in the entire situation at a glance—the dirty drawing room with its musty, unused smell, the old Lord whose madness was increased by drink, the cold and trembling child in rags. When she looked up at him at last with green eyes, luminous with trust, he hated the errand that had brought him. Captain Montgomery had traced the Bramwell family to Wales to tell them of Perceval's death.

He gave the girl her brother's sapphire ring, and put his arms around her when she started to cry. Caroline flinched from his touch. The Captain drew back, thinking he had frightened the child or offended her delicacy. But then, his eyes flashing with anger and sudden understanding, the young Captain firmly removed her shawl and took a good look at the flesh that was exposed above the neckline of her ragged dress. He pulled the cotton fabric from her body and swore under his breath to see the welts on her back.

Captain Montgomery had pulled her to him very gently then. He was careful not to touch her back, and encouraged her to lay her small head against his broad, strong chest. He stroked her hair and talked to her quietly.

"My dear child," he said, "be strong, because I promise you, I'll be back. If there were no war, I should take you with me now, but I cannot."

At these words, the child's sobbing became more piteous.

"Oh, if only there were no war!" he cried, choking a sob. "Why fight Napoleon when such villainy exists at home?" He held her close. "But I promise you, little Caroline, I shall return for you."

He repeated this promise to Lord Asbury adding, "And when I return, if I find you have touched her again, I shall kill you. And that is one promise I shall be most happy to keep."

Then he was gone.

The days turned to weeks, then to months, and then almost three years had passed, but Caroline went on feeling the comforting warmth of the stranger's smile. She mourned grievously for her brother and sewed his ring into a little pouch that she wore next to her heart. But she missed the gallant Roderick Montgomery even more than she missed Percy. After all, it was hopeless that her brother would ever be restored to her, but Roderick Montgomery had said he would return.

Lord Asbury took the promise seriously as well. Although Caroline continued to live like the lowliest of servants, he never again raised a hand to her.

The little girl grew into a young woman without becoming fully aware of the changes in her body or in her sentiments. When she wandered the desolate landscape dreaming of her promised rescuer, Caroline noticed but did not understand the warm flush that invaded her fragile body whenever she pictured the young Captain riding up to the door. When she remembered the shelter of his arms, hot but joyful tears would well up in her deep green eyes.

He told me to be strong, she reminded herself, day after day.

I'm glad he didn't come today, she would tell herself at night. *I've become such a Homely Joan, I shouldn't want him to see me now.*

She longed for him with a sweet anguish, her sweet and brave rescuer. He was for her a pattern-card of all that was noble in a man. His image helped her remember there was a better, more beautiful world somewhere outside the confines of Pemberton.

The child who was born to dress in silks and satins had no fantasies of living like a lady of quality. In Caroline's dream, the Captain took her away and she ate good meals at a table and slept peacefully in a warm dry bed at night.

What more could she want? To have the Captain talk to her from time to time. And smile at her and pat her hand.

Maybe he would even teach her Latin. Then she could take a look at Virgil and Ovid. Oh, there was so much she wanted to read!

It was raining pitchforks and shovels over Pemberton. The storm came in through the broken roof and through all the cracks and crevices of the old building and pelted the two occupants of the Hall without mercy. Lord Asbury didn't notice; he was snoring off the effect of the jug of porter. Caroline didn't notice either. She had found a relatively dry spot, and was reading poetry aloud by candlelight, one small hand cupped around the flame to protect it from the draught.

> Of Truth, of Grandeur, Beauty, Love, and Hope,
> And melancholy Fear subdued by Faith

Her voice echoed quietly beneath the crash of the storm.

> Of blessed consolations in distress . . .

and the voice broke off suddenly only to be raised again in a cry that could barely be heard over the moan of the winds.

CHAPTER TWO

"Caroline! Chit! Where are you?"

Lord Asbury's bellowing voice rang through the house. With some trepidation, Caroline lit a candle at the fire, mounted the stairs, and followed the shouts to their source. She found her uncle in the drawing room. Caroline had entered this room perhaps five times during her life at Pemberton Hall, and to her sentiments it was the saddest place in the house, as it still held the air of a home that had once been gracious. The faded Aubusson carpet was still on the floor, though stained with damp and mildew. The rosewood piano stood on three legs beneath a particularly bad spot in the roof; Caroline's uncle used its box as a catch basin for rainwater.

"Supper will be served soon, milord," she said in a barely audible voice. Surely the delay in the evening meal was what had made the old madman fly up into the boughs with anger.

"Supper?" He spat on the abused carpet. "My dear, we have a guest."

A tall figure stepped into the circle of light thrown

by the wax taper, and Caroline's head reeled with combined hope and fear.

Was it? No, it couldn't be. And yet it must be.

The man standing before her was surely Montgomery, and yet he was not the man she remembered. He stood tall and stiff, a raven-black cloak over his shoulders. In the half-light she could just see a glimpse of riding boots and tight fawn-colored breeches. But the difference in his appearance had nothing to do with his being out of uniform. His face was transformed. The lean brown face was now of palest white, while the scar that ran down one cheek stood out even whiter—if such a more white color could be possible. His gray eyes, which had smiled at her before in spite of their shock and anger, were now icy cold. She had sustained herself with the memory of a kind and vibrant gentleman. The Montgomery who stood before her was a cold being whose face revealed nothing but bitter pride.

"Is she to your liking?" asked Lord Asbury while Caroline stood trembling. "And what of you, chit? You are my own flesh and blood, and I shan't sell you to a stranger if you do not wish to go."

"Sell me, sir?" murmured Caroline in bewilderment.

The gentleman stepped forward and took her hand in his grasp. "I am Captain Montgomery. You remember me, don't you, child?"

"Yes, sir," she replied, hanging her head in anguish. Her thoughts were confused between her desire to protest that she was not a child any longer, her wish to be gone along with this stranger and far from Pemberton Hall, and her wish that he would disappear so that the real Captain Montgomery, the dashing officer of her dreams, could return in his stead. How was it possible for her rescuer to be such a disappointment?

"Don't look so out of curl, chit," continued Lord Asbury. "Very few ladies of quality ever have this opportunity. You are about to hear exactly what value a gentleman places upon your person. Well, Captain, how much money do you offer?"

Anger brought a tinge of color to Montgomery's cheeks. "I'll give you a thousand guineas, my lord, and I'll see you in Newgate yet."

The old man paced the worn carpet as if deep in reflection. At last he faced the man in the cloak and gave his reply. "I am an honest man in my dealings, Montgomery," he said, his lip curling in an exaggerated sneer. "I have heard that one thousand guineas will buy the finest thoroughbred at Tattersall's, so I could not accept more than eight hundred for the brass-faced chit."

Montgomery drew a bag from beneath his cloak and threw it at the madman's feet. "Count your gold at your leisure," he said. "Pack your things, child," he added in a softer voice.

Child! thought Caroline, both warming to the designation and rebelling against it. A child was someone to be cared for and protected, and she'd been in need of protection for so very long. But at the same time, the advantages of childhood had been torn from her. After the ordeals she had been through and the household responsibilities that had been thrust upon her to assume, Caroline felt entitled to the respect due a full-grown woman. She didn't expect to be treated like a lady. She wouldn't quarrel with someone who considered her base-born, but she wouldn't be considered an infant.

"Where are your things?" repeated Montgomery.

"Stand where you are!" ordered Lord Asbury. "She has no things," he explained. "And surely you won't be gone without my blessing . . . I know you London rake-hells, and I warn you, if it is your intention to seek your pleasure with the chit tonight and have her back on my doorstep in the morning, you will offer me the gravest provocation. I sell her to you with the understanding that I shall never see the creature again."

"No, you never shall," agreed Montgomery. "I'll stake my life on that."

The implications of her uncle's speech were lost to the inexperienced girl, but Montgomery's reply cheered her hesitant heart immensely.

He put an arm around her. "We'll leave in the morning," he said.

"What?" cried the madman. "I do not run an inn. Neither one of you belongs to me and you'll be gone directly. I won't have you under my roof tonight!"

"You'd send the child off with the sunset hours ago?" cried Montgomery, but then let the subject drop. He thought of the cold whipping winds outside, yet reckoned the elements to be less dangerous than the old man. And with the full moon high in the skies, traveling at night would not be altogether impossible. So rather than argue, he determined he would do well to accept Lord Asbury's edict.

As he led Caroline to the door, they heard her uncle call after them, "You will admit I made no statement as to her virtue. Most likely she's lifted her skirts for every miner in Glamorgan, but you shall not . . ." The rest of his parting speech was lost as Montgomery helped her up to the saddle of his black stallion, untied the horse from the post of the house, and jumped up behind her. Only the rook-rattle clamored a farewell.

The stallion at least hadn't changed. It was still Jupiter, the proud beast that had impressed Caroline years earlier almost as much as its master. On that first visit, Montgomery had reined up the prancing steed, waiting for a stableboy to meet him. This time he'd known better than expect to find servants about.

Neither Montgomery nor Caroline cast a backward glance at the ruined Hall as they rode away.

The mountain mists showed as light rainbow rings around the full moon, and fell upon the riders in a chill and penetrating drizzle. They rode across the somber landscape in silence, except for the sucking sounds made by the horse's hooves coming free of the mud. Caroline sat sidesaddle while Montgomery held her before him, wrapped in the folds of his raven cloak which provided some, though insufficient, protection from the wet and cold.

Caroline had no fear of the steep and obstructed way before them. She had no doubt that the man who had claimed her from Pemberton Hall would see them through the journey safely. Her concern was for the future. What would the silent Captain Montgomery do with her? She would gladly work in his kitchen, for she was certain his servants were treated with a courtesy her uncle had long forgotten had he ever known it. But his frigid manner frightened her. She had gladly cast in her lot with him, but only because the life she left behind was so wretched. She was already disappointed, for her rescuer did not deign to address a single word to her, and in this, he was no more personable than the Lord Asbury. Should she die of cold and exposure in the mountains, such an end might well be the best thing that could befall her, she thought. As if he sensed her thought, Montgomery pulled her close to him and wrapped his arms more closely around her slight and shivering frame. The warmth of his strong arms sent a tingle of sensation through her body, and then for an instant, a feeling of heat coursed through her. In that moment, she experienced a combination of feelings—comfort and security, and a sudden crying need she did not understand. Feeling Montgomery's hands cupped over her rounded breasts, she moaned softly, and with a confused fear, she felt her nipples unaccountably stiffen and strain. The disturbing yet pleasing sensation was over in an instant, as Montgomery dropped his hands and drew back so suddenly, she almost fell from the saddle.

"Gracious heaven!" he exclaimed. "How old are you, child?"

"Seventeen, sir," she replied. "I shall be eighteen in May." The dark night hid her flush and her confusion.

"Eighteen?" he repeated stupidly, in a mixture of bewilderment and annoyance. "I had no idea . . ." he mused, then recovered himself enough to say, "then you must not call me 'sir,' but rather by my name which, as you know, is Roderick."

He didn't seem to notice her failure to acquiesce or to protest, so engrossed was he with his own thoughts. But after a bit, Caroline broke the silence to inquire quietly, "Where are we going, sir?"

"If the horse can carry us as far as Cardiff, we shall certainly find a chaise for hire there, and then . . ." Montgomery left the sentence unfinished. He had intended to take the child to his London home, but it was an entirely different matter to carry off a young woman. Caroline was of gentle birth, and Montgomery knew he would have to treat her as such, but her upbringing had rendered her rude in appearance and ignorant of city manners. He, himself, having passed most of his youth in the Army, knew little about propriety or how to comport himself with a lady. Now he felt Caroline's life had been thrust upon him, but unwelcome as the burden might be, Montgomery's sense of honor would not have allowed him to relinquish it.

The horse picked its way carefully up a hill much steeper than any Caroline had known, and she threw herself forward over the wet and tangled black mane to keep from falling backward. The way was slippery and insecure. At her back, she felt the Captain, leaning close against her, his breath warm on her freezing cheeks. When they reached a clearing where the roads forked, one fork leading across a broad meadow and the other into a forest, she wondered if her companion knew which way to go. He hesitated, then directed the horse to the forest, glancing up at the moon, and hoping its light would penetrate in the closed and dusky woods. Fortunately, it was late November and the leaves were no longer on the branches, but rather lay wet under Jupiter's hooves and they rode on, listening to the muffled sound of their passage over the damp carpet.

"Oh, sir!" cried Caroline, suddenly. "We *must* pass by Merthyr Tydfil." A sudden jolt on the saddle had pressed the binding of her book into her thigh, and reminded her of Wordsworth's ballads hidden in her apron. She had been carrying the book with her for over a month, awaiting an opportunity to go to town and return it to the Society. When she explained her predicament, Montgomery laughed.

"An honest and commendable sentiment," he said warmly, "but I'm afraid we have more important tasks ahead of us. I shall see the Society receives some recompense, but you can hardly expect me to worry about a book of verse at a time like this."

"But you don't understand!" Caroline had been so very grateful for the kindness of the people at the Society, she had always been most scrupulous in returning her books. The Captain's lack of concern and his condescending attitude upset her, but she had to admit to herself the justice of his way of thinking. Besides, she was quietly pleased that she had been able to make him laugh. There was still a trace of her dream hero, then, left behind in this cold man's shell.

A light smile played over her lips as they moved steadily between the trees, occasionally passing through a rill where water splashed in melancholy fashion over smooth stones. Their bodies moved in rhythm with the horse's steps, and despite the cold and her uncertainties, Caroline felt herself being gently lulled to sleep in the Captain's arms.

She woke up to shouting. She was choking in the wet silk of the stallion's mane, clasping the beast's neck as it reared and whinnied. Behind her, Montgomery was whispering urgently, "Can you keep your seat, child? I cannot hold you, the pistol, and the reins," and she was sobbing, and five or six men—two with muskets—had cut off their way.

Footpads! thought Caroline.

She screamed as one man pointed his weapon directly at the Captain and braced himself as he pulled the trigger.

There was no explosion, and the silence seemed to thunder in her ears. The musket powder was wet, and while the attackers and the Captain tried to exchange gunfire, neither sound nor bullet would emerge from any of the firearms on the scene. When one of the men drew a knife, the Captain drove Jupiter right into the midst of the attackers.

Caroline's fear turned almost to pity when she saw the helplessness of the would-be robbers, and when the man with the knife fell beneath the stallion's hooves. The others drew back, and the Captain spurred Jupiter on, in a reckless galloping course through the night that left the footpads far behind.

But just when both were breathing a sigh of relief at

their escape unscathed, and Montgomery had reined the stallion in to a pace more appropriate to the rocky, obstructed path, the beast stumbled, sending Caroline flying over his neck. Montgomery reached for her desperately, but too late.

Caroline opened her eyes to find herself in a large but lumpy bed. She sighed and stretched. This wasn't like the bed she'd slept in at home in Yorkshire, but it was surely the best night's sleep she'd known in many years. She was probably dreaming, she thought. Anxious to continue the dream, she rolled over, her eyes shut. But the scratchy feel of a poor sort of woolen blanket against her bare skin kept her from falling again into sleep. Something strange was certainly happening, because Caroline had begun to realize she was not dreaming.

A hand pressed itself against her forehead. "Are you awake, Caroline? You still feel flushed."

This time her opened eyes looked into the gray eyes of Captain Montgomery. He was bending over her in bed, and adjusting his cloak over her body. "I asked them for more blankets and didn't even get a civil reply," he said.

"My clothes?" she asked, in confusion.

Fortunately for Caroline, her knowledge of worldly matters was so thoroughly inadequate that her situation was not as frightening or embarrassing for her as it would have been for another maiden of her age. She knew modesty from her mother, because even in early girlhood, a child knew to hide her nakedness. And so it was unsettling to think that someone—perhaps even this man she barely knew—had removed her clothing without her even being aware of it. And while the child had observed the coupling of beasts in the barnyard—

an observation which Percy had wisely advised her to keep to herself—it had never struck Caroline that any comparable intercourse occurred between human beings. She had heard and read vague references to "physical union," and there had been her uncle's incoherent ravings about lifted skirts, but most of what her uncle said had made no sense to her. And even though she had some awareness that some men and women participated together in some mysterious activity, it had never occurred to her that such activity would take place in a bed.

And so, for Caroline to find herself in bed in a strange room with a man bending over her was no cause for alarm.

"You were soaked through to the skin, child," said Montgomery. "I had to remove your clothing for your own good," but his tone grew cold as he noted her inappropriate composure. Though he could not let himself credit the madman's words—"every miner in Glamorgan"—Captain Montgomery was not pleased to see how easily the young lady accepted his presence at her bedside. He had expected that he would have to reassure her that nothing had happened, and that only the circumstances of her accident had forced them to repair together to the nearest inn.

Caroline was completely ignorant of these considerations, and now her innocence worked to her detriment. She was only aware of the look of displeasure in the Captain's steely eyes. Slowly, memory returned: the night, the footpads, and her own fall from the stallion. That was it. He was disgusted with her failure to keep her seat. No doubt he'd been in a hurry to return to London, and his willingness to assist her had turned into a more difficult project than he had anticipated.

"Captain Montgomery," she said quietly, "please accept my apologies. I can see you are displeased with me, and only wish there were some way I could repay your kindness to me. You have shown me a courtesy I neither expected nor deserved . . ." She leaned toward him earnestly, and her well-shaped shoulders emerged from the blankets.

Montgomery sprang back, his eyes now flashing a cold fire. Had he really wasted his pity on such a one as this? Her words about not deserving his courtesy, her hint that she wanted to repay his kindness—all this meant only one thing to him. The chit was nothing but a light-skirted wench after all. He knew very well what service she was offering in repayment. And while he still sympathized with the terrible tribulations she had suffered, he felt he had been tricked into treating her with undue respect. The Captain had seen too much of people who were not what they pretended to be, and this latest instance roused his anger.

"On your sick bed, and your mind turns to such matters already?" he exclaimed.

"I should think that any time and any place would be right to thank you for taking me under your protection," said the hapless girl, ignorant of the worldly meaning of "protection."

"Then I'm your protector, am I?" he asked, and he flung himself roughly onto the bed beside her. "So I needn't have spent the night sleeping in a chair, you say?"

Grabbing her by the shoulders, he planted a bruising kiss on her mouth. "Mr. Jones downstairs thinks I've bought myself a doxy for the night, and so I have," he continued, "though at a higher cost than I believe customary."

"Why are you so angry with me?" gasped Caroline as tears came to her beautiful eyes. Her obvious terror and confusion should have convinced any man that she was being misjudged. But Montgomery's judgment was clouded by the warring passions within him: resentment, outrage, and the powerful attraction that had taken hold of his senses when he had removed Caroline's clothing. It had only been with the greatest, most painful self-restraint that he had kept himself from possessing the beautiful woman who had slept peacefully through the night. And all the while, the brazen chit had expected no such courtesy. Well, he would wait no longer.

His grip was brutal at her throat as he tilted her face up toward his. "What have you to say, woman?" he asked, but at this moment, through his excitement, at last he saw the expression on her face as her utter shock and confusion turned to rebellious anger.

Caroline had not the faintest idea what this man was trying to do to her, but the violence in his attitude made her defend herself with a fierce pride. Her strength had only begun to come back following her total collapse, but she struggled and freed a small hand. Her broken nails left a jagged scratch down Montgomery's face.

Convinced of her innocence, and almost too late, the Captain sprang back to his feet and stumbled to the chair, burying his head in his hands.

"I hate you!" cried Caroline, helplessly, still not understanding what had happened or why. "Why?" she asked piteously. "Why? Why?"

While the Captain was silently questioning himself whether he was fit for human society, Caroline was wondering if she would have done better to remain at Pemberton Hall.

CHAPTER THREE

"Caroline, can you forgive me enough to listen to what I must say?" asked Montgomery at last. They had spent hours in silence, she in the bed, the Captain in his chair, until he had hollered downstairs to have a bowl of soup sent up.

Caroline had not allowed him to feed her and had not even looked at him, though she did accept the steaming bowl. Her spirits rose with each spoonful of hearty stock in which turnips and carrots had been simmered. It was only when she'd finished the last spoonful that he'd approached, taken the empty bowl from her hands, and spoken.

"I'm afraid that I shall have to talk to you in a way that a gentleman should never talk to a lady," he said slowly, "but nothing I can say can be any worse than what I've already said."

"Don't trouble yourself, sir," she said coldly. "As you well know, I'm not a lady."

"Caroline, my dear," he interrupted, "it's just such talk as that which caused the problem. For your own good, you must let me—as best I can—give you some notion of what I thought every schoolroom miss must surely know."

"And I'm no schoolroom miss, either," she reminded him.

"Don't make your situation worse, Caroline," he ordered her sternly. "Your position in society will be difficult enough for you without your being rag-mannered as well."

"Yes?" she asked petulantly. The very idea of her having a position in society was ludicrous.

Montgomery remained seated in his chair, unable to think of a way to begin the promised lesson.

"Caroline," he began at last, "do you know anything of . . . country matters?"

He was alarmed to see her eyes light up in delight.

"That's what Hamlet and Ophelia talk about!" she exclaimed.

"But do you know what Hamlet was referring to?" Montgomery asked, smiling in spite of himself.

"I may not have spent time in the schoolroom," cried Caroline, "but I do understand what I read!"

"Hush now, hornet. Not so loud. But I'm not convinced you do know what I meant by the term."

"I was born in the country," she said, stalling for time. Caroline was not going to let this odious man catch her in her ignorance.

"The way of a man with a maid?" he asked. "Does that mean anything to you?"

"You are a fusty tutor, sir," she answered, "to press me with questions, laugh at my ignorance, and give me no answers." But faced with his continued uncomfortable silence, Caroline softened toward the man. His whole attitude had changed since his strange attack upon her person. Also, he had roused her curiosity to an exceptional peak, and she was eager to know what it was he was so reluctant to tell her. To encourage him, she changed her tone. "Captain Montgomery, please do not be afraid to speak. As you have observed, my upbringing has been of a rough and crude sort. I'm not likely to fall into a spasm or have an attack of the vapors, whatever you may tell me. Perhaps it is best for you to simply forget that I am Percy's sister. Speak to me the way you'd talk to a comrade in Egypt . . ."

"I hardly expect any of my comrades in Egypt needed a talk of this nature," he objected drily.

She sighed. "Well, I don't know what the nature *is*. Just talk and don't be afraid. Neither one of us seems to be the ordinary sort of person, and I did survive your unaccountable behavior of this morning, after all . . ."

"All right," he said.

"But why don't you look at me? And why don't you begin?" she asked as he paced the small room and avoided glancing in her direction. "Oh, what a hobble we're in!"

"More than a hobble, my dear. Much worse than that," he warned. "And where did you learn such words? One night out of your uncle's care—if a word such as 'care' can be used to describe his use of you—and you resume the speech of a young lady of quality . . . How am I to explain?" At last, taking a resolution, he plunged into the subject. "To begin with, do you realize that I have brought you into very improper surroundings?"

"I suppose so," she said, "but this inn is so much more cheerful and comfortable than Pemberton Hall. And really, you had no choice after I went flying over Jupiter's head. There must be no other habitation for miles and miles."

"I'm glad that you appreciate that I wished you no injury by bringing you here. But the problem remains that good intentions don't signify. It is very difficult for a lady to stop at an inn—even one of much better repute than this place—without danger to her good reputation. While this place happens to be of so low a character . . ." He shook his head ominously. "Then, to make matters worse, I stayed here in your room because I was more willing to risk your reputation than to leave your side for a moment in such a place as this. We are in a place where a penny will buy enough of Mme. Geneva's brew to render a man unconscious, and for tuppence, besides your gin you're welcome to a pile of straw to sleep off the effects. Anything could have happened to you here, Caroline, if I'd left you alone."

"Then in all this you did right," she said reasonably. But her voice grew more agitated as she reminded him again of his strange outburst and how he had hurt and frightened her.

"Yes," he sighed. "Which brings us back to the point I was trying to broach . . . Do you know why a maiden's reputation is sullied if a man spends a night in her room?"

"Because it's not proper," she replied promptly.

"Do you know why not?"

"Good gracious, Captain Montgomery. When I lived at home with my parents, there were hundreds of rules about what was right and what was wrong, and maybe I'm just a goosecap, but I never understood the reason for *any* of those rules."

The more Caroline regained her composure, the more the poor Captain was cast into the doldrums. Was he really going to have to go through with this lesson? To Caroline, his obvious discomfort was terribly amusing, and as the conversation proceeded, her spirits rose higher and higher. It had been so long since she'd been able to simply sit and talk with another person.

"Caroline," he began again with a dry throat. "Men have certain physical needs—and women do, too, even ladies of quality . . . And when a husband and wife are alone together in the bedchamber, their love makes them do . . . well, they kiss, they touch each other, they do certain things, you see."

"Yes, of course," said Caroline agreeably, encouraging him to continue.

"But there are times . . ." How could he explain this in such a way that she wouldn't hate him for his attempt, and a way that wouldn't leave her with unconquerable feelings of revulsion for intimacy? Montgomery wanted no loving intimacy with the girl, but if he were going to try and marry her off and provide for her future happiness . . . "when a man feels these needs. And if he isn't in love, or doesn't have a wife, he may pay some immoral woman to satisfy him."

"And you mean they do the same things he and his wife would have done?" she asked.

"Yes, Caroline . . . but even if the, uh, proceedings are the same, the feeling is very different. And Caroline, sometimes a man will even keep such a woman in a house and provide her with money and clothing so that she will always be available to him . . . for such purposes. I'm telling you this because such a woman is said to be 'under the man's protection' which makes that a phrase you would be well-advised to avoid when describing our relationship."

To his immense surprise and relief, Caroline broke into happy peals of laughter. "What a cabbage-head I am!" she gasped between laughs. "What you must have thought of me!" Her gaiety was followed by a sudden hush. She blushed deeply and looked out at him under downcast eyes. "And I'm doing it again, I fear," she whispered. "I collect this subject is not one for funning conversation, and here I am laughing like a brass-faced creature. Oh, Captain! First you carry me off in my rags, and . . . what you must think of me still!"

What an exceptional young woman, he was thinking. It was really remarkable how her healthy young spirits had not been broken under the years of misfortune. She was still proud and happy and quick-witted. There was not a trace of self-pity on the bright face before him that flushed over and over again, in succeeding waves of joy, embarrassment, and a lingering touch of fever.

Caroline sat a moment, her brow knitted in concentration. Suddenly, bits and snatches of conversations overheard and half-forgotten were coming into her head, memories of things seen and not understood.

"Captain Montgomery," she asked at last, "these proceedings—are they what cause babies to be born?"

When he nodded in assent, she clapped her hands with delight. "Oh, I knew it! I guessed! And," she persisted, "does this whole subject refer to what's under my skirts?"

This time it was the Captain's turn to blush red, while Caroline quickly and helplessly apologized for her hasty and immodest words.

"Captain Montgomery," she continued once that gentleman had recovered his composure. "I begin to see what a predicament we find ourselves in, and I think perhaps you should share with me your thoughts on how we are to extricate ourselves."

Montgomery looked at her in surprise. He was accustomed to giving orders in the field that were obeyed without question. It had not occurred to him to discuss strategy with the young lady whose green eyes had turned thoughtful and whose demeanor seemed chaste and serious in spite of the fact that she lay naked under the blankets as she addressed him. He already knew she was a patient creature and one who made the best of circumstances that could not be helped. Her calm tone now implied a maturity beyond her years, and suggested a quick intelligence.

"Very well," he agreed, almost to his surprise, and added, "but first you must drop this habit of calling me Captain Montgomery. As you know, my name is Roderick, and considering the intimate nature of our conversation, it seems unnecessary to treat me with such formality."

"But that conversation was the inevitable product of our circumstances," she replied. "Its unfortunate necessity gives us all the more reason to maintain a certain distance."

"You are right, Miss Bramwell," he conceded, and Caroline felt a perverse vexation that he had been so quick to comply with her suggestion and drop the use of her Christian name. He also complied with her other request and briefly sketched out their situation.

"The innkeeper is ignorant of our true identities," he explained. "He thinks you are . . . well, as we discussed. I think our stay here will remain secret enough. The problem is what is to become of you. If you can trust and forgive me for what happened earlier, I pray you will accept my offer to take you to London. Merthyr Tydfil is far away. I shall present you as my ward, an orphan of gentle birth, which is not altogether far from the truth. No one need know that you were orphaned almost four years ago. I shall bring my elderly cousin, Lady Annabelle, to town as your sponsor, and I warrant we'll have a fine match made for you within months of your first coming out."

Caroline considered these plans in silence. "It is all very kind of you, Captain Montgomery," she said, "but if matrimony is the ultimate object, it seems to me that as the man who compromised my reputation, you should marry me yourself."

He started in surprise, and was only reassured by the mischievous laughter in Caroline's eyes. "But there is no way you can be presented, Miss Bramwell, until you learn the manner of a lady. And ladies do not broach the subject of matrimony, even in jest, with gentlemen." After an uncomfortable pause, he added, "And anyway, I'm not the sort to marry."

Once again painfully aware of her fresh young body which the blankets and his cloak could hardly hide or disguise, he paced to the fireplace and found, much to his relief, that her sodden clothing had thoroughly dried.

"We shall continue this once you are dressed," he remarked, and taking a seat, he shut his eyes. "You may tell me when it is all right to look." In spite of his gentlemanly intentions, Montgomery could not control the workings of his memory and imagination which proceeded to picture Caroline's form in such exquisite detail that he might as well have abandoned all attempts at courtesy and looked his fill.

"Open your eyes, dear friend," chirped Caroline's sweet voice after an interval that seemed to last a century. "As you can see, I am quite ready to be presented at Carlton House." And she executed a dainty pirouette in her apron and ragged dress. "Really, Montgomery, aside from my ignorance of proper behavior and lack of suitable attire, just look at my hands. You can hardly pass me off in society as I am."

He hardly noticed the calloused hands she held out to him, taken as he was by the fact that once she had restored some measure of propriety between them by getting dressed she had directly begun to speak in terms of greater trust and intimacy.

"Really," she continued, "you rescued me from a most desolate and miserable life, and need not lift me up to heaven to make me happy. If you can help me find suitable employment in pleasant surroundings, I'm sure I should be happy enough. I can cook. Or I could be companion to some lady—especially one who would like me to read to her aloud. I think I should like that very much, in fact . . ."

"No, Miss Bramwell," he insisted, abiding by her previous wish that they maintain their distance. "You are much too good for a life like that. You deserve admirers and a home and family of your own. You deserve more than kind treatment and pleasant surroundings. You deserve real joy. Haven't you waited long enough? I wouldn't say this if I didn't believe we can accomplish what we set out to do."

"But what do you propose to do?" she exclaimed laughing. "Hide me somewhere until my hands heal and hire me a tutor who will teach me what a young lady must know? Please, let's not dream of attaining such impossible and unlikely goals."

"Caroline!" he cried. "That's just what we shall do. I shall spirit you home with me and not until you are ready to face the *ton* shall I send for the Lady Annabelle. It may be a reckless gamble. If anyone learns you are living beneath my roof before Lady Annabelle's arrival, our work will have been in vain. But what have we got to lose?"

"Oh, please. Do be serious. I'm told London is full of gabblemongers. How will my presence remain secret for long? Your servants will know and they will talk. And who shall we find to teach me manners and who will hold her tongue? It seems unlikely that your elderly cousin would play such a role."

"Indeed, she would be the last person I should confide in," Montgomery admitted. "But the problems are not insurmountable."

"Of course not. If you keep me locked in a tower and if I never speak a word, the servants may never realize there is a female in the house."

Montgomery's mind was racing. The young lady was making an impression on him that grew stronger by the minute. He was intrigued by her strength, by the self-respect she'd retained after years of ill treatment. *She's far better than I am,* he thought. *I return from the war, and cannot let my scars heal. My treatment of her this morning just proves how unable I am to stop from thinking the worst of all I meet.*

He was anxious to plot a strategy that would establish her again in her rightful place.

It didn't seem fair for her to have to go through so much pretense. Her low position was not her fault. But he knew the *ton* only too well. Unless Caroline was prepared, it would be like throwing her to a pack of wild dogs.

"They wouldn't be as likely to remark your presence," he said, "if there were another woman installed in the house—under a thin veil of secrecy—as though she were my, uh, my mistress."

"And do you have such a lady in mind?" asked Caroline, a catch in her voice as she tried to keep the smile on her face.

"Yes, by Jove, I do!" Montgomery reached for Caroline's hand and squeezed it lightly in his enthusiasm. "Emma! She'll be perfect, and I know she'll play along with us."

"Who is Emma?" asked Caroline.

"An actress of great promise and little money. She's a kind, bright, and delightful sort of person, but not the sort one would normally present to a lady of quality."

"Which we both know I am not," interjected Caroline. "Tell me more."

"I shall send word to Emma immediately. A man on horseback can travel more quickly than we will, and can carry word for her to meet us outside of London. We shall travel in a closed carriage and she will join us."

"What about the coachman?" Caroline objected.

Montgomery pondered the matter, then answered, "We shall engage one who speaks only Welsh. His gabble will never travel as far as the English ears of London."

"Won't we have to change horses and coachmen on the way?" she asked.

"Yes. But at least our origin will not be traced. It will be almost impossible to connect you, once you appear, with the girl who boarded a carriage in Cardiff."

Montgomery spoke in such a reasonable voice that the fantastical plot began to seem less fantastical.

But Caroline was still not convinced. "What makes you think that Emma will want to do this for us?" she asked.

"It's wintertime," replied Montgomery. "The Drury Lane Theatre is still in ruins from the fire. It's no season to be traveling through the provinces. Emma will be low on funds and facing the unwelcome necessity of accepting a protector. We are friends and I believe she would welcome the opportunity to play this role. . . . while you slip secretly into the house, I shall establish Emma in the house without quite as much discretion. The gabblemongers will be busy talking about how she has secretly come under my protection. Then when I order clothes from the best dressmakers, no one will wonder why. And when the servants hear feminine chatter, there will be no mystery and no speculation. And as far as teaching you how to find your way in society, Emma will be a much better teacher than a real lady could possibly be. To a real lady, her behavior is second nature. Emma's profession has taught her how to imitate and simulate. She'll be perfect. That is, if you don't object to so inappropriate a companion . . ."

"Inappropriate! Oh, I should love to meet an actress. I don't care what the *ton* thinks. I believe there's hardly a more noble way to spend a life. But better yet, Montgomery, do you think once I am able to appear in public you might take me to the theater one evening. I should dearly love to go!"

The two regarded each other a moment in amazement.

"Do you really think this enterprise will succeed?" asked Caroline, suddenly hushed.

They stared at each other in silence, both struck at the same moment with the realization that they were actually committed to an exceedingly strange and uncertain course of action.

"I rose to captain, you know," he said at last, "and most of my success was due to good fortune."

"I hardly credit that," she replied warmly. "I'll lay your courage and talent were . . ."

"We can hope Providence still smiles on me," he concluded. Then he asked, "Caroline, do you think you can stand being a prisoner? It might be months, you know, until you can leave the house."

"When I lived at Pemberton Hall, an occasional escape from the house was all that kept me alive. I trust your home will not be as gloomy," she answered.

"It is not extremely luxurious, but I'm sure you will

find it a more pleasant abode than your uncle's," he agreed readily. "And it will be winter, after all. You'll be happy to stay indoors away from the cold. And by the time spring comes, you will emerge with the first flowers."

This speech brought a pretty flush to her cheeks and a girlish giggle to Caroline's lips. "Montgomery," she said, gaily, "it's as though the bad times never happened. I can no longer remember what it was to be unhappy." But Caroline was not really as forgetful as all that. The image of a young Welsh girl suddenly forced itself into her cheerful mind. "Montgomery," she asked tentatively. "I shall need an abigail, shan't I, if I am to be a lady?"

"Yes, indeed," he replied. "But we shall have to wait. There's no one we can trust yet, much as I warrant you could use some assistance."

"And Emma will need someone, too," Caroline insisted. "Someone who will be quite loyal to us all . . ."

"And where are we to find such a jewel?" asked the Captain.

"In Merthyr Tydfil," answered Caroline. "Her name is Mary Williams and the poor thing is forced to work in the mines. I should so like to help her, and I am certain we could rely on her."

Montgomery considered the suggestion in silence. "I don't know, Caroline," he concluded. "I absolutely refuse to head back in that direction with you now. But let us wait and see how our plot proceeds, and I promise you if all goes well, I shall send someone to Merthyr to fetch the girl if that will make you happy."

"I don't know why you are so very good to me!" cried Caroline.

Surely life could not have suddenly turned so perfect, leaving her without a serious care in the world other than the tension and excitement of the dangerous gamble. She had a new, fine friend, and would spend afternoons with a shocking wonderful actress and she would dress in muslin and lace and meet all the dandies of London and go to the theater and perhaps even win at the game and end up married to a gentleman.

But dismal thoughts began to crowd her poor overworked brain. "My father was not very lucky as a gambler," she recalled. "I may very well lose, too."

And a still more ominous thought crept into her mind at the thought of matrimony.

"Montgomery?" she asked, her voice trembling just a little. "I was thinking of what happened this morning."

"Please, Caroline," he begged. "Don't dwell on my conduct . . ."

"No, Montgomery. It's not that. It's just that when a husband and a wife join in those proceedings," she hesitated, seeking the right words, "is it always so very unpleasant for the wife?"

The Captain hung his head in shame and unhappiness.

"Caroline," he said, quietly, "I turned to you in anger this morning. But when a husband and wife lie together in love, it is very different. I promise you, it is different. . . ."

He turned his face so that she should not see the tear falling down his scarred white cheek.

CHAPTER FOUR

"Let me draw the curtains, Miss Bramwell, or all our plotting will be in vain." Montgomery was repeating his request for perhaps the tenth time.

"Oh, but we're still far from London, are we not?" objected Caroline, her eyes gleaming as she watched the countryside from the window of the carriage. The cold brown November aspect could only have delighted a person of melancholy disposition or one who had been shut away in solitude for altogether too long. She sighed with pleasure derived from the ride and from the warmth which the hot brick at her feet provided her lower extremities. "There's simply no one around at all," she argued.

"That doesn't signify," he replied patiently. "A coach or rider might appear at any moment. Besides, you must accustom yourself to the habit of secrecy."

"Very well." She feigned a pout and a petulant flounce back against the faded squabs, but her eyes were still laughing with pleasure.

The long and difficult journey had been effected

with the minimum hardship. Montgomery had shown part of the skill that had made him so valuable in the field—he had loaded the carriage with adequate provisions as they had determined it best not to stop for refreshment in any public place. While they had not dined luxuriously, neither had they suffered from hunger and thirst.

"But you're not being fair!" she cried out when she saw it was Montgomery's intention to continue to survey the road through a small raised portion of the curtain.

"We shall ride right past Emma if I don't keep watch for her carriage," he reminded her.

Much to his relief, once deprived of the enjoyment of watching the passing countryside, Caroline was soon overcome by the fatigue brought on by the relentless and monotonous journey, and soon fell asleep on the seat. Montgomery was glad to be freed from the duties of conversation. For although Caroline was by far the most delightful of the young ladies he had known, Montgomery was unaccustomed to spending time in chatter. All in all, he found a talkative companion to be rather a strain on his nerves.

The two travelers had been together for a fortnight, stopping only to change horses, and as the days had passed, Caroline had necessarily grown even more disheveled than at the journey's start. Still, as the carriage proceeded on its way, Montgomery could not avoid turning his gaze from time to time away from the road. He noted how peacefully the girl slept for all the jouncing and jostling, and he was not unaware of her beauty.

When Caroline next opened her eyes, it was to see a striking young woman stooping her tall and regal frame to climb into the carriage. The hood of her fur-lined cloak fell back revealing a mass of golden curls falling about her lovely face which was just a little flushed from the cold.

A second carriage was pulled over by the side of the road, and at a wave from the beauty's gloved hand, the coachman set the beasts atrotting.

"Well, Roderick, I've done as you asked," said the woman in a pleasing voice, "and now I hope you will tell me the meaning of this little adventure." Her puzzlement was reflected in her violet eyes, and she smiled at Caroline in a friendly yet quizzical way.

"I'm glad to meet you," said Caroline without waiting for Montgomery to present the two. "I'm Caroline Bramwell, and you must be Emma." Dressed in rags as she was, Caroline fully expected disdainful treatment from anyone who was not already apprised of her story, and so she was impressed by Emma's friendly manner.

"Yes, I am," Emma agreed, "and I hope that you have a better notion of what you are doing here than I do." Her first impression was equally favorable due to Caroline's natural and candid tone. Caroline's ignorance of social custom made her greet the actress with the same regard she would have shown a lady of unblemished repute.

Montgomery explained the predicament and the strategy and Emma's eyes opened still wider with surprise, disbelief, shock, and delight. She hugged Caroline warmly when she learned of the girl's tribulations, and promised to do all she could to help.

"And as for you, Captain," she said, teasingly, "your reputation would surely be cast into utter ruin should anyone know what a sentimental gentleman you are, after all. Still leading Crusades for the side of justice and right . . . I don't see why you work so hard to hide that side of your character."

"This is a matter of duty and honor. Sentiment doesn't enter into it at all," replied Montgomery coldly.

Emma merely stifled a laugh and patted Caroline's hand. Then, looking into the girl's green eyes, she said softly, "We shall succeed, Caroline. And then, you and I will belong to different worlds. But in the meantime, I promise you we shall be the best of friends."

Caroline was not as confident about the future. But for the moment, she concluded, life was almost too good to be true.

Still, she found it impossible to hide her vexation at being forbidden to look out the window. "How can you deny me a first glimpse of London?" she demanded, but Emma firmly grasped the little hand that was reaching toward the curtains.

To bolster support for her part, Caroline quoted Wordsworth: "This city now doth, like a garment wear/ The beauty of the morning, silent, bare," and her companions could scarcely restrain their mirth.

"It's nighttime now, my dear," Montgomery pointed out quite correctly. "And I'm sure I can't remember a beautiful morning in all my London days . . . cloaked in noxious vapors of coal is more like it."

"Don't ruin it for her completely," Emma objected. "London may not be as pretty as a poem, but you will love the city just the same," she assured the frustrated girl.

"You'll have your fill of it soon," added Montgomery sternly. "You agreed to abide by our rather difficult conditions and I was convinced you were not such an addle-pated chit as to throw your chances away, spurred by reckless whim."

Caroline was abashed by this scolding, and secretly pleased that the sounds of London could not be shut out by the curtains. It was like passing through a dream in which an entire wonderful world is shrouded in mists, all but invisible. Most visitors from the country would have found the clatter of London, even after dark, noisy beyond belief. But Caroline's experience was of Merthyr Tydfil. By comparison, the sounds of busy London were much faster and more feverish but did not assail the senses so roughly. The buzz and rumble and shouts of London at night were pleasant to Caroline's ear as a distant waterfall.

The dream continued upon the arrival at Chelton House, the London residence that had come to Montgomery through his mother's family. Under cover of darkness, the Captain escorted Emma up the steps while poor Caroline trotted along behind them carrying the actress's reticule and bandbox. She looked for all the world, they hoped, like the lower sort of serving maid who might be employed by an actress who had not as yet played any roles of note.

Montgomery greeted and then summarily dismissed the servants who came to welcome him home. He stood the while with an arm flung around the actress who stared straight ahead in a pose of proud indifference. The Captain then led the two girls upstairs.

"Won't they wonder about us?" asked Caroline nervously.

"Of course," responded the Captain.

In his own home, he seemed more sure of himself than ever.

"But they are generally discreet, and I don't fear their speculation. Their talk may give rise to enough scandal-broth over Emma here, but I'm sure they didn't even notice you with us."

"I'm so sorry you must be subjected to this on my account," said Caroline, turning to Emma shyly.

"My life has been a subject for the gabblemongers

before," said Emma wearily, but quickly covered her feelings with a cheerful smile.

"Please forgive the appearance of the rooms," Montgomery interrupted, "but I spend hardly any time at all here and the furnishings remain as they were when the place was occupied many years ago by my parents. In fact, the only room I've done over is the kitchen, and that at the insistence of Mrs. Gregory. Since she has so little occasion to exercise her culinary abilities, due to my infrequent stays, I felt it wise to humor her and accede to the demand."

"But it is all quite grand!" insisted Caroline as she followed up the stairs, running her hand along the light mahogany handrail and admiring the balustrades in which flowing scrolls of acanthus were cunningly worked in the heavy wood. She had had no idea that Captain Montgomery was so rich. His riding attire had certainly given no indication of this kind of wealth. She was slightly intimidated, but also relieved that his generosity toward her would not cause him any real financial hardship.

She caught only a glimpse of the oak-paneled drawing room. Caroline knew nothing of current fashions, and could tell only that the furnishings and appointments were of the finest quality and, unlike those at Pemberton Hall, had been maintained with scrupulous care.

As they climbed still another flight of stairs, Montgomery assured his female companions that the third floor would be declared off-limits for the servants "except when we require them and specifically request their presence."

"So we're to be quite isolated," commented Emma, somewhat drily. "It's a good thing I trust you."

"I'm sorry that I cannot offer you a front window,

Miss Bramwell," continued Montgomery, teasing, "but I know you would develop the unfortunate habit of looking out into the street and would certainly be remarked. So you'll have to be confined to a back room. You'll find it quieter, anyway."

So saying, he showed Caroline into a bright and spacious bedchamber. Floral designs were painted lightly over the pale yellow walls. The fireplace was so covered with Chinese trinkets and little jars, the exquisite objects seemed to blend right into the ornamental carvings of the mantel itself. As for the bed, "Why it's fit for a princess!" Caroline exclaimed. Four-postered and canopied, the mahogany bed was screened by imported bed-curtains painted in the tree-of-life design.

Emma interrupted the girl's happy gushing to say, "Aren't you going to carry my things next door and help me get settled?"

When Caroline responded immediately with an apology, and a prompt exit from the bedroom, Emma's face clouded with pity. She had been speaking in jest, and was shocked to see the extent to which Caroline had become accustomed to obedient service. Emma took her reticule from the girl's hand and exchanged a look with Montgomery, who knew he dared not assure the actress that at least in some matters, Caroline was not so obliging.

"You needn't go into the hall," said Montgomery evenly. "The two of you share a sitting room, and your chambers connect through it."

Calling Caroline back, he opened a door set in the painted wall and revealed a charming room, and beyond it, a dove-gray bedchamber with "flocked" wallpaper in imitation of the Chinese style.

"Now I imagine you ladies will wish to rest. And if you insist you are not fatigued, I shall insist that you rest anyway. Because our unexpected arrival has caused a terrible clamor downstairs. The formidable Mrs. Gregory is being assailed by the fidgets because she fears we shall call for supper before she is ready. So if you will both be so good as to collapse for an hour or two, I shall call for a bath for Emma, and then she may request a second tub of water prior to supper. That way each of you will take a turn. Then, I shall arrange to have the covers laid in the sitting room—for two, of course—and Caroline, you will join the party once we have been left quite alone." With these words, Captain Montgomery took his leave.

"Yes, I think I shall sleep for a while," said Emma, "and you, dear, had just as well learn to start taking orders. Roderick is a good and compassionate man, but he brooks no contradiction or interference."

Caroline gave Emma a quick impulsive hug and retired to her fairyland chamber.

Captain Roderick Montgomery figured prominently in her dreams. Once again, they were riding together on Jupiter's strong back, but this time through meadows filled with springtime flowers and under a bright and warming sun. Once again, she was wrapped in his raven-black cloak, and in his arms. A strange and pleasing tremor ran through her as his strong gentle hands moved again over her breasts, and this time did not draw away in surprise. His fingers brushed gently, then stroked her through the fabric of her fine dress which grew flimsier and yet gauzier in her dream. But as his grip upon her became tighter, and she grew aware of his hot and rasping breath, Caroline recoiled in horror and fear. Jupiter stumbled, the Captain cried out in surprise, and she lost her seat to go off in a terrifying, sickening flight into a wild and dizzying unknown space. She woke up with a pounding heart.

This dream put Caroline in a shaken and subdued state that had not entirely left her when she joined the other conspirators for supper. The delicious aromas that rose from the plates helped dispel her sense of impending disaster. It had been years since she had sat down to a good meal. In fact, the peasant soups and bread on which she had supped at the wretched inn had been far more nourishing and agreeable than her usual fare at Pemberton. For though it had been Caroline who prepared the meals, her uncle had kept close watch over kitchen expenditures and she had never dared to do more than sample the meals she prepared for his palate.

"You see, I could smuggle a dozen young ladies into the house and Mrs. Gregory would never be the wiser," smiled Montgomery. "I request a meal for two and she provides a table from which a regiment could sup."

The different courses had been set in covered dishes upon the sidetable, Montgomery having instructed the footman he wished no interruption during the meal. "Of course, they all think the worst, but even their fertile imaginations will not divine the truth," he chuckled.

Emma thought to hush her host, thinking his easy talk was too frank for Caroline's ears. But she kept her silence, noting Caroline's manner becoming less hesitant and more cheerful. As for Caroline, it was not just the first bite of pigeon pie that restored her good mood; it was seeing the Captain smile and laugh. Perhaps the dashing officer of years past was not entirely changed after all.

She smiled at him warmly, taking in his impressive appearance. For Montgomery had come to this first meal in formal and elegant attire, from the starched shirtpoints of his collar to the Dresden ruffles on his sleeves. And Emma was relaxed and gracious in sprig muslin and violet ribbons threaded in her hair. If Caroline's appearance was at all ridiculous or disconcerting in contrast to all this splendor, neither Montgomery nor Emma let any such feeling show on their faces.

Montgomery served Caroline a generous portion of pike on her Wedgwood plate—not the common Wedgwood, but rather the fine line of pottery used by the aristocracy. He suggested she try the sauce, a delightful and buttery concoction of anchovies and walnut pickle. It proved most pleasing, yet unduly strange, to Caroline, who was unfamiliar with such niceties of the fine table. She had considered herself a passable cook, but her uncle had liked his meals ample and plain. The world of sauces—except for simple stewed apples to go with the madman's roast goose—was a mystery to her.

"However does Mrs. Gregory make this?" she inquired with enthusiasm.

"I have not the slightest idea," answered the amused Captain, passing her a platter of roasted sweetbreads.

"You're going to make the poor child sick!" chided Emma. She didn't wish to curtail the girl's enjoyment, but guessed correctly that Caroline was not used to digesting such rich fare. "In the last hundred years, I daresay more people of the best families have died of overeating than in duels."

"Well, I certainly shall not die in a duel," Caroline retorted, "and I cannot live forever, anyway. So I shall take my chances. And some more sweetbreads." With such words, she put an end to the debate and happily helped herself from the platter, and then to some currant pudding as well.

The Captain sat back easily, poured himself some claret, almost unaware of the general sense of contentment that had stolen over him.

Emma's voice broke the quite spell. "I know this is

only a charade and it is not my place to make demands on you, Roderick, but I do hope that tomorrow you will dispatch some fellows to bring my trunks around. If we take up the skirts a few inches, Caroline and I are almost of a size, and until you make better arrangements for her, I shall gladly let her wear my dresses."

Caroline's grateful exclamations to Emma were soon transferred to Montgomery when that gentleman revealed the last dish of the evening and passed her a fresh apricot tart.

Emma tried to draw his attention back to practical matters.

"Very well, very well. I shall send for your things in the morning, and I'll stop by the shops from St. James's and Bond streets to Leicester Square and I'll let them all know, in the strictest confidence of course, that you may charge what you wish to my account. And I hope," he added, "that you will take advantage of my generosity directly. I don't want to keep Caroline waiting."

"Will you be able to accompany me?" asked Emma. "I know I'm not a lady of quality, but even so, I dare not visit the shops alone in the afternoon."

"Oh, bother!" exclaimed Montgomery. "I don't begrudge either of you a penny. You may spend all you wish and buy what you like, but I haven't the time to spend on ladies' matters."

Caroline wanted to quake before his displeasure, but Emma remained quite calm. "Don't set up your bristles, Roderick," she said. "Just do try and be reasonable. There is really no need for such haste, you know. I don't have to visit the shops tomorrow. Caroline will wear my clothing, and once you have provided us with an abigail—you can do that, can't you?—she can accompany me on a shopping expedition in the morning hours when I shall feel ever so much safer."

"As you think best, my dear," he replied carelessly. "Just as long as I needn't concern myself overmuch with your doings."

This exchange set Caroline to thinking. A feeling of unease set in, and she tried to tell herself it was due to the effects of the heavy meal.

In fact, she realized she was quite downcast at Captain Montgomery's attitude. For all his generosity and kindness, it was becoming quite clear to her that he felt no personal involvement in her situation. Use my wealth but let me be, was what he was saying to them only too plainly.

He had already done altogether more than could have been expected of any virtual stranger. Caroline had been unable to believe that such favors would be bestowed simply out of a sense of honor. And following the intimate nature of their talk at the inn, though she had never looked upon him as a lover or suitor, she had certainly come to think of him as a close and dear friend. It was painful to suspect that he had no real regard for her as an individual. She was a damsel in distress and entitled to aid. Clearly, the Captain felt he had wasted enough of his time in resolving her problems.

Her feeling of senseless rejection was deepened by her belief that her presence had been helpful to the Captain's own emotional state. Hadn't she made him laugh and smile and talk? Hadn't he begun to seem like the man she'd dreamed of for those long and dreary years? Did he really prefer to hold himself aloof from the small and pretty joys of daily life and friendship?

His gray eyes seemed so cold and distant at times. A mist seemed to cloud her own green ones and a sigh escaped from her lips.

"You poor thing!" cried Emma, throwing her arms

around the girl's frail shoulders. "After all you've been through and that dreadful long journey, we're keeping you up entirely too late. I'm sure this is all very different and frightening to you, but you'll feel fine soon. Just wait until the sun comes pouring in your window in the morning."

"It's a back window, you know," said Caroline, with an attempt at jest.

"Yes, but that's to keep out prying eyes. The sun, at least, *will* find its way in."

Emma helped Caroline to bed, and Caroline noticed, to her surprise, that the Captain remained seated at the table. She'd expected him to take the first opportunity to escape. When Emma bade her good night, Caroline saw Montgomery still waiting, and before Emma closed the door, she caught the searching look he turned on Emma's face.

Caroline pulled the coverlets up to her chin, wondering if some sort of proceedings were to take place in the dove-gray bedroom, in the four-poster bed almost identical to her own.

CHAPTER FIVE

In the morning, Caroline had been awake and dressed for an hour when at last she heard loud footsteps in the sitting room.

"Your chocolate, uh, Madam," announced the footman awkwardly, and Caroline heard a knock that must have been on Emma's door.

"Thank you, and good morning," came Emma's sprightly voice. "Please just set the tray on the sidetable."

However are we going to keep this game going? Caroline wondered to herself, pitying the servants who had to serve invisible house guests.

She listened to the retreating footsteps, heard the creak of an opening door. Then Emma's whisper, "Caroline, dear, are you awake?"

Caroline opened the door to find Emma in a white cambric morning dress that had become only slightly creased from the journey, folded into a surprisingly tiny bundle in the bandbox.

"There's plenty of chocolate for us both," she continued, "but only a single cup, so we'll have to share." She poured, giggled, and handed the cup to Caroline. "This is hardly how things are managed at fine dinner parties. I don't see how I am to teach you."

Caroline took a warm, delicious sip, and passed the cup back. "I hope you don't mind sharing with me," she said shyly. "I must look like a carrier of gaol-fever."

They laughed gaily, then Emma held her finger to her lips as footsteps were heard to approach again. Caroline bolted from the room and hid behind her door, thinking that deception was an awful bother.

The knock on the door was followed by Montgomery's voice. "May we come in?" he asked, putting a marked emphasis on the word "we."

Emma gave her calm assent, and Montgomery appeared in the doorway. Behind him, she could see the men with her trunks.

"Oh, Roderick, you're even better than your word!" she exclaimed, and nodded readily when he asked if the men could carry her belongings into her chamber. "I'm so glad to see my clothes have arrived," she added loudly in order to share the news with Caroline.

Young Miss Bramwell's impatience knew no bounds until at last Emma threw open the door to her hiding place.

"Unpack and get dressed, and when Mrs. Gregory has some breakfast ready, I'll carry it up myself," said Montgomery, wisely withdrawing from the scene of feminine merriment.

But the tray of bread, tea, and plump oysters was delivered upstairs long before the girls were ready to eat.

Emma's modest wardrobe seemed like a queen's trousseau to Caroline. The newer dresses had somewhat lower waistlines than those that had been carefully mended and preserved from earlier years. "I have to dress well in my profession," sighed Emma, "and I would thoroughly enjoy it if only my pockets were somewhat plumper." She showed Caroline a fringed shawl of real silk. "A gift," she explained, and Caroline discreetly pressed her for no further explanation.

Some of the dresses were so old, they looked straight from the schoolroom. Caroline chose these to try on, not wanting to borrow Emma's best. The two friends tried on clothes in front of the glass in Emma's room.

The dresses hung on Caroline's malnourished frame, but the flowing lines of the style helped disguise the imperfect fit. And the antique ruff which covered the neck properly during the daytime helped fill out the bosom, which was more ample in Emma's case than in Caroline's.

"It's a fairly good fit, at least for in here," Caroline agreed, "and if you buy clothes to your size at the dressmakers, I can adjust them easily enough myself so that I'll be somewhat presentable when I first emerge from my cage." She smiled inwardly to think that her fumbling experiments with needle and thread back at Pemberton were to prove useful in her new life.

Poking her head out into the sitting room, and ascertaining that no one was in sight, Emma hurried out and brought the breakfast tray back into the bedchamber. In the meantime, Caroline straightened the tilt-top tea table which stood by a wall of the bedroom and pulled it over to the bed so that the two friends could sit side by side and breakfast off its black-and-gold lacquered surface. Emma also retrieved the early morning chocolate cup and rinsed it out with water from the bedside pitcher.

"What luxury!" she cried. "A separate cup for each

of us!" Dressed in their knickers and petticoats, the friends sat down on Emma's bed and made short shrift of Mrs. Gregory's breakfast.

It was only when they had unpacked and put the clothing away, and Caroline was dressed in pale green and, in spite of the schoolgirlish puffed sleeves, was feeling more like a lady than ever before in her life, that she realized Montgomery had not joined them but had left them to eat alone.

"Don't be surprised by that," Emma counseled. "This entire project is so very unlike him. That's a man with no time for friendships or flirtations."

"He is rather mysterious," agreed Caroline, "and so very different from when I first met him. Although I was younger then, and I suppose he made a kind of fairytale impression on me. I can't help but think that he must have been through some terrible experiences in the war in the east. I don't really dare ask him."

"I'll tell you as much as I know," said Emma, "but I'll wager no one understands him well. He quite dislikes being called Captain, you know, and never appears in uniform. Some would have it that he came home in disgrace, and it was only through his political influence that our dear Montgomery was not stripped of his rank altogether. Others say he continues to advise the government closely in military matters and took off his uniform in disgust over Army politics. He's been accused of being everything from a reactionary to a dyed-in-the-wool Bonapartist." Emma smiled at a sudden thought. "In fact, just the other day I saw his likeness tacked up in a cartoon shop, with the tricolor stuck in his hat."

"But that's disgraceful! How can they get away with such slander?" demanded Caroline.

"There was more," giggled Emma. "They even had a page of instructions protruding from his pocket, with Bonaparte's signature at the bottom! It's ridiculous, of course. I've never even heard that Montgomery frequents Holland House."

"What, or where, is Holland House?" inquired Caroline.

"Lord and Lady Holland live there, on the road out toward Kensington. There is usually an assortment of artists and radicals and French sympathizers at their dinner table, but I know many of them and would hardly call them traitors. And as for Montgomery, he spends much more time with a French Countess—de Lescaux I think she's called—who advocates the raising of a new Royalist army. That's hardly a Bonapartist position."

Caroline considered this information nervously. She didn't like the idea of Montgomery involved in political intrigue. "There *are* traitors in England, you know," she said, "and one cannot be too careful. Remember, I spent the last years in Wales where the memory of the French invasion is still most vivid."

"But Caroline, dear, then you must realize the Welsh suffered more at the hands of our own government when the spies hurried down to seek out Dissenters than they suffered at the hands of the drunken French convicts who landed ashore."

"You sound like a radical yourself," observed Caroline in amazement.

"Please, it's hardly as bad as all that. But much of this is common knowledge to people who read the opposition newspapers along with the *Times*," Emma defended herself. "Anyway, I do think you should be a little cautious before pointing an accusing finger and crying treachery. Why, do you know that the government had spies following Wordsworth around the countryside, filing reports that even he was a French spy?"

This news about her favorite poet, whose work had sustained her through many difficult hours, came as a shock to Caroline.

"Was such a report really published?" asked Caroline. "It's hard to believe I wouldn't have heard of it, even if it did appear in some opposition publication . . ."

"Oh, no. It hasn't been made public," replied Emma. "Coleridge told me about it. He was under surveillance, too, at the time. It seems that Wordsworth and his sister would go out into the fields with camping stools and she would sketch while he composed poems. And some ridiculous top-lofty gentleman decided they were drawing maps to send to an invading French Army."

Caroline's amazement grew, but now she was less impressed by the dubious dealing of the government than by the fact that she was sitting with someone who knew Coleridge personally.

"He's a bit of a wateringpot, actually," added Emma, "though it hardly seems a proper designation for a man. Still, what else shall I call someone whose tears flow so freely?"

"It must be wonderful to know such people!" Caroline exclaimed. "And you will have so much to teach me before I venture out. I begin to realize the extent of my ignorance."

"Oh, you're not ignorant. Not at all," Emma hastened to assure her. "There's no reason for me to share these tidbits with you, except for pleasure. A lady of quality isn't expected to know about politics or the private lives of artists. In my profession, however, I've often found myself in such places at such times as gentlemen are wont to talk freely about their matters. And of course, Mrs. Siddons and Mrs. Powell hear a lot more of the gossip than I do. . . ."

"Then I should much rather be an actress than a lady," declared Caroline. Being a lady was not such a wonderful situation after all, she reflected. Montgomery was planning to deliver her from one gaol to another. The Lord of Bedlam would simply be succeeded by another keeper—called a husband—and she could only hope the new keeper would be gentler than the old.

"Don't be a goosecap," said Emma sharply.

"Oh, I'm sure it's not easy work," Caroline hurried to add, "but I do have an excellent memory, and . . ."

"Caroline, dear, if you have an opportunity to rise in this life, you must grab at it. My life is gay at times, but still, there are days and nights when I go hungry. You have experienced those pangs yourself, so you know it is no romantic game to suffer. And though I'm young, it is hard not to think about what the future holds. Even should I achieve greatness, it is hard not to fear the poverty that can overtake one so quickly upon retirement from the stage. I see my friends drifting into unfortunate liaisons as they attempt to put some money away, or in the hopes of securing a piece of land here, a mortgage there . . ."

Even these practical words could not fully convince Caroline, who threw her arms around her companion. "But Emma, you are the best friend I've ever had," she said. "I would so much rather spend my life among people like you . . . I don't give a button for all the antiquated flummery that fashionable society holds in such high regard. I shouldn't like to spend my life using fine muslins and lace to cover up my appalling ignorance and lack of interest in the world around me."

At the same time, she vowed privately to herself that

if she should be rich one day, she'd see to it that dear Emma should never be in need again. For it was her opinion that besides being friendly and kind, Emma was also a virtuous person who had more or less resigned herself to a future in which virtue would be a luxury beyond her limited means.

Emma was not aware of these silent reflections, but Caroline's speech reached her heart and made her even more determined to see that her new friend give up all thought of jeopardizing a successful future. "I dare say," Emma argued, "that there exist gentlemen with the same disregard for convention that you profess yourself. Although I trust they hold their views in secrecy. You are a beautiful woman, Caroline, and will have your choice of London's eligible young men. If you are discriminating and careful, surely you will find yourself one who will admit you into his thoughts and rejoice in your ready wit."

Caroline sighed, somewhat reassured, but still feeling that she would much prefer to suffer economic privation with Emma than live a dreary life with some proper husband. She was quite accustomed to a poor standard of comfort, and kind words held more value to her than a purse of golden guineas.

"But if our scheme fails," she said, pursuing her thoughts, "would you then help me begin a career on the stage?"

"We'll worry about that some other time," said Emma. "I'll not give my agreement, because you are just so reckless as to ruin your chances in order to force my hand. I still hold that you'll find a man with whom you can live in complete charity." Then, shrewdly, she added, "Someone quite different from Montgomery. That one will admit no one—male or female—into his confidence."

Caroline's blush told Emma that the young woman had indeed conceived a great affection for her rescuer. It was only to be expected, thought Emma, but she could not imagine a man less likely to fall in love than Captain Montgomery. The gabblemongers had him closely associated with the Countess de Lescaux who had managed to escape Paris with her head still connected to her slender lily-white neck. But Emma believed this liaison had as much basis in truth as the story that she herself was the new object of the Captain's passion.

To cheer Caroline up, she proceeded to rattle off a stream of amusing tales concerning the more bohemian of the writers she had known. Caroline was especially delighted, although a little shocked to hear that William Blake and his wife read *Paradise Lost* aloud to one another in their garden as naked as Adam and Eve before the Fall.

"I've never read any of his works," she hastened to assure Emma after she admitted having heard of him by name and reputation.

"As for Sheridan," continued Emma, "I'll never forget the night the Drury Lane caught fire. It was just about two years ago and I was horror-stricken. All I could think of was where would I find work if it burned to the ground? My fear proved to be quite justified. I did a tour of the provinces, but just imagine, with Covent Garden and Drury Lane burning down within five months of each other . . . ! Well, there's a sight too many actors without work. We fight each other bitterly for what roles we can find. And of course there's been considerable scrambling and tumbling about in search of protectors.

"But dear old Richard took it all quite calmly, even though the building was his own property, you know.

He simply watched the flames, then took a seat at the Piazza and called for refreshment. As people remarked on his behavior with surprise, he merely lifted the glass to his lips and said he should surely be allowed to take a glass of wine by his own fireside."

"Can that really be true?" asked Caroline. "Were you actually there?"

"No," admitted Emma, "but I find it quite in character. The loss of the theater and a great deal of money would not have troubled him quite so much as long as the incident provided him with the opportunity for a *bon mot*."

The day passed in such conversation, and the ladies ate their way through nuncheon, dinner, tea, and supper, without the Captain making an appearance. Emma, who was accustomed to a certain freedom in her comings and goings, began to chafe under the restrictions of sitting all day upstairs, but sympathy for Caroline kept her from stirring. She knew that once her illicit presence was generally known, she would be free to wander the house and to go about out-of-doors as well. Poor Caroline would have no such luxury, and Emma wondered how the girl would bear up under the strain.

"I hope I shall be able to go out tomorrow," commented Emma at last. "Is there anything I can bring you?" she asked, hoping to soften the blow.

"Oh, yes!" cried Caroline. "Please, if you could bring me some books to read. How I wish you could smuggle me a tutor as well. I wish it were possible to take real advantage of this enforced solitude. Do you know what I've always wanted to do? To learn Greek."

Emma laughed. "That is not the sort of lesson the Captain expects you to learn this winter."

"But I must have some entertainment."

"What a remarkable thing to say!" Emma grew more impressed with Caroline by the minute. "I should hardly have thought the study of Greek to be so entertaining."

"Anyway, who knows what the Captain expects." Caroline had turned glum at the thought of his absence. Then feeling guilty at her own ingratitude, she forced a smile. "I've never been so happy," she assured Emma. Her heart skipped a beat at the lie. For at Pemberton Hall, her young soul had grown almost deadened to grief. Here, in London, beneath the Captain's roof, Caroline found herself growing more sensitive again. Yes, she was happy, but underneath it all, she was dissatisfied. Caroline was only too aware of the anguish that assailed her with each thought of her protector. For although Montgomery had forbidden her to use that word, she could think of no better.

Her long indolent day left Caroline with little desire to sleep. Nothing like laziness to keep a person awake, she thought. There was no sound in the house, and at last, no longer able to resist the temptation to explore, Caroline sprang to her feet. She pulled on a pair of Emma's bootees, covered her bare shoulders with a shawl, and after listening for a moment at the door, stepped out on tiptoe into the hall.

She didn't even dare carry a candle, but moving with the utmost stealth, began to descend the curving staircase, feeling the edge of each step carefully with her foot.

She soon became convinced that she was engaged in a fruitless and risky endeavor. The chance of discovery was great, and in the dark, her tour of the house was not terribly interesting. Still, it felt wonderful to be able to move about freely, and at past two in the morning, she couldn't seriously expect others to be about.

But a sudden clatter of boots on the stairs made her draw back and hold her breath. Montgomery rushed past her, so close that she could smell strong liquor on his breath. Thinking it a miracle that he had not seen her, Caroline waited for his footsteps to die away, then returned as silently as she could to her comfortable and charming prison cell.

CHAPTER SIX

"But I thought you said it was all politics," protested Caroline, putting aside the issue of *The Examiner*, "and here I find a poem by Byron."

"Are you complaining?" asked Emma. "I thought poetry was to your taste."

Caroline paced the room, now picking up a book and now putting it down. The days of inactivity in the carriage had made it necessary for the girl to regain the use of her stiff legs. Her knees had become positively locked into position until Caroline had thought, for one panic-stricken moment, that she would require a physician. That would mean the end of their secret, and she had burdened Montgomery too much to see their plans go awry from the start. "I just don't know what to look at first," she exclaimed.

To Emma, this state of nervous energy seemed more a sign of good health than of imminent collapse and it made her smile.

Emma had persuaded Montgomery to accompany her on a shopping expedition after all, and had brought back a collection of books, newspapers, bonnets, slippers, and samples of the velvet, satin, and muslin which the dressmakers were busy converting into frocks.

Now she took Caroline by the hand, had her sit in the walnut cane chair, and began to brush her thick black curls. Emma had always found that a session of vigorous hairbrushing helped to calm her own nerves before a performance and hoped this would help Caroline relax.

"But I thought I was masquerading as *your* abigail," protested Caroline, trying to take the ebony-backed brush from Emma's hand. "You mustn't be so good to me," she added. "You and Captain Montgomery are spoiling me so." Her pampered state of the moment made her think again on the future that was being planned for her.

"Emma, do you believe in love?" she asked.

Emma's hand stopped, poised for a moment in midair. "Are you thinking of the Captain?" she asked at last.

"No," said Caroline, "or maybe I was . . . but not in the way you think—that is, if you think that I'm—that I have some sort of affection of that sort for him."

"You'll have to explain yourself a little better than that."

Caroline's jet-black eyebrows drew together in concentration. "Emma," she said, "I've never talked about things like this with anyone. It's been so long since I had anyone to talk to about anything. I hardly know how to put my thoughts into words. I've certainly had lots of thoughts all these years . . . but I feel things and can't express them. It's almost like talking a foreign language, so please be patient with me, and press me if I don't make myself clear."

Emma squeezed Caroline's hand, and could not keep

from wondering how long it would take until those poor fingers were white and soft again.

"I know the Captain wants to see me properly married off, and that's very kind of him. But it seems as though it would be just odious and awful to live with a man I didn't love. Perhaps that's why I envy your life, Emma. I feel I'd be so happy to be able to earn my own way in the world."

"But what makes you so sure you wouldn't love your husband?" asked Emma gently. "Just because you haven't yet met the man? You haven't met many nice people, and once you come out, I'm sure you'll be dazzled by so many young blades, your only problem will be deciding which one you like best."

"What about you, Emma? Is your good advice only for my benefit, or do you follow it yourself?"

Emma would have preferred not to discuss her own heart. But she knew so many details of Caroline's private life, she felt she must reply honestly as a simple matter of mutual trust.

"I'm rather fond of a man I know from the theater," she admitted. "But he takes no notice of me, so, in a way, I'm happy to be in hiding here."

Caroline clapped her hands. "But Emma, just wait until he sees you in the best clothes the Captain can buy!"

"I hope he's a better man than to be swayed by externals," she replied coldly. "Anyway, I fear he'd take a dim view of a girl forming an irregular attachment. And he will, of course, believe me to be protected by the Captain. That will detract from the beauty of my new satins and laces."

"But I thought theater people were not so concerned with such matters."

"To his credit, I believe Edward holds to his standards," said Emma quietly.

"Oh, you must forgive me then!" exclaimed Caroline as tears of distress surfaced in her green eyes. "I'm so sorry. If I had known that you would be putting yourself in a bad position by helping me this way . . ."

"Don't think of it," said Emma kindly. "Much as I love you, Caroline, if I'd thought I stood a chance of capturing Edward's affections, I expect I would have refused to go along with this scheme."

Caroline sighed. "Still, I'm sorry. But look how you prove my point. What happiness have you gained by being in love? I'm really not at all sure I should want to love anyone." Before Emma could protest, she went on. "I mean, love is supposed to be a good thing, is it not? But then, I think of my uncle . . ."

Emma reprimanded her: "Now that you're safe with us, you shouldn't think of that monster anymore."

"But that's just the point," sighed Caroline. "He is a monster, I suppose, but he became that way not through sin and wickedness. It was love that drove the man from his wits. At least so my mother told me . . . Back in Yorkshire, oh, many years before I was born, he fell in love with a neighbor's daughter. But her parents objected to his suit because he wasn't moneyed enough for their tastes. Off he went to seek his fortune, and the attachment was strong on both sides, you see. The girl refused many suitors, waiting for her true love to return, even though years passed and she was no longer quite so young. At last, one day, my uncle rode into town a rich man. But the influenza had carried the poor girl off just two months before. It was after that he went into Wales and went on making money and living more and more like a beast."

Emma resumed her brushing of the black tresses, because for the moment she could not think of any reply to the sad story.

Outside the window, sparrows chirped on the bare boughs of a plane tree. She listened to them while she thought.

"But Caroline," she said at last. "With your limited experience, you must think your uncle's life follows a common pattern. While it's true that many people have suffered agonies over love, many have known great joy. And very few have been driven to such depths. It seems more likely a morbid streak in your uncle's personality that must have led him to such an ending."

"And there are quite a few morbid streaks in my family," said Caroline softly, thinking of her father.

"But not in you, my dear. Why even Roderick has remarked on how you must have a great and abiding love of life to have come through your ordeals in such good spirits . . . Anyway, whatever you think of the bridegroom who has yet to appear, don't you wish to have children?"

Caroline blushed at this question, but led on by her trust in this new friend, seized the opportunity to learn more about a disturbing subject. "Emma," she asked, "I hope you will not think it wrong of me to ask. But if you know anything about the proceedings which led to the birth of a baby, I should be most grateful if you would explain it to me."

Emma regarded her in amazement. "I was to accompany you and teach you how to dress. I had no idea this was to be part of the bargain." But she was immediately sorry for the surprise in her voice when she saw how this threw Caroline into greater embarrassment and confusion. And so she went on to explain, to the best of her knowledge, what she understood of physical love.

Caroline listened attentively, and in spite of Emma's

delicacy and her assurance that all this was quite normal and not at all unpleasant, she found herself reacting with distaste. No wonder such things were kept secret, yet she didn't fail to see the humor of the situation.

"It's terrible not to know these things!" she exclaimed. "One can make such terrible awkward mistakes out of sheer ignorance." Her words poured out in a jumble, her embarrassment compounded by the giggles she could barely repress. "Why, I've noticed a swelling in the Captain's breeches on several occasions," she spilled the story, "and honestly believed it to be due to a war injury. I was on the point of asking him about it more than once."

After their laughter had subsided, Emma remembered how the conversation had begun. "You agreed that your thoughts about love had something to do with him . . ." she began hesitantly.

Caroline explained herself. "He seems to have closed himself off to love. And yet he is such a good person . . . it certainly makes me think it must be better not to love and end up like the Captain than to love deeply and end up like the Lord of Bedlam."

"But that's like saying you'd rather die of consumption than of typhus, when what you should be thinking about is living!" exclaimed Emma.

"No, that's an unfair comparison," objected Caroline. "What I really want," she began . . .

"Is to study Greek," shot back Emma, and then broke into smiles. "That reminds me of that scene from *The Rivals*. Oh, do wait here just a moment!"

"And where do you expect me to go?" asked Caroline, in a voice that was tart and yet brimming with affection.

Emma returned shortly with a book she'd found among those in her trunks, and flipping through its well-thumbed pages, quickly came upon the passage she sought. "Here, my dear. Though I hardly take my cue from Mrs. Malaprop."

Caroline scanned the page quickly, and then gaily demanded a command performance.

"But I only walked on as a servant in the production," insisted Emma, "and anyway, I'm still too young, thankfully, to portray dreadful silly old aunts like Mrs. Malaprop . . ." Nevertheless, she promptly broke into the speech without reference to the open page before her. "I would by no means wish a daughter of mine to be a progeny of learning," she explained in that babbling rush of dignified nonsense that characterized certain ladies of good breeding. "I don't think so much learning becomes a young woman; for instance—I would never let her meddle with Greek," a significant glance and lowering of the brows at Caroline, "or Hebrew," and Emma went on ruling out the other "diabolical instruments" in such an overbearing, self-satisfied, and yet well-meaning tone, that Caroline was soon laughing freely.

"But you don't believe that yourself for a moment!" she cried. "Oh, I do hope Montgomery's cousin is nothing like Mrs. Malaprop, but please, let's read the play together from the beginning."

Emma was willing, and they divided up the roles, the male characters and the female. Emma gave the book to Caroline, insisting that she herself had heard the play performed so many times she had it by heart in its entirety.

"And I plumed myself with having a good memory," said Caroline, much impressed. "But I see now I'd never be good enough to join your ranks."

"Necessity will work wonders for you," laughed

Emma. "We are paid little enough, and forfeit a night's salary should we 'dry up' and forget a line."

The ladies soon entered into the spirit of the play so entirely they quite forgot to keep their voices down, and didn't even notice Montgomery in the doorway, or the smile that played briefly over his lips as Caroline, playing an old servant, waved her arms and shouted orders to an "impudent Jacaknapes . . . you little, impertinent, insolent, kitchen-bred—"

"I believe that's the end of the scene," commented Montgomery drily, a scowl now replacing the smile. "I've overheard the servants, and they are terribly impressed with Emma's abilities as an actress. You change your voice so skillfully, they could swear there were two people up here instead of just one." He delivered this warning in as courteous a manner as possible, admitted Caroline to herself, and so she quietly obeyed when Montgomery told her to get quickly behind her door, as the footman was on his way up with the leg of mutton.

"The servants also believe me to be passionately in love with you," she heard him add to Emma, "taking all my meals in your rooms."

It seemed to Caroline, with her growing sense of what was proper speech between men and women, that Montgomery should not have spoken of love and passion, even in fun, to a woman unless they were actually on such intimate terms. Or unless such matters were so far removed from his mind, he used words like that without a second thought as to their meaning.

When Caroline emerged, Emma was seated at the table alone.

"This will certainly confuse the staff," commented Emma. "My passionate lover sees me served and then runs off to eat at his club!"

Why does he avoid me so? thought Caroline, uneasy

to realize how disappointed she was to find Montgomery gone.

The winter passed. Although her window faced back, the room was sufficiently elevated for Caroline to see through the naked branches of the trees to an occasional pinnacle rising from some unknown church, to the warm red brick color of distant buildings. The sky was usually sooty and yellow, but the sun went down in an eerie wintry magnificence, almost more lurid in color than the brightest sunsets in the countryside. Day after day, she watched the snow fall, then melt, then fall again.

At night she could hear the clatter of hooves on the streets, and the chant of the Charleys as they patrolled the streets: *Twelve o'clock and all's well.* When she echoed the words, she sometimes felt she was warding off a terrible disaster that hung over her head and the heads of those she loved.

Emma assured her she was not the only person of note who had chosen to stay hidden and out of the public eye. The Prince of Wales himself was in retired seclusion after an uncertain incident.

"He says that he sprained his ankle while teaching Princess Charlotte the Highland Fling," whispered Emma, "but *on dit* that he was soundly thrashed by Lady Yarmouth's husband."

Caroline's eyes opened wide in shock. How could anyone dare to "thrash" the Prince? "Have they taken him under arrest?" she asked.

"Yarmouth? And admit the story is true?"

"But why would he . . . ?" As understanding dawned, Caroline cried out in frustration. "Oh! When am I going to learn the ways of the world!"

"You are already much changed," said Emma

mildly, "and I hope you will not change so much as to be like all the others."

Caroline's ill-used hands had grown soft again, but now they learned new injuries as she pricked herself with her needle, altering the gowns and frocks that had been sewn to Emma's measurements.

She saw almost nothing of Montgomery, except for one evening when he presented her with a necklace which she tried to refuse. A large emerald was set in silver, surrounded by smaller stones. There were earrings to match. And though he pressed the gift on her, there was no warmth to his voice or smile on his face. He seemed unaware of the shiver that ran down her spine when he lifted her black curls and touched her neck as he fastened the catch for her.

He had given her another present, even more precious. For Caroline had been in residence for about a month when a young woman burst in through the open door, her fresh face shining and happy.

It was Mary Williams, scrubbed and dressed in a new frock and apron, and clumsy in an endearing way. Her joy, when she saw Caroline dressed in a beautiful gray velvet gown and sitting quietly and peacefully in her sitting room, knew no bounds.

"Oh, Miss!" Mary cried. "You look ever so beautiful and so much happier. The Captain have explained it to me, and I'll do anything to help you, Miss. I can't believe you remembered me, Miss, just like that . . ." She gushed on and on, silenced at last when she realized Caroline was simply smiling at her, but not saying a word.

Mary gave her a probing, concerned look. And Caroline, who had learned something of the world by now, blushed at the implication. She had been sitting up by her window, comfortable and warm, absorbed with her own thoughts and her needlework, looking for all the world like a woman dreaming on her unborn child.

In the meantime, word was being bruited about through the household that Mary was the replacement for the "unsuitable" lady's maid who had accompanied Emma upon her arrival and been promptly dismissed.

Jupiter had been retrieved from Wales along with Mary and was now home in the stables. This seemed to lift Montgomery's spirits, but it was hard to tell because he was rarely at home. He spent the holidays with friends on a country estate, and was back in London for a week before Caroline so much as saw him.

Emma was still a dear friend, but she and Mary sometimes spent much of the day riding in Montgomery's carriage, being seen, and patronizing the fashionable shops. So Caroline was very much alone.

She'd put on weight, much to Emma's delight, and it began to seem her dresses would have to be altered back to the original size dictated by Emma's figure. It was no wonder, with nothing to do all day but read and eat, and with Mrs. Gregory's cooking. When it wasn't a roasted lobster, it was tench with a pudding right in its belly. Or rabbits smothered with onions, or mutton chops. And Mrs. Gregory put the most amazing things inside a pieshell: mince, eels with currants, veal scallops stuffed with spinach, artichoke hearts baked with dates and orange peel, pigeons. Every day there was tea with dainties or macaroons.

Caroline had grown to enjoy these treats so much, she realized Emma had been quite right: she should be most sorry to have to ever live in poverty again.

Mary grew daily more skilled in dressing Caroline's hair and due to her outings with Emma she soon knew her way around London quite well.

One day was so much like the next, though, that at

times Caroline felt like a sleepwalker. Life went on for everyone else, but for her it was all unchanging. Emma and Mary told her how beautiful she looked, and as the most bitter cold weather passed, she took to wearing satins and laces instead of velvets. It was one mark that time was passing, but how slowly, how slowly.

One day Mary dashed upstairs laughing to show Caroline a new treasure—a snowdrop she had found in the garden. Now that she had proof that springtime was really arriving, Caroline found herself in a sudden panic. She had waited and waited, but now that Emma would be going, and the formidable Cousin Annabelle taking her place, she was frightened. Caroline had longed to be allowed outside, but now she feared to face the *ton*. Girls from the provinces were treated badly enough by the ambitious socially prominent mamas and by their intriguing daughters. Reputations were lost over trifles as it was. How would she be able to hold up her head among people like that? Even as a respectable daughter of a Yorkshire country gentleman, Caroline knew she would have met with scorn. And she doubted that her parents would ever have dreamed of launching her into the select circles that Montgomery seemed to take for granted.

She thought she'd give anything to be riding Jupiter once more, with Montgomery's cloak about her shivering shoulders. She'd give anything to be seeing Emma for the first time, bowing slightly as she climbed into the carriage. She called to mind the happy expression on Mary's face, the first day that the girl had burst into the room. Oh, to go backward instead of ahead!

The road thus far had been exciting and filled with special moments, but now that spring had come, Caroline was afraid she didn't have the courage to follow her road through to the end.

"Aren't you glad, Miss?" asked Mary.

Caroline assured her she was overcome with happiness. If she'd admitted the sight of the flower had upset her, poor Mary would have been cast into the doldrums. These days, more and more, it seemed polite behavior meant hiding her true feelings.

But what a foolish time to despair! Caroline recalled that in all her worst moments, someone had appeared like a guardian angel to help her. From the anonymous gentleman who'd kept her supplied with books to read to Captain Montgomery who'd done much more than could ever have been expected. She had to count herself a very lucky girl, and it was mean and ungrateful not to be smiling.

The first daffodils were bursting from the earth like so many little flames of sun when Montgomery's letter was dispatched to the Lady Annabelle, and a week later they had her reply. She would be glad to be sponsor to his young ward, and would arrive in town the afternoon of the fourteenth.

"So you must arrive that night," said Montgomery. "I shall go to fetch you, and the servants will welcome my cousin to the house."

He ordered up a supper that was fit for a celebration, but Caroline and Emma were hardly in a festive mood.

Mary had taken on the job of serving at table, which was irregular, but suited the other servants who preferred to stay away from the sinful third floor. It was one thing to establish a mistress in lodgings, after all, and quite another to install her under your own roof!

So it was Mary who carried in course after course, starting with three kinds of pâté, ranging from an old-fashioned liver-currant spread enlivened with nutmeg, to two new and garlicky recipes that had been circulated by a French prisoner-of-war trying to ingratiate himself with his English "hosts." The oyster-lamb casserole was topped with asparagus, the turnip steamed in wine and stuffed with apple. There was boiled cod with oyster sauce, roast beef with pudding, roast goose, and a cold tongue.

The ladies barely touched their food, much as Mary urged them to eat. But the abigail had formed a close attachment to Emma, too, and found it hard to keep from crying at this last evening together. Mary, who had found life full of miracles since being freed from the mines, couldn't believe that the brave and rich Captain Montgomery could simply accept the rules of society. Though she would never have dared or wished to argue with him, the thought of separating two ladies who were such bosom friends seemed cruel and unnecessary. Caroline was of the same opinion, but Emma, who knew more of London, was resigned.

Once the dishes had been cleared, Caroline could contain herself no longer. "I can't believe we shall never see one another again!" she cried, throwing her arms around her friend, but still restraining her tears.

"Of course we shall see each other," Emma reassured her, stroking the black hair she had once spent the morning brushing. "Roderick will take you to see me at Drury Lane when I am famous as Mrs. Siddons, won't you, Captain?" she demanded of Montgomery who stood uncomfortably by the fireplace staring at his highly polished Hessians as though he expected to find a spot on them. "And when I play Desdemona, while I lie across the bed, dead and gone, I shall open my eyes for an instant and wink at you up in your box."

Caroline smiled at the thought, but her distress was still evident. "But someday, if my position becomes finally secure, do say that we shall do as we like and see one another again."

"I hope so," whispered Emma, unwilling to mislead her friend with too many false hopes.

Caroline hugged her warmly, then ran into her bedchamber and locked the door.

Then Emma and Montgomery could hear her crying in great and pitiful abandon.

CHAPTER SEVEN

Before dawn on April fourteenth, Montgomery led Caroline out of doors for the first time in almost four months. He had apologized greatly for the inconvenience she was about to suffer, but Caroline was so pleased to be away from her room, that no discomfort would have plagued her overmuch. Silently, he helped her step up into his carriage. The mornings were still frosty and cold, and she sat muffled in the raven cloak of which she had such strong and compelling memories.

Montgomery returned with some hot bricks for the floor, and Caroline settled herself on the floor as well without waiting for him to remind her. She was sure he would be pained to have to make the request. Although the carriage was closed, the horses had yet to be harnessed. The footman, the coachman, and the stableboys would soon be about, so this additional precaution had to be taken to keep Caroline from view. Also, the conspirators had decided not to cover the windows. No one must suspect a mystery.

She lay cramped and uncomfortable, wondering how she would survive the next several hours, and yet excited that the last stage of her life-in-hiding had begun. Montgomery threw a carriage rug over her form, and tucked it gently around her. His lips brushed her forehead lightly. "Good luck," he whispered.

Caroline felt herself flush and was glad Montgomery had softly disappeared again. She drew the cloak more closely around her, felt the bricks warm and comforting beneath, and settled in for a wait.

In the meantime, the script was proceeding inside the house just as Emma had planned and rehearsed it.

At five thirty in the morning, Mary ran down to the kitchen in tears. Mrs. Gregory was making herself a cup of chocolate, and raised her eyebrows uncertainly at the girl who burst into the kitchen and collapsed in a chair. Because Mary had been lodged upstairs, almost secretly, and led a life removed from the servants' hall, there had been a certain amount of gossip and resentment about her. But Mrs. Gregory's reserve and possible hostility were soon melted by the sight of so many tears. Mary was not a great actress, so Emma had taken advantage of the girl's real distress and had given her lines that were so close to the truth she should have no difficulty in giving a believable performance.

"What's wrong, my girl?" asked Mrs. Gregory, still keeping her distance.

"Oh, what's to become of the young Miss?" wailed Mary. "He's sending 'er away, out there in the cold!" Mary was thinking of poor Caroline, wrapped up like a parcel on the floor of the carriage, even though she knew the lines were meant to refer to Emma. "What's to become of 'er?" she cried.

Mrs. Gregory was moved to see such loyalty in an

abigail, misplaced though it might be. She recalled that Mary had not arrived in the house together with the actress creature, but rather had been fetched—who could say why?—all the way from Wales.

"Dear girl." The cook put a wide hand on Mary's heaving shoulders. "What could you expect, what with the Lady Annabelle coming to town. The Cap'n couldna very well keep the woman upstairs what with his cousin takin' up residence here. Your young lady will do aright for herself, for that kind always does get by."

"She was kind to me," cried Mary, "And now I'm to remain behind to serve another while she is out in the cold."

While Mrs. Gregory gave the girl a cup of chocolate and tried to ease her mind, Jenkins, the butler, was watching as the groom hitched up four greys, and more significantly, as Montgomery marched stiffly down the steps.

"Well, are you coming?" he asked snappishly, turning his head. The actress followed. There were tears at the corners of Emma's eyes, but she held her head proud and high.

The expression on Jenkins's face did not change, but he noted the proceedings with an inward chuckle of satisfaction. So he's packing his lightskirt off and away, he thought, *before the old dragon moves in.*

Once Emma had climbed into the carriage—struggling first without assistance in mounting, and then propelled by a rude shove to her hindquarters which surprised the watching servants into gales of unbecoming laughter—Montgomery turned back to the house.

"Jenkins," he said sharply. "I've already asked that the Pink Room be made ready for Lady Annabelle. However, my ward will also be arriving from Wales. Please see that Lily prepares the Green Room for her use. I don't know how many—if any—we'll be for dinner, but let Mrs. Gregory know we'll be three for supper."

"Yes, sir," said Jenkins, and the young master was gone.

Montgomery's next step was to dismiss the coachman. "I'll take the ribbons myself," he said. And the man happily absented himself. His employer was surely in one of the foulest of moods ever.

By then, Mary and Mrs. Gregory were very much in charity with one another. Mrs. Gregory was especially pleased with Mary's honest exclamation, "It will be good to be 'ere with the rest of you! It's been so long since I 'ad a friend to be with!" Mary's happiness at being a legitimate part of the household at last was as sincere as the real tears she was shedding in worry for her mistress.

Jenkins stayed at the front window to catch the last glimpse of Emma's profile, haughty and unbowed, as she was being driven back to the streets where the Captain had found her. He shook his head with satisfaction.

And Caroline was enduring the terrible jostling and bouncing of the vehicle. The plan seemed so desperate at this point. Surely such measures could only be warranted in a matter of life and death. But the Captain and Emma had both assured her it would be worth it in the end.

It was open daylight by the time Montgomery dropped Emma at the lodgings she had occupied before joining in his scheme. He had continued to pay her rent throughout the winter, so that she should have no trouble returning. There were people on the street and faces at many windows, all remarking Emma as she marched away from the carriage, shivering under her pelisse.

It's going to work, she was thinking. *It's going to work.*

The tears began to pour down her lovely cheeks just before she reached the shelter and privacy of the door.

Caroline could hear the bustle of people in the streets, the snorts of horses, the clatter of other vehicles around them. She scarcely dared to breathe. *Don't think about it,* she ordered herself sternly, but anxiety kept her pulse racing. Soon, she thought, soon, they would leave the city behind. Soon, on an empty stretch of highway—if only they found themselves quickly alone on the road!—Montgomery would rein the horses to a halt and then turn the carriage around for the return trip to London. Then Caroline would be able to sit on the seat like a human being. They'd return as far as the Rose and Thistle—a coaching inn of the finest quality, and there they would take a table just as the stage from Cardiff was leaving for the last leg of its London route. Caroline was to appear a disembarking stage passenger, and Montgomery, the gentleman sent to accompany her home. They were counting on confusion, on many travelers being served luncheon, and on many trunks being unloaded. They would partake of their meal in full public view and would linger until the messenger reached them with word that Cousin Annabelle was safely installed in the house. It would all be so easy.

But the shouts and noises of the city were still all around her, and it seemed that hours had already passed since Emma had walked out of her life. Emma had reached beneath the rug and squeezed Caroline's hand for a moment before she'd gone on to play her part, walking back to her old life of hard work and much insecurity.

Running risks seemed to bring out affection in people, thought Caroline. Emma squeezing her hand. And more important, Montgomery leaning over to give her courage with a soft, chaste kiss.

"I should hate to see a day," said Montgomery, as they sat over their neck of mutton at the Rose and Thistle, "when in some future world, we send women out to fight our wars." It had been so long since they'd spent any time together, and now, conscious of the shared risks of their adventure, the Captain and his young "ward" felt warmly one to the other. "All the same," he continued, "if I'd had soldiers like you and Emma, and even Mary, under my command, I expect we'd have won the war by now. I don't know how you'll fare in your first skirmish at Almack's, but in my opinion, you've already earned your medals."

These compliments made Caroline's face glow, and Montgomery looked upon her proudly. The months of rest and proper diet in his home had worked wonders. She had been a beauty before, but now . . . She was radiant. Her face had filled out with no more gaunt hollows. Her skin was still white as milk, but before it had had the pallor and dryness of the sickroom. He had not seen her shoulders bare in months, but as he'd adjusted the rug about her, he'd felt them plump and warm, no longer skeletal and frail. Her simple traveling dress, with embroidered ornamentation, had stood up well. It was no more creased than one would expect of a frock that had been through a more conventional journey. Her black hair was still her crowning glory, now more lustrous than ever.

For her part, Caroline was thinking how handsome he appeared in his blue satin coat and modish yellow breeches. Most of all, though, it was his smile that transformed his lean face. It had been so long since she'd seen him smile.

As if sensing that this was a moment in which she could expect him to be indulgent, Caroline took a deep breath for courage and asked a favor. "I know you've done too much for me already, but I was thinking, I would appreciate it so much if you could do something for Emma."

He nodded, pleased that the girl's nature still looked so quickly and consistently to the good of others. "Emma will be well paid for her part in this," he assured her.

"Oh, I was sure you would be generous. But what I was thinking," Caroline went on, "I collect it's a very uncertain life in the theater. Rather than money or jewels or whatever it is you think to give her, wouldn't it be a good idea to buy Emma some shares in the theater?"

"Shares in the theater?"

"Yes. They must be looking for investors to rebuild the Drury Lane, aren't they? If she had some shares, then when she has no role, or when the day comes that she retires from her profession, she can still share in the profits. And she does love the stage so. This way she'll always be a part of it . . ."

"I don't know that women have held shares in a business like that before," he replied, somewhat amused, but also somewhat impressed by the astuteness of Caroline's reasoning. "However, I'll see what can be arranged."

This answer completely satisfied Caroline, who remembered how Montgomery had expressed doubts about bringing Mary to London and had made no promises, and then gone to considerable trouble and expense to grant Caroline's wish.

Neither of the travelers had begun to grow impatient, when a young boy appeared with a message for Captain Montgomery.

"Well," said the Captain, standing, and offering Caroline his arm, "my respected cousin is in residence. Shall we go?"

"Yes, Captain Montgomery," she replied demurely. "I am so anxious to meet my guardian's dear relation."

"I sometimes forget Emma is the actress," chuckled Montgomery.

"Emma? Who is she?" asked Caroline, the words catching a moment in her throat.

Caroline's second trip into London was far more exciting than the first. The prospect of meeting Lady Annabelle was even more nerve-shattering than the thought of hiding upstairs. She wished Montgomery had allowed her to sit up on the box beside him because there were so many questions she wanted to ask about the cousin. But it was time for ladylike behavior now. Although she was free at last, there were other rules to obey, and Caroline sat proper and straight alone.

This second trip was also her first real chance to see the city that had been her home since November.

Even before they reached Westminster Bridge, Caroline could see St. Paul's—its gold cross and its dome, striking and dominant, rising above the city and right against the sky. There was the Tower, and now the brick buildings and church spires that had appeared in so different an aspect from her window. Her eyes were drawn again and again and again to the Tower. She too knew what imprisonment was like, but she had been well-fed and gently treated, and her confinement was a prelude to happiness rather than to merciless justice.

Montgomery had no sooner reined up the coach than the coachman came running out to see to the horses.

Caroline looked at Chelton House for the first time in calm daylight, and was glad to see its simple elegant proportions, its carefully joined white stone, and its classically simple portico. Many of the homes they had passed in the fashionable part of town had been ornamented with heavy Gothic touches. Although she knew even the Prince of Wales favored some Gothicism at Carlton House, for some reason, Caroline could not help but think it a barbarous style, and the thought of barbarity brought her uncle readily to mind. She'd never had a real chance to look at Montgomery's London house before, and had not completely known what to expect.

As they entered, and the servants greeted them, she was pleased and relieved that no one seemed to associate the well-dressed young lady before them with the pitiful ragged creature who had once appeared carrying an actress's reticule.

Mary was so pleased to see her, her face lit up in a bright and happy smile that Caroline feared would surely give them away. But Mrs. Gregory, Jenkins, Lily, and the others were too busy scrutinizing the new guest to notice the reaction of an awkward little abigail.

"And Miss Caroline's trunks?" asked Jenkins as Montgomery began to direct his ward to the drawing room where Lady Annabelle was taking tea.

"They will be delivered later," replied the Captain, and Caroline didn't dare throw him a quizzical glance, although she knew very well she hadn't any trunks. If Montgomery expected the plan to succeed, he really ought to advise her of the stories he intended to tell.

Caroline had no further time to wonder about the handsome, yet distant, man who stood rigidly beside her, because the next moment she was being introduced to Lady Annabelle, an aging caricature who sat straight and proper, careful not to let her own stiff back touch the high back of the caned Restoration chair.

At first glance, Lady Annabelle seemed harmless. Her hoop skirt, bustle, and white powdered wig bespoke the fashions of a much earlier time, and gave a hint that the old lady had lost touch with reality. The diamonds and pearls which dressed her hair style in the most elaborate fashion failed to hide the fact that the wig was set awry on her aged head. But the piercing blue eyes were sharp and alert, and Caroline rightly guessed that appearances were deceiving. Lady Annabelle appraised the girl slowly and Caroline knew her "sponsor" would not miss very much.

"You look very fresh, my dear, for a girl that's been traveling all the way from Wales," were the first words Lady Annabelle spoke. The words came out in a comical cracked voice; the observation was astute. "How long *were* you traveling, girl?"

Montgomery hadn't prepared Caroline at all to answer such questions.

"After the first few days," she replied, struggling to keep her tone even, "I quite lost count of time."

"Really," added the Captain, "I find the worst part of a journey by stage is entering London with the noise and crowds. You know you've reached your destination, and yet it seems to take an eternity until you are finally handed down again to terra firma at the appropriate stopping-place. On the open road, rutted though it may be, one rides in relative peace. That's why I met Caroline's coach at the Rose and Thistle, so she should at least make the last part of the journey in relative comfort."

Lady Annabelle reflected, then appeared to accept this story. "Though I dare say, the young lady's beauty had something to do with your haste and concern."

"I'm glad she meets with your approval," said the Captain. "I know your discriminating taste, and should feel sorry indeed had I asked you to sponsor someone you considered a Homely Joan."

The old lady reached and lifted Caroline's chin. "Come closer, dear," she ordered. Then, "Yes, you are a beauty, but that doesn't mean you meet with my approval. It takes more than a pretty face . . ."

Whatever Montgomery's shrewd cousin suspected, at least Caroline reasoned she could never guess the truth, that Caroline had been living in the house for over four months, that only that very morning she had been smuggled out and wrapped in a rug, only to be returned, transformed, in the afternoon. The thought made Caroline want to laugh.

"I'll expect your respect, young lady," added Lady Annabelle. "I congratulate you on your ability to control your mirth. I know my appearance amuses many of your contemporaries, but if I choose to remember my youth—or my mother's youth—that is my affair. You'd do well to keep it in mind that I still have great influence over a number of ladies I believe you will want to meet. Even Lady Jersey and the Countess Lieven dare not criticize my fashion of clothing or speech, and they extend certain courtesies to my friends."

Montgomery added nothing to the conversation. When Caroline stole a glance at him, he sat formal and distant, lost in his own thoughts. Exhausted, and at a loss, Caroline used her long journey as an excuse to be allowed to retire to her room.

It was Lady Annabelle, rather than Montgomery, who coolly took the role of head of the household, by ringing for Mary and directing her to show Caroline upstairs.

"The Green Room, milady?" asked Mary, bobbing

an awkward curtsey. A narrow smile curved on Lady Annabelle's face. The abigail was unpracticed and fresh from the country—the perfect choice for the inexperienced young lady.

Oh, it would be amusing to watch the faux pas Caroline was certain to make. And it would be equally amusing to see how she would extricate herself, if she could. Her beauty would help.

Lady Annabelle took Caroline by the wrist and detained her a moment. "Thanks to my friends, you won't wait long for a voucher to Almack's. Other girls from the best of families won't gain admission so easily."

"I hardly think my ward is ready for Almack's," argued the Captain.

"Roderick, dear," The old lady smiled a cruel smile. "I have full confidence in her. Don't you?"

Caroline left the room, hoping to miss Montgomery's reply.

"Wherever did you find that curious little girl?" asked the old woman's high voice, loud enough so that Caroline and Mary could hear her from the hall.

"I told you," replied Montgomery absently. "Her brother was with me . . ."

"No, no, you muttonhead," scolded the Dragon. "Not your ward, I mean that poor rustic little abigail."

And if Mary was displeased to hear herself called a poor rustic, Caroline's heart sank to think Montgomery looked upon her as a "curious little girl."

"I wish Miss Emma was a real lady," cried Mary once they'd reached the safety of the Green Room. " 'Twas a sight better 'aving *'er* around."

"I don't know that a real lady is the nicest thing in the world to be," sighed Caroline, and let Mary undress her and brush out her dusky ringlets until she relaxed enough to look around at her new room. The Green

Room was more old-fashioned than the chamber she had occupied on the third floor. Caroline knew little about how to date the furnishings, but the bed hangings were a clue. In the Green Room, these were of linen. Flowers and birds and fish were embroidered lavishly and boldly in chain-stitched silken floss. The linens obviously dated back to the time before cotton was allowed free entry into England. Caroline was amazed that the curtains and canopy smelled fresh and the fabric remained strong, for the manufacture surely dated back to the previous century. Whoever had purchased the furnishings of the Green Room, and the artisans and workmen who had created them, were probably all long dead.

"Do you want to sleep, Miss?" urged Mary.

"No," Caroline replied. "It's just I have such a headache . . ."

"No wonder, Miss. I was so afeared you'd choke the life out of you this morning. I worried fer you, Miss."

Mary encouraged Caroline to sit back on the bed and she piled pillows behind her head.

There was a knock at the door. "Your trunks have arrived, Miss Caroline," advised Jenkins.

Caroline was still wondering what trunks, when two large boxes were conveyed inside. She nodded to Mary who opened the latches, and then Caroline soon jumped out of the bed to join the girl.

"Oh, 'ow beautiful, Miss! I didn't know you 'ad such fine things!" cried Mary.

Nor did I, thought Caroline silently. She lifted a satin dress shot through with gold threads. From a hatbox she removed a bonnet with its curling ostrich plumes. It was beautiful, but Caroline questioned herself whether it was not better suited for a person of more years than herself. She blushed at the sight of the next dress, pale green with flounces of lace, and silk embroidered roses. Seed pearls clung to the petals like dew. Even without trying the gown on, she could tell the bodice was cut much lower than she would consider proper. No, how could anyone think these items came out of her wardrobe?

Mary pulled out a white satin petticoat, with an embossed silver trim. Most shocking of all was a small casket which Caroline opened to find full of jewels. She shook her head, almost trembling. She would happily wear Montgomery's emeralds, just for the memory of how his hands had felt on her bare neck. Her brother's sapphire still rode near her heart. But how could she wear these diamond armlets and brooches? What did she need with chains of amethysts and ruby earrings set in gold filigree?

" 'Ow beautiful!" exclaimed Mary, beside herself. "An' these be all yers?"

"No," answered Caroline simply.

"But then why are they . . ."

"Apparently Captain Montgomery has had them sent."

" 'E must love you, Miss," said Mary, holding the earrings to Caroline's delicate earlobes and admiring the effect.

And I thought I knew nothing of the world, Caroline reflected. *Poor Mary knows even less. She hasn't yet perceived that appearances and gestures tell us so very little.*

"I can't wait to 'elp you dress for dinner." Mary was so very eager, so easily made happy.

"But I shan't wear any of these . . ." Caroline began to protest, but then reconsidered. She wouldn't want Montgomery to think she was ungrateful for the gifts. Besides, as she looked at the new dresses, she couldn't help herself. Her own enthusiasm for the new wardrobe began to grow till the touch of the satins and silks transported her into a fairyland with almost as much ease as Mary had been carried away in rapture.

Mary was delighted by her mistress's change of heart and helped her into a loose violet satin tunic. They laced it up with the amethyst chains.

"This would look so lovely on Emma," commented Caroline. But Mary just laughed and held up the hand-glass.

"Miss Emma is quite beautiful, Miss," she argued respectfully. "But look in the glass. She never looked so beautiful like you do now."

Will Montgomery think so? Caroline wondered hesitantly. Did she want him to? She wasn't sure. She only knew that she felt so much happier herself when he was smiling and at ease. Now with Lady Annabelle in the house, they might never again have the opportunity to be friends, talking quietly and hopefully, as they'd done over luncheon at the Rose and Thistle.

She descended the stairs slowly.

Lady Annabelle was waiting. She smiled maliciously when Caroline appeared. "How very elegant for a quiet supper at home!" she exclaimed. Her compliment hurt Caroline more than a direct criticism would have done. Lady Annabelle had changed her clothes, too. Now she was dressed in a simple frock. Her elaborate wig was gone, and in its place, a house cap. "The best thing about being home," she continued, "is that one can relax and dress simply. Cleanliness and simplicity, that's what true beauty is all about. Don't you agree, dear?"

"When you can't think of an answer, best just to smile," Emma had said once. So Caroline smiled.

And kept the smile frozen on her face, even though Montgomery chose not to join the ladies for supper.

CHAPTER EIGHT

In spite of Lady Annabelle, the next few weeks were a real delight to Caroline. She was free at last to travel about London, and as Lady Annabelle was often indisposed and chose to remain behind, sometimes she was able to leave the house accompanied only by Mary. Then she could breathe freely and enjoy life to the utmost.

Gloves were fitted to her hands and boots to her feet in the finest shops, but Caroline much preferred walking and exploring to buying. Her new respectable status made it possible for her to visit booksellers and make her own selections rather than rely on what others might bring her.

One morning on St. James's Street, a laughing crowd caught her attention at number three.

"They look a lusty lot, Miss," warned Mary, who tried to restrain Caroline from going closer to determine the cause of such jollity.

"Don't be an addlepate," said Caroline. "After the

dangers we've both faced, how can a few merry gentlemen in their cups make us turn our steps?"

In the front of the Berry Brothers establishment hung two huge scales, and in one of these sat a young dandy with windswept hair, clad in modish yellow skin-tight breeches. He held his head proudly over an impeccably creased white starched cravat, and he was taking a pinch of snuff with an elegant-mannered gesture. George Berry, the wine merchant and proprietor, was loading cases of fine imported wines into the other scale while the dandy's companions were betting on how many cases it would take for the balance to be even.

"Is this 'ow porter get to market in London?" marveled Mary as they drew near. "Weighed in the balance like tea?"

Caroline was perplexed, too, but then hit upon the answer. "The balances *were* for tea!" she exclaimed. "Smell the air, Mary! You can still smell it. This must have once been a coffee and spice shop."

Caroline's remark aroused the interest of a haughty gentleman. He helped himself to snuff from a jeweled enameled box with a gesture that lacked the grace of the young dandy but was intended to show off the Dresden ruffles on his cuffs and the large glinting diamonds on his fingers. His shirtpoints were so starched and high, they rose against his fat, hanging jowls. Looking straight at Caroline, but ostensibly addressing his remark to a companion, he spoke in a loud whisper that reached Caroline's ears: "Keen as a good hunting dog, that one."

Without hesitation, he stepped forward and presented himself as Lord St. Clair.

"Are you new to London, Miss Bramwell?" he asked upon learning her name. "You must be, because I cannot recall seeing you before, and yours is not a face that would be forgotten."

"I am visiting with my guardian, Captain Roderick Montgomery, and his cousin, Lady Annabelle," she answered modestly enough.

St. Clair responded with a peal of laughter. "Is the Lady Annabelle still so . . . original?" he asked.

Disagreeable though St. Clair seemed to be, Caroline warmed to him at once to see he was not awed by too much respect for the old Dragon.

"Come now," urged St. Clair, in response to Caroline's smile, "you are new to London and so must follow the rules of St. James's Street."

Still more rules?

"It is customary to weigh each young lady come to town upon her arrival," he said, gesturing to the scales where the dandy was seated. Caroline was quite aware the man was lying, but the thought of taking a seat on the balance caught her imagination.

A spirit of rebellion had begun to color Caroline's acts. Lady Annabelle was clearly trying to make her feel uncomfortable. Caroline knew that even if she catered to the woman's every whim and behaved like a perfect pattern-card of decorum, Lady Annabelle would find her lacking. So rather than appear merely inexperienced and foolish, Caroline had resolved to be shocking. She would let the woman—important though she might be—see that Caroline Bramwell would not be intimidated.

Caroline did not fear Montgomery's displeasure either. If he were angry, perhaps he would take some time to talk with her. Even his voice raised in anger would be preferable to his neglect. Caroline missed him, because since his elderly cousin had arrived at

Chelton House, Montgomery no longer considered Caroline his responsibility. He saw that she had everything money could buy, but he simply had no time for her anymore.

And if she gave rise to so much scandal-broth that she ruined her prospects, Caroline was not too concerned. High society no longer seemed like something to aspire to. With Montgomery by her side, she wanted to prove herself his equal. But with only Lady Annabelle for a companion, Caroline simply didn't care what the *ton* might think of her.

She looked St. Clair directly in the eye. "If it is custom, I can hardly refuse," she said in a demure voice that provided an effective contrast to her bold eye.

"You are unseated, Wentworth," cried St. Clair, "for the lady will take your place."

The men looked around at Caroline with astonishment.

"No, no," interrupted Caroline, and St. Clair smiled to see how easily he had embarrassed the girl and how cruelly she'd become aware of her error. "Pray be seated, Mr. Wentworth. I shall be weighed, but not against casks and bottles. I shall match my wit—or my weight—against any man or woman."

"You mean you'll be balanced with Wentworth, here, Miss?" asked the proprietor, his eyes agog. George Berry was accustomed to the pranks of the gay blades who frequented the vicinity, but no lady—not even Harriette Wilson or any other of the fashionable lightskirts—had ever joined in.

"But the fight must be fair," continued Caroline. "I must insist that Mr. Wentworth remove his boots, as they give him an advantage."

"Next we'll be seeing mills for the ladies," commented an observer with disapproval.

"Miss, you can't do this," whispered Mary.

"Oh, but I shall."

Caroline watched while two friends knelt and pulled off the highly polished and buffed Hessians from Wentworth's legs.

"Be careful where you put those, man!" Wentworth was losing humor with the situation. "And I hope your hands were clean. You have no idea how hard I work to keep my Hessians from shaming me . . . Shall I remove anything else, dear lady?" he asked.

"I believe that will do," said Caroline agreeably.

Then, while young Mary wrung her hands, Caroline let herself be helped into the scale. The balance jounced a few moments, then settled with Caroline a good foot higher than her competitor.

"But who is to be the winner?" demanded Wentworth. "We never did set our terms, whether the winner was to be the heavier or the lighter."

"The winner is obviously the bird who flies higher," answered St. Clair. "The lady has triumphed."

"A generous concession," said Caroline pleasantly as she was helped back to the ground. "But I expect you believe the real winner to be yourself."

Mary did not know whether to laugh or cry as she followed Caroline down the street. "I dearly 'ope they don't 'ear of this back at the 'ouse," she repeated, while Caroline just as repeatedly assured her that London society kept no secrets.

That afternoon, at fashionable five, Caroline was seated beside Lady Annabelle in that distinguished person's carriage riding through Hyde Park. They exchanged smiles and nods with other elderly ladies, snubbed the people Lady Annabelle said it was necessary to snub, and were aware of many curious stares. Caroline felt the eyes of many men upon her, and drew her shawl higher, partly because the weather was still a trifle chilly and also because her new dress was cut, she thought, too low. None of the intrigued young gentlemen dared approach the carriage, however, while Lady Annabelle sat in proud guard.

The buds had begun to come out in leaf on the trees. New grass was beginning to poke its way through the soft earth, but the ground was not barren thanks to some grass that had remained green beneath the snows.

Lady Annabelle said little, but at least she was not antagonistic or critical. Caroline knew that word of the morning had not yet reached her ears. She began to feel very foolish. By the time the storm broke, the incident would have lost its flavor. The fun would seem so terribly insignificant compared to the trouble her little prank was bound to cause.

Caroline shrugged. Surely, after all her years of unhappiness, she was entitled at last to do as she pleased on occasion. But that's not the way life is in London, she reminded herself.

Caroline was awakened that night by the sound of knocking at her door. "Come in," she responded automatically, and to her surprise, it was Montgomery who entered the chamber. She knew at once why he had come, for as soon as she lit her lamp, she could see the angry sparks in his eyes. He'd heard about the morning in St. James's Street even if his cousin had not.

"Sir, a gentleman doesn't enter a lady's bedchamber," she said coldly, her heart beating wildly with guilt and other feelings she couldn't name.

"I've seen you with the covers pulled to your chin before," he said, scowling. He closed the door behind him. "Besides, today you proved you are no lady."

She began to speak, but Montgomery cut her off. "I

won't even speak of ingratitude, but think of my family's good name! All these months you've been living under my roof. Even before that, I left important matters which had been entrusted to me and spent weeks retrieving you from Wales. I acknowledge your situation has been difficult, but now, when you are free, how could you behave in such a way? Jumping onto a set of scales as though you were to be sold by the pound?"

"Most unfortunate," said Caroline, "considering you've already paid your eight hundred guineas for me." She paused, then added weakly, "Lord St. Clair told me this was a custom that one must abide by."

"And I'll wager you knew better," snapped Montgomery. He paced the room, not even looking at her, trying to keep his voice down. "You have the sense of a cook-maid, but more wit than a cabinet minister. You knew better."

"It's no wonder I've the sense of a cook-maid when you consider that's what I've been most of my adult life," was her rejoinder. Her voice was cool, but Caroline was seized with agitation. It had been days since she had seen the Captain, even in company, and over a week since they had spent a moment alone. She had dressed in the fine clothes he'd sent her, but when he was not there to see her, the dresses shot with gold embroidery seemed more mockery than generosity.

"And it's a cook-maid you shall end." Yes, his tone was mocking enough. "Though I'd say you haven't reached adult status yet. This was the act of a willful child, and now my family must face the consequences. You've even made the Betting Book at Brooks's—fifty guineas against twenty-five that Lady Annabelle drives you forth from the house when she learns your true *measure.*"

Like many a guilty person, Caroline quickly grasped at the opportunity to turn the situation around. "The Betting Book? And you, sir, criticize my behavior, an embarrassing faux pas, I'll allow, but something I did without intending any harm to your illustrious name, while you gentlemen of the *ton* find it fashionable and proper to spend your nights drinking and gaming."

"You'll not get off so easily, my dear," he warned her. "I begin to wonder if you have not some morbidity like your uncle, that prevents you from behaving as one ought."

This was a sore point with Caroline, and one that almost left her without rejoinder. But no, she would not be outdone. "I'll own, dear sir, that my family is no pattern-card of respectability. But there's another lesson I learned from my parents, and that is, that more good families have been ruined by wagers and gambling than by a young girl's indiscretions." Her voice wavered in an imitation of distress that would have done credit to Emma, but Montgomery's sympathies were not engaged. She backed further and further against her pillows as he approached and bent over her with a threatening glare.

"I shall scream for assistance," she whispered, and he clamped a strong, hard hand over her mouth. His cold eyes penetrated into her heart and she fiercely longed to beg his forgiveness and promise to make amends. But his roughness angered her, so that, frightened and guilty as she was, Caroline was too proud to admit he was in the right.

"Do we understand one another at last?" he asked, and his hand set her lips free.

She glared back at him, hating his distance, his arrogance, the way he treated her, the way he abandoned her to the company of his cousin. Yes, he had done much for her, but she'd never asked for his favors. He had carried her to a new life, and could at least treat her civilly. She wasn't going to fawn on him or press herself to obey his every command.

"Stand back, sir," she said, her eyes flashing like a cat's in the lamplight. "The smell of gin makes me faint."

He recoiled as if hit. The hatred in her voice had been barely disguised. Then, "Don't put on those missish airs with me," he growled, but stood back all the same. "Don't call for your smelling-salts in front of me," he added at the door. His tall figure cast an even taller shadow in the flickering light. "Remember, my dear," he said, "I know what you are."

She choked her tears of hurt and rage in the pillow. What an unfeeling monster he could be. Precisely because he did know her past, as he had so cruelly reminded her, was all the more reason for her to expect kindness from him. They had shared so much. She had trusted him—not just with her honor, whatever that concept might signify. In some intangible way she couldn't express, she had trusted him.

But he was an inhuman monster without feeling. It was awful to think how stupid she had been to love him.

To love him as a friend, she amended her thoughts.

A girl had to be mad to love him in any fashion, she thought. *As a friend*, she reminded herself again, *as a friend, only a friend*, as she cried her way into a world of uneasy dreams.

CHAPTER NINE

Days went by and there was no change in Lady Annabelle's manner. Caroline would have concluded that Lady Annabelle remained ignorant of the escapade, except for a remark she let fall at nuncheon. "They raise some high-spirited fillies out in Yorkshire," she said. "Is that where you said you were from, dear?" And when Caroline began to review her family history, Lady Annabelle made it clear she had not really been soliciting an answer to her question.

Perhaps the old woman's apparel was the way she herself showed her scorn for convention. Caroline wondered if she had won the Dragon's affection at the same time that she had alienated Montgomery. It was also possible that Lady Annabelle was glad to see Caroline misbehave because it gave her a chance to demonstrate her own power: the girl *she* was sponsoring would have to be given another chance. But sometimes, Caroline caught a strange, self-absorbed look in the woman's old eyes and then she thought that Lady Annabelle was simply bored and unhappy and would welcome disaster as much as success—anything to make the day a little different.

"I am having a dinner party," announced the dowager one morning.

Caroline put down the book she was reading, and when she realized in annoyance that she had failed to mark her place, she decided that Lady Annabelle could not make her interrupt her reading and then allow the subject to drop. So in a tone that was more irreverent than hesitant, she ventured to ask, "Am I invited?"

She thought she detected a momentary twinkle in the icy blue eyes before the Dragon recovered her stony dignity.

I do amuse her, Caroline reflected. *Whatever Montgomery thinks, I haven't wrecked everything yet.*

"The dinner party is for you," replied Lady Annabelle. High rank apparently encouraged people to develop the strangest skills. Lady Annabelle, for example, had the unusual ability to keep all warmth from her voice, even when giving a compliment or promising a treat. "I shall invite some dear friends of mine," she continued, "who are certain to be among your severest critics. Perhaps some will prove to be allies. That remains to be seen, but it's as well you meet some here in a setting somewhat less trying than your presentation ball."

"My what?" Caroline was astounded.

"If I'm to be your sponsor, you must come out properly," shrilled Lady Annabelle as though she anticipated problems. "I was so pleased I never had a daughter," continued Lady Annabelle in a calmer voice. "I knew I should never want to have to introduce a girl of my own into society. So I truly hope you will find yourself a husband without further ado and let my cousin and myself be freed from such chores."

Caroline was abashed. Her shame at having to rely on the generosity of others was combined with surprise at Lady Annabelle's cutting candor. "I know I've put you both to great inconvenience," she said. "Captain Montgomery doesn't even speak to me anymore, so I'm quite aware that he has had his fill of caring for a ward. But you've been so diligent and stayed so close to me—it seemed so willingly—that I hadn't guessed the extent of my imposition."

Lady Annabelle arched her thin eyebrows. "You can be made to scrape and bow on the shortest notice, can't you?" she asked. "Where's your pride, girl?"

Her words about scraping and bowing brought the servants to her mind. She rang for Mrs. Gregory, complaining all the while that Montgomery had seen fit to equip his London house with only the barest skeleton of a service staff, and that had she known, she would have brought proper servants with her from the country.

Mrs. Gregory was not soon enough in responding to Lady Annabelle's summons, and so the Dragon worked up a temper and took Caroline storming downstairs with her.

Mrs. Gregory hardly glanced up from the dough she was kneading as they clattered down the stairs. She was tall and angular, with so little flesh on her bones that one would never have guessed she could be so accomplished a cook. Mrs. Gregory was dour and rarely smiled. Caroline knew the woman would not bother to remind them that it was not always possible for a cook to drop her work and run upstairs without ruining a meal in preparation. It was beneath the woman's dignity to justify herself. Anyway, she was a woman of few words. In fact, the cook was of so uncompromising a temperament and so formidable an appearance, that Caroline had to restrain herself from calling her "Lady Gregory."

The strain of hurrying down the stairs had expended much of Lady Annabelle's energy, so that by the time she arrived in the kitchen, she was huffing and panting for breath rather than fuming and raving. Mrs. Gregory went calmly about her business. A murmured, "Yes, milady?" was the only indication she gave that she was aware august visitors had descended into her domain.

Caroline was the one who found it hard to contain herself, for this was her first visit to the kitchen of Chelton House, and she was amazed by what she saw. It was far different from the rude kitchen in Wales which had been her home.

"Good gracious, Mrs. Gregory," she cried, "whatever is this and how does it work?"

For the fire that burned in the kitchen was not an open fire, but rather looked like it was in an oven. And though the old-fashioned brick oven built into the wall was obviously not in use, a smell of baking filled the kitchen.

" 'Tis a Bodley Range, Miss," replied Mrs. Gregory, suddenly showing an interest. The young lady's curiosity was gratifying. "The range is closed over the top so the fire heats the surface, do you see?"

Indeed, a kettle of water was boiling on the hot plate that covered the range. Back in Wales, Caroline had heated water in a cauldron that hung over the flames. In the same way, her breakfast cakes had been made on a cast-iron griddle that was suspended over the heat. Ladling the buttermilk batter into the griddle had been hot and frightening work, though she'd grown accustomed to burns and scorched clothing.

"But the Bodley Range has been in the best kitchens

since 1802," remonstrated Mrs. Gregory. "I don't know where you've been."

"Where the rest of us have been, I dare say," snapped Lady Annabelle. "My cousin Montgomery is one of the few fools to try every new invention on the market. I note you still use the old turnspit and don't try roasting meat in that pitiful small fire."

Even the old turnspit was a revelation to Caroline. It was rigged up with pulleys and chains, and as Mrs. Gregory explained, the rising heat from the fire caused it to turn "without human intervention."

"I require twelve scuttles a day," continued Mrs. Gregory. She had been questioned about the subject nearest to her heart, and was not going to let her listeners escape without the full story. Like many uncommunicative persons, Mrs. Gregory needed only the right encouragement to release a flood of words. "It's a job to clean it out, but I don't have that task, of course, and the closed range is the better for not releasing all the soot into the sky. It's the open ranges that are to blame, my good mother said it many a time, for in her day, or rather when she was a girl, for she's not in the ground yet, surprising though that be, you heard no talk of these London fogs such as we must put up with these days . . ."

Lady Annabelle sighed. The worst of it was she had no intention of sitting in the kitchen, and her elderly legs would not hold out much longer, especially with the exceptional heat that filled the room.

"I'm not terribly interested in the history of cooking ranges in England," she said, cutting short the speech, "and Miss Bramwell has matters waiting her attention upstairs." With these words, she dismissed Caroline. "I am here to discuss the menu for tomorrow, Mrs. Gregory," she said firmly.

Caroline headed upstairs alone, wondering if Montgomery, too, had a key, if there was a simple question she could ask which would make him speak with enthusiasm and without restraint.

The dinner party took place the next night in the long formal dining hall.

There had been serious disputes between the Lady Annabelle and the affronted cook over the former's insistence on a patriotic meal.

"No Frenchified cooking, I'll have you to understand," the Dragon had insisted, striking the pâté and the escallopes de veau from the menu. "There will be no garlic," was the definitive command.

"It will be mutton chops and souse and common beer, then. As you wish." Mrs. Gregory's tone could not hide her contempt.

Lady Annabelle flew into as much of a rage as her health and station would permit. "Souse? You'd serve pickled pigs' ears to Lady Seften and Countess de Lescaux, would you?"

"Oh, so you'll be inviting a foreign lady?" The cook's neutral question pointed up the contradiction in the lady's all-British stance.

"Yes! And she will see that the greatest nation on earth needs no assistance from any other country to serve a feast worthy of the angels."

"Ah, the angels! Well, if it's to be ambrosia we're to eat, I doubt its origin is to be found on our blessed isles." And Mrs. Gregory turned her back and proceeded to baste a joint.

"Insufferable!" muttered the Dragon as she mounted the stairs, hiding her conviction that dinner would be superb.

Still, the Lady Annabelle was never easily satisfied.

At the last moment, before the arrival of the guests, she had two extravagant girandoles moved into the room. "Hideous things, actually, but we have to let them see this is a house of quality," she grumbled. "Since Montgomery never entertains at home, I'm sure people have some notions about Chelton House which are unworthy of our good name." Still not satisfied, she went on to oversee the installation of a costly epergne in the corner. It was a particularly ornate work in silver, with double pagoda roofs. Caroline was relieved once the epergne had been left in place to suit the lady, because the tiny silver bells which hung all around it had tinkled mercilessly while the piece was being moved. Rather than being musical in nature, the jingling had cut right through Caroline's head into her nerves.

As the guests were introduced, Caroline tried to figure out where she stood in Lady Annabelle's estimation. The Dragon was shrewd, if eccentric, and Caroline was sure each invitation had been issued with great forethought.

Lady Seften was the only member of the Almack's cabal to appear. Reputation painted her as the kindest, most friendly of the Grand Seven. The fact that Lady Annabelle had invited her rather than Lady Castlereagh or Lady Jersey indicated a concern for Caroline and an unexpected sensitivity. Or perhaps a lack of confidence. Caroline's tentative feeling of gratitude passed quickly enough when Lord St. Clair was announced. Was Lady Annabelle hoping for a scene? Even Montgomery searched his cousin's face for some sign. Caroline clamped her jaw and stared straight ahead, dreading the encounter. But when St. Clair entered, he gave not the slightest indication that they had already met.

I suppose that's the most important rule in the world of the haut ton, thought Caroline sadly. *Whatever you may think and whatever you do, just never speak candidly or frankly and you'll be all right.*

It was this restriction that kept her from being happy. All the years with her uncle she had yearned for a companion. Briefly, she had had Montgomery. Embarrassing and frightening as it had been for her in the low-life inn, Caroline now looked back on the days there with great nostalgia. And she longed for Emma with all her heart. For Caroline knew she'd misbehaved, but she didn't take her indiscretions seriously. It would be easy to follow the rules if it were just a matter of not going here or there, or not doing this or that. The only real strain was swallowing her words and holding back, all the time, from speaking her mind with someone in full confidence.

The name of the Countess de Lescaux was familiar, but it was only when the woman herself entered and planted a fond yet casual kiss on Montgomery's cheek that Caroline knew where she'd heard of her. Emma had said the Countess and the Captain had been mentioned together in the scandal columns in a romantic context. The Countess wore her customary black. She had said she would remain in mourning for her executed family and for her country until *Buonaparte* had been destroyed. She always referred to Napoleon disdainfully by his Italian name. Her mourning did not preclude her attendance at all social functions, nor from decorating her black clothes with the most costly exquisite laces and ornaments of jet. She claimed to have escaped with her life and *sans* her fortune. Perhaps, thought Caroline bitterly, that was why she couldn't afford enough fabric to cover her body properly. The Countess's snowy orbs thrust their roundness and curves out over the top of her décolleté.

"Since she's come to England," Emma had reported,

"they say the only people who've seen her out of black are those who've seen her wearing nothing."

Caroline shyly let herself be presented to James, the young Marquess of Holtsford, who kept his chin resting on his narrow chest as though he were continuously scrutinizing his cravat, and to the Duke of Enbridge. His Grace was of Lady Annabelle's age, twice the girth of the portly St. Clair, and given to ponderous silences which Caroline found much preferable to the portentous utterings she'd expected from one of his rank and overlarge presence.

Mrs. Gregory showed that simple English fare could be up to the mark with an outpouring of kitchen creations—mince and pigeon pies, poached salmon in dill ("*Irish* salmon, my Lady," the cook had said with exaggerated courtesy), a fine roast beef with two puddings (Yorkshire and orange), diced beets, and spinach and cabbage salad done up in all lurid and colorful vegetable splendor. The goose was accompanied by a dish of stewed prunes and cinnamon, and Mrs. Gregory had prudently withheld the fact that the liquid the prunes had stewed in was in fact wine crushed from grapes that had never known English soil.

Montgomery, the Countess, and St. Clair were deep in conversation. At her end of the table, Caroline had to try her best seated between the tight-lipped Duke and the graceless Marquess. She wondered if young James was typical of the young gentlemen who were to court her and win her heart. While she exchanged pleasantries, she strained to overhear the political discussion that, against the rules of polite society, had broken out at the other end of the table.

"If you must criticize my countrymen," purred the Countess with only a trace of an accent, "if you please, say their names correctly. The man is Changeur. Louis

Léon Changeur. I do not like him, but my sympathies wander in his direction each time I hear him labeled 'Charmilly'."

"But that is his name!" thundered St. Clair, so that the assembled company no longer had to strain to hear his words. In fact, it was now impossible to avoid at least aural involvement in the debate.

"Charmilly is a different man altogether, I assure you," replied the Countess. Points of color had come to her high cheeks and accentuated her pallor, but she retained a composure that was beyond her opponent. "They have in common—what? Three letters, nothing more. Is it not so? I knew the other, the Charmilly. This Changeur is a different gentleman."

"A tradesman, not a gentleman," corrected St. Clair, and the Countess shrugged, so that it seemed her breasts would surely pop out over her dress.

"What is this disagreeable chatter about tradespeople?" demanded Lady Annabelle with imperious disdain. She had clearly meant to put an end to the topic, but the Countess believed the question was meant in sincerity and hastened to reply.

"This Mr. Changeur, he is financing construction on the Great West Road."

"Just beyond Holland House, it is necessary to add," St. Clair tried to make his argumentative voice sound fraught with significance.

Caroline searched her memory, and recalled that Holland House was the center of the Opposition, and some said, of Bonapartist sympathy.

"The building," continued St. Clair, growing red in the face, "promises to be large enough to accommodate at least one thousand persons. The meaning is apparent to anyone who is not blinded by traitors' tongues."

"How can one be blinded by a tongue, dear sir?"

asked Lady Annabelle. "It must be dreadfully uncomfortable."

"There are many people in London, some with quite unimpeachable background," intervened Lady Seften, "who lack decent accommodation. Isn't it true we have one million residents within the walls? It would seem a residential plan in Kensington would be of great value."

"You deceive yourself, Lady Seften." St. Clair was not above berating the gentle lady. "This is not residential accommodations that are being prepared. There is only one reason anyone would make such an investment. Charmilly is constructing barracks for the occupying army he expects to invade our shores as soon as he is ready. And the enemies here in our midst will open the gates of our city to him. Mark my words."

There was a moment of embarrassed silence, in which the Countess's voice penetrated like a jeweled dagger. "The name is Changeur, my noble friend." The words were mild, the voice charged with venom.

The Marquess bestirred himself to turn to Caroline. "And you, primrose, what think you of all this nonsense? Can I at least be assured that you have better things on your mind than foreign agents?"

Primrose indeed, she thought. But Caroline took the opportunity to express her own thoughts, and ignored the implications of the Marquess's speech.

"It seems we, as a people, are only too ready to seek out traitors in our midst," she replied. "Our great poet, William Wordsworth, who has vastly added to England's greatness in the world of letters, even he was followed and suspected and investigated as an agent for the French. I hold that speaks poorly for our government and for ourselves."

A hush followed, and all eyes around the table turned suddenly to Caroline's face.

"Wherever did you hear that, dear child?" demanded the Duke, breaking his silence.

Realizing her error, Caroline sat frozen in confusion. Her information came from Emma, a person who no longer existed in the world in which Caroline now found herself.

"Don't embarrass the girl just because I've been too free in repeating gossip." Montgomery came to her rescue.

"Strange. I never saw anything of it in the papers," commented St. Clair, who prided himself on his familiarity with all events, whether international or purely social in scope. "I suppose though, Montgomery, that you still keep *artistic* company."

This oblique reference to Emma made Caroline's heart skip. Eyes around the table turned swiftly to Lady Annabelle. Everyone was wondering whether the dowager knew of her cousin's recent entanglement. Lady Seften's kind eyes looked on Caroline with nervous concern, and then critically at St. Clair.

A lady fine as I am must be protected from even casual reference to a creature like Emma, thought Caroline bitterly. *And yet she is the best friend I've ever had.*

Lady Seften's social magnetism and force were now proved: her glance in Caroline's direction seemed to set the pattern, and within instants, all the guests had turned to the young girl.

The Duke of Enbridge rose to the occasion by asking a polite question of the young lady who'd become the focus of attention. "And why," he asked, "do you think the government maintains such vigilance?"

Caroline knew he was merely trying to revive the conversation and move it away from "artistic" matters. She knew she would put herself in the wrong if she answered in earnest. The correct thing to do would be to blush prettily, say "I don't know, Your Grace," and let everyone congratulate her on her attractive innocence. But Caroline was irritated both with the assembled company and with the idea that ignorance is attractive in a young woman. Or rather that *feigned* ignorance is attractive. She had learned most unpleasantly the disagreeable consequences of true ignorance.

Caroline took a deep breath and plunged ahead. "Because by branding as French traitors all those who dare criticize our policy, or those who live or think freely, with respect for all of nature and for all fellow men, the Government believes they can forestall or diminish the clamor for reform."

"A most unusual speech to come from such a charming young lady," said the Countess, smiling a thin and artificial smile. "This hardly sounds like your teaching, Roderick."

Lady Seften once more stepped into the breach with her gentle voice. It was hard for many people to conceive how she had made her way into the cold and lofty circle of ladies who ruled London's *ton* without losing her good-natured ways. Emma had said it was her ability to organize when others were scheming, her willingness to work when others were busy with malicious gossip. But now she proved that she could deliver a setdown on occasion.

"But my dear Hélène," she addressed the Countess, "it was you who introduced the subject with your remarks on behalf of the unfortunate Mr. Changeur." Then Lady Seften turned to smile at Caroline with evident concern in her eyes. "But tell me, child. Where *do* you get your ideas?"

"I have read in *The Examiner*, my Lady," replied Caroline almost in a whisper.

Montgomery's laughter broke the tension but did nothing to ease Caroline's mortification. "So Leigh Hunt has an ally right here under my own roof. A veritable nest of radical vipers this house has become . . ."

Lady Annabelle suggested the company withdraw for a hand of whist, and brandy for the gentlemen.

"I always have luck with the Captain as my partner," said the Countess meaningfully, and Caroline watched glumly as Montgomery gave the beauty his arm.

"To think one of my own kin should prefer dishes from across the Channel," commented Lady Annabelle quietly in Caroline's ear as they followed.

It was strange, thought Caroline. She had proved such a disappointment to her gallant rescuer on horseback, but at the same time, she had won the confidence of the formidable old Dragon.

CHAPTER TEN

"May is the right month for a primrose to make its appearance," announced Lady Annabelle.

Caroline blushed with annoyance at this sly reference to the Marquess of Holtsford.

"That seems so soon," objected Caroline. "Especially since I did not do you and Captain Montgomery any credit at dinner."

"And from what I see of you, I collect you'll embarrass us more, rather than less, as the days pass. So it's best to present you at once and get it done with."

The words were stern, but Caroline had to admit she merited as much. A fine job she'd done with all the kindnesses that had been shown her. Was she really so bad? Apparently she was, because when she did wrong she *knew* she was doing wrong, yet a perverse impulse always seemed to make her go right ahead.

"You will scotch all of our hopes for you, young lady, if we but give you time," said the Dragon, but she patted Caroline's hand as she spoke. "Still, we'll have you married by crook or by stile," Lady Annabelle assured her.

She'd probably meant to be kind, but Caroline sighed. Yes, she would be punished soon enough. If she ended up marrying the Marquess, what a dreary life he would lead her!

"How old are you, child?" asked the old lady, as if with an afterthought.

Caroline shivered. She'd heard the question before, in the same words, but asked in a tone of shocked surprise, when Montgomery, his arms around her, had suddenly realized she was a young woman and not a mere girl.

Impatient for an answer, Lady Annabelle rapped against the scalloped tea table. "What? Don't you know your age?"

"I'll be eighteen in May," Caroline murmured.

At this, Lady Annabelle smiled. "Why then, it's perfect. We shall have the ball for your birthday, just as it should be."

"I'm glad to know I've done something properly," commented Caroline.

"In this case, the credit goes to your parents and not to yourself," was the Dragon's proper put-down.

The sennight passed in a flurry of cleaning and preparation. Montgomery took an additional staff to prepare the ballroom which he alleged had never been used even during his parents' lifetime.

"You are the first young female we've had in the family for half a century," he explained. "No daughters, no brides . . ."

"A warlike tribe is what they are," interjected the Dragon, shaking a bony finger. "You can't imagine what lengths a woman must go to for a little attention from a Montgomery . . . I turn myself into a ridiculous old hornet, and you, poor child, had to lose your parents and a dear brother to make a claim on the Captain's honor. We Montgomerys work on the principles of honor, loyalty, respect, and fear. Why, the heart, the very organ of the body that they say is the seat of affection, it's been bred right out of us, isn't that so, Cousin?" she demanded.

"I never stopped to think about it," replied Montgomery. Shutters of ice seemed to slam down over his eyes. "But if it's true, I dare say we're the better for it."

"A fine speech to make to a poor girl who's about to enter the grand whirl of romance," was Caroline's sarcastic rejoinder. To survive among these people, she would have to remain detached from her feelings. Could it really be possible to make a jest of deep longings? To deny mysterious bonds and say they were of no importance whatsoever—to deny they even existed?

Lady Annabelle continued to administer an occasional jesting set-down and to plume herself on her indifference to social festivities, but as the days went on, she threw herself more and more into the preparations. Caroline's ball was giving her the chance to experience her long-suppressed romanticism. And while Caroline winced to think what hideous decorative effects the Dragon might supervise, she soon learned that Lady Annabelle could show excellent taste when she so desired.

"The company will be small and select, but the party will be memorable," she pronounced. "It will be easier on our nerves not to invite *everyone*, and the questions of acceptance and rejection will keep our friends puzzled and gossiping for weeks. I have plans . . ."

The night finally came, although the invitations were almost withdrawn at the last moment when a disgruntled clerk assassinated the Prime Minister, and Montgomery judged the planned celebration to be unseemly.

"But my dear cousin," shrilled Lady Annabelle, "by those terms we should banish all gaiety and social intercourse until Bonaparte is defeated once and for all. I hold that we fight the French and these sordid assassins best by showing them they will not disrupt the fabric of our lives. You men of politics are too hasty to turn a tradegy into a crisis."

And so the scheduled date remained unchanged.

Caroline sat in her room while Mary dressed her hair. How she wished Montgomery would put in an appearance. How she needed someone she could talk to! At least Mary was somewhat aware of her story.

"I'm eighteen, but the number doesn't seem adequate," she allowed.

"I don't know that I understand you, Miss," answered Mary, putting down the silver-backed brush and regarding her mistress's thoughtful eyes in the mirror. "You are in the very bloom of youth . . ."

"No, it's not that I feel old, that I feel fifty years or one hundred. It's more . . . it's as though I've lived through several lives, and this is but one of them. It hardly seems worth celebrating."

Caroline's musings became silent, and Mary guessed she was thinking of darker days in Wales.

"I agree with you, Miss. Eighteen is but a number, but you 'ave a reason for celebratin' when you think of the days—or lives, as you call 'em—which are all behind you now."

Later, as she entered the ballroom, Caroline wondered at Lady Annabelle's intuition. It wasn't the beauty of the room that dazzled her—the rose and silver hangings, the tubs of primroses and boughs of silver and green. But through the door that had been reserved for Caroline's entrance—somewhat too grand an idea to have a special entrance, Caroline had thought helplessly—Lady Annabelle had instructed the workmen to build a small copy of the New Bridge. The tiny figure that gracefully crossed the bridge, dressed in the traditional white silk coming-out gown, looked like a princess from a fairytale. The silver embroidery shimmered under the soft lights. The facets of the ruby and diamond stones around her slender neck shot fire into the air, and to Caroline, everything seemed reflected and magnified hundreds of times, not only in the high-framed mirrors, but in the crystal drops of the chandelier, in the glasses on the sideboards, in all the eyes upon her.

"That's the bridge in Wales she crossed to come to us," Lady Annabelle explained to the guests, until some had heard it several times. "Today, she crosses another bridge, and will be welcomed as warmly as when she first came into this house." There was something defiant in the Dragon's voice, as though she dared anyone to challenge whether Caroline had really been so delightful an addition to her life.

"It's like you be crossin' a bridge," had been Mary's last words as Caroline left her room.

Touched by this truth, which Lady Annabelle had then rendered in solid form, Caroline felt happy at last, and her shy pleasure colored her cheeks more perfectly than any artifice could have done.

The guests were all enchanted, though the walls of the newly opened ballroom did hear many whispered comments about the unusual nature of the presentation. What precisely was the true relationship between the Montgomery family and the girl from Wales? Or was it Yorkshire? And lovely though she seemed to be, had she means of her own, or was the gallant Captain also throwing her a dowry? Without one, no one could possibly expect any of the gentlemen present to make an offer. Not an offer of matrimony, at any rate.

The dancing itself was subdued, as Lady Annabelle had forbidden the waltz. "Call me a fusty antique if you will," she'd said in a voice that admitted no argument.

Caroline had no objections however. She'd learned to dance from Emma, and while she had enjoyed whirling around the room to three-quarter time, she knew she would not want a strange man to hold her about the waist. At least, certainly not the men with whom she was spending most of the evening. The Marquess of Holtsford wouldn't leave her side. He insisted she call him James, and made several remarks on the primrose theme. Aside from that, he kept silent and stared downward. Caroline realized that he was not examining his cravat, as she had surmised on their last meeting, but rather keeping watch over his hands, for it seemed whenever he was not concentrating on his long fingers they twitched nervously in the most appalling manner.

To escape from the unfortunate Marquess, she found herself paying more and more attention to Robert, the future Lord Warwick. This young man was polite and earnest, and his light-blue eyes faced her directly, as they were not needed to keep troublesome digits under control.

Lady Annabelle nodded at her approvingly, and Caroline tried to find Montgomery in the crowd. Surely that was his strong back and his well-shaped legs on the other side of the room, but that gentleman seemed to be leaving. When she saw the black dress on the man's companion, Caroline turned resolutely back to Robert Warwick. So, Montgomery would slip out with the horrid Countess right in the middle of her presentation ball, thought Caroline. He hasn't even common courtesy to give me, she thought bitterly, and fought to keep the emotion from showing on her face.

Her somewhat forced conversation and the alarmed flush on her cheeks seemed normal for a miss from the country on her first presentation to the *ton.* At least that is what young Warwick thought, and was unaware of the warring sentiments that wracked the slender body encased in white silk.

His interlude with the Countess Hélène must have put Montgomery in good humor, because he made an unexpected appearance to join Caroline and Lady Annabelle for breakfast. That was how Caroline interpreted the faint smile that played over his lips, only to vanish along with the warmth in his eyes whenever he realized he was being observed.

"Let me congratulate you," he stiffly gave Caroline his blessing. "A splendid début."

When Caroline tried to excuse herself after the meal, Montgomery detained her.

"Don't hurry off, Caroline. There is something you must see." Taking her hand firmly in his, Montgomery led her outside to the stables. "Now that we've introduced you to society, it will be up to you to cultivate these friendships. It will help when you can ride out in Hyde Park with the others." With these words, he presented the girl with a beautifully groomed chestnut gelding whose tail was docked and whose coat was burnished like fine metal, but satin soft. The horse was not as magnificent as pitch-black Jupiter, not as regal as the greys which pulled the carriage. But the gelding seemed spirited and strong, and Caroline guessed it was her perfect match.

"I hope you do know how to ride," added Montgomery awkwardly, misreading her speechlessness.

At this, Caroline threw her arms around him and kissed his cheek, only to feel him grow rigid with surprise and push her away.

"Oh, I'm so sorry," she managed to say, utterly crushed. "It's just that . . . it was Percy who taught me to ride so many years ago. And just now, it's as though you were my brother . . . I didn't think."

"You'll need a riding dress," he said, passing over the embarrasing scene. "I'd hoped to accompany you, but I have pressing matters to attend to this morning, so perhaps Lady Annabelle can . . ."

Caroline wasn't fooled by his lame excuse. He had intended to take her shopping, but her show of grateful emotion had ruined it all.

She tossed her head carelessly, and didn't try to hide the fire in her humiliated eyes. "I'm in no real hurry to meet with your friends in the Park," she said caustically. "Whenever your cousin wishes to go out, I shall attend her." What was wrong with this man? The gesture of affection she had shown him, quite innocently, had quite upset his balance, while he allowed the Countess great liberties in public view. If a ward couldn't plant a chaste kiss on her guardian's cheek, well, something was very wrong!

Yet, she wondered, *had the kiss been that chaste*? *Was it the kiss of a ward to a guardian*? *No, it wasn't*, she concluded. *But it was the kiss of a sister to a brother. Montgomery really did stand in the stead of father and brother to her now, but she had loved her father and Percy dearly, and they had loved her in return.* She longed for a lost world of simple affections, and told herself it was a terrible mistake to dream she could recapture such with this cold and odious man.

"Aren't you going to name him?" Montgomery broke into her thoughts.

"Who?"

He regarded her curiously. His dark eyebrows drew together, but his expression was more hurt than thunderous. "Your gelding."

"Oh, am I to have a choice?" Her temper, restrained for so long, flared along with the flashes and sparks in her eyes. "Haven't you already given him a name? I thought everything was arranged, and I need only be obedient and then I shall have the happiest life any wretched little cook-maid's ever known."

He grabbed her by the wrist and twisted her around. When she lowered her green eyes, he lifted her face and forced her to look at him. "You're not a wretched little cook-maid, Caroline," he said.

"No, I guess not. Just an ungrateful one." His touch had not only subdued her, but had melted her anger away. She herself was ready to melt.

Why couldn't he always speak to her kindly?

There was some sort of feeling, surely, in those deep gray eyes.

"I know you've been under a strain," he continued, "but if you must make missish scenes, please confine them to more private places."

She wrenched herself free. So that was all! He was concerned with her spirits lest an outburst make her less attractive in the public marketplace.

"I understand, Captain," she said spitefully, hating him with all her aching heart. "We can't let the scandal-broth have it that the Montgomery family offers rotten meat in the market."

From the doorway, she called back to him. "Name the beast yourself!" and Montgomery flushed with shame and rage in front of the stableboys while Caroline ran upstairs, dizzy and drowning in violent tears.

At nuncheon, Caroline sent word that she was indisposed. She didn't want Lady Annabelle to see her red swollen eyes. Besides, she felt so reckless and wretched, Caroline doubted she'd be able to curb her sharp tongue if she had to spend any time with others.

The Dragon, however, was soon begging admittance at Caroline's door, anxious to see the girl's condition for herself.

"Too much punch last night, I warrant," she remarked, but her keen eyes didn't seem to miss much and Caroline assumed the elderly lady realized the cause of the upset was emotional rather than physical.

"You should be better by Wednesday, I hope," added the Dragon.

"Wednesday?" As usual, it seemed, some plans had been put into action without anyone informing Caroline.

"Yes, dear, last night was a brilliant success. You did so well for yourself, your voucher to Almack's has been granted. It was delivered by hand only an hour ago."

"That's good news," said Caroline without enthusiasm. Almack's had certainly been a goal to be attained, but she had not been looking forward to her debut appearance there.

"Good news if your taste runs to stale cake and lemonade. A preposterous way to spend an evening, my dear . . ."

"People hardly go there for the refreshment," Caroline commented.

"Then you think you'll enjoy being looked over by dandified blades who think they're attending a cattle market in the countryside," sniffed Lady Annabelle. "And by the nasty old dowagers like myself who are hoping you'll embarrass yourself. And by old men whose wickedness makes them appear even more foolish than we all know them to be."

"What I meant," explained Caroline, "was that the meager fare offered the dancers is hardly the most unpleasant part of the program." The description supplied by her sponsor had only served to confirm Caroline's own worst fears about Almack's.

"Captain Montgomery is most anxious to have your future settled, you know," added Lady Annabelle.

Caroline fought back tears and a constriction in her throat that seemed sure to choke her. "Yes, I should think he would be," she murmured faintly. "And I shall do my best not to disgrace either of you."

Lady Annabelle laughed in surprise, but Caroline's words were spoken in sincerity. In all the years she had been mistreated by the Lord of Bedlam, she'd never raised her own voice in anger or fought back with insults or caustic speech. She'd been quiet and mild and only tried to do what was expected and stay out of her uncle's way. Then, along came Captain Montgomery, the first person in ever so long to treat her kindly, shower her with gifts and attentions, and she responded in so abysmal a fashion.

"I trust I'll soon be out of your hands," she concluded.

"You sound as though you've already selected a bridegroom, my dear!" cried Lady Annabelle. "I thought you had a girlish *tendre* for my cousin, but I see I was wrong. Some young blade has taken your affections very quickly, I dare say." Caroline's scarlet flush didn't disabuse the old lady of her mistaken notion. "Enjoy your youth, dear, but please be careful with your heart. Whoever your young gentleman may be, don't give him your heart too easily."

"I won't," Caroline assured her truthfully. For her resolution to find a suitable marriage partner with all possible haste had nothing to do with giving her heart.

CHAPTER ELEVEN

"Miss, oh Miss, please excuse me, Miss." Mary came bursting into the Green Room and Caroline looked up with amusement. Her abigail didn't mean to intrude, but the girl's excitement was riding roughshod over her own sense of decorum. "There's been a letter for me. I mean, there be one. Here it be, Miss."

"Who is writing to you?" asked Caroline, to whom the sender of a message was of infinitely greater importance than the mere fact of the message's existence.

"But I don't know, Miss. That's why I come to you!" Mary thrust the paper into Caroline's hand, but at the last moment found it hard to relinquish her own grasp on the treasure. "I hope you don't mind, Miss," she said, still holding on, "but seeing as how I don't read . . . and I'd much rather have you look at it than Jenkins if it be something of a personal nature . . ."

"I understand, Mary," said Caroline gently, and smiled with such reassurance that the girl was at last able to deliver the paper wholly into Caroline's possession.

"Why, this letter is from America!" exclaimed Caroline. Mary gasped and her hands flew to her mouth.

"Oh, it will be my brother Daniel!" she cried. "Please, Miss, tell me it be my brother Daniel."

The missive had indeed been dispatched by a Daniel Williams, and upon hearing this, Mary burst into tears of joy.

"I didn't know you had a brother in America," said Caroline curiously.

"Nor did I, Miss. And what does he say? Oh, Danny, my Danny, he really went and done it!"

It transpired that Mary's brother, almost of an age with her, had often talked of running away from the mines to seek his fortune in America. Without money, the only way to accomplish his plan was to secure paid passage by contracting himself to an unknown and distant employer.

"I never thought 'e'd really go," wept Mary. "But what do 'e say?"

Caroline was happy to be able to be of assistance to Mary, but she felt more strongly than ever the tragedy of people who couldn't read or write.

If I were to receive so personal a letter, I shouldn't want anyone else to read it first, she thought. In fact, it was a nervous need for privacy that had made Caroline withdraw to her room. Tonight was to be her first appearance at Almack's and she had felt agitated all day.

But turning her attention again to Mary, "Your poor mother," she said. "How does she get on with two of her children so far from home?" Caroline had been thinking of family feeling. What she meant was, didn't Mrs. Williams miss her young ones?

Mary blushed. To her, the question referred to the wages that the Williams children brought in to the impoverished household. "The Cap'n sends her part of me wages, and," she admitted, "it seems 'e's added to the sum from time to time."

How generous and good Montgomery could be! Caroline wondered again at her guardian's nature. Such generosity had to indicate a generosity of spirit, she argued to herself. Unless it was simply that Montgomery set no value on his wealth. It seemed that not his money—nor anything else—gave him pleasure. It didn't seem right.

"Miss?" Mary's shy impatience communicated itself, and Caroline read aloud:

> Dear Sister,
>
> This will let you know I am well in the free Commonwealth of Massachusetts, of late the Colony. Mr. Hendricks set me to clearing forest for him all winter and it was cold and hard work but the air here be fresh so a person can breathe it. Which is not the way you will remember at home. I have me a house built of logs on Hendricks land.
>
> Sister, this letter I be writing to you with my own hand.

That was clear enough, thought Caroline. There were many misspellings among the scrawled words in the childish hand.

Mary gasped with increased excitement and looked over Caroline's shoulder to get a closer look of the characters her brother had drawn himself.

> Mr. Hendricks teaches me. He says I can be of use to him with the reading and writing once I get it. And 'twill serve me when I go on my own.

> I hope you are well with the mistress from Pemberton. If she treat you ill . . .

"Oh, no, Miss!" Mary was aghast, but Caroline just laughed.

"Danny is just looking after you, Mary," she said. "He has no way of knowing whether you are happy here or no."

"But I am, Miss. I wish I'd let Jenkins read the letter!" Mary buried her scarlet face in her hands.

"Hush. Now listen to the rest."

> . . . come and join me here. A John Cox in London is captain of ships. He don't sail on them no more. But if you ask for him—he that has one leg only—at the East India Company wharf, he can help you. So I did hear from others what came over on the ship with me.

"Well, that is information I do not need," declared Mary stoutly.

"You don't have to fly up in the boughs for my benefit," Caroline assured her. "There's more:

> Do not worry for me, Mary. People tell fearsome tales of the Red Indians, but I have met one or two and not at all savage.

He signs it 'your loving brother.' "

Mary hesitated before accepting the letter back from her mistress.

"This certainly seems like a lucky year for starting new lives," said Caroline.

"I want to keep this forever," Mary said softly, hugging the letter to her bosom. "But you mustn't think it's to 'ave the name of that one-legged cap'n."

Caroline hugged her tear-stained maid. It was strange, she thought, how good news could make a person weep as much as bad news. "It's all right, Mary," she said. "And now, unless you plan to run off to America in the next hour, what I'd really like is a good hot bath."

"The carriage is ready, Captain Montgomery."

"Yes, I know. But my ward isn't."

Caroline overheard the exchange between Jenkins and her guardian as she hurried down the broad staircase. Oh, why did Montgomery have to be in his usual bad humor tonight? Facing the *ton* at Almack's would be difficult enough. *If only,* she thought, *if only I could count on a smile, on some sort of support from him.*

She regretted that she'd allowed Mary to fuss over her curls for so long. She hadn't meant to be late, and now Montgomery had his bristles up.

But when he caught sight of her, and of her pale green satin petticoats showing beneath a charming sprig muslin, with deep-green velvet ribbons woven through the gown, and ribbons of the same fabric threaded in her piled hair, Montgomery could not keep himself from smiling, and moving forward to take her hands.

"You look beautiful, Caroline," he said appreciatively, and his finger ran to the emerald necklace around her neck. He lifted it lightly. "I was thinking of your eyes when I chose this," he said, "and I see I matched the color well."

Why couldn't he always be this way?

As he let the stone drop back, his fingers brushed the hollow of her throat, and for a moment, she felt as though the floor beneath her had opened.

"I thought we were late and you in such a hurry,"

complained Lady Annabelle, whose head was crowned with ostrich feathers which seemed to double that lady's height and which waved and bobbed frantically when she moved. "Now we know the season has truly begun, and I, for one, am ready for winter's return." She continued talking as they left the house. "And help me up into the carriage, Roderick, that's right, but careful now with my gown. When the face and body are wrinkled, all the more reason to see the gown isn't creased."

Montgomery helped Caroline up next, then took the seat beside her. He wore his best blue coat and white waistcoat. His cravat was white on white, and while the points of his collar were properly starched and fashionably high, they didn't reach the height of modishness that marked the dandy.

Montgomery, Caroline thought approvingly, dressed with enough heed for fashion to show his respect, but he was not so frivolous as to concern himself overmuch with its more refined dictates.

She had not even expected him to accompany her on this first dance at Almack's. And now, here they were sitting side by side, in perfect good humor, and thoroughly pleased with each other, looking more like man and wife than guardian and ward.

Although who would want to marry a man of such changeable and brooding temperament, I really don't know, Caroline told herself. And it was a complete mystery as to what kind of woman could get through to that impregnable heart. Unless the awful Countess had succeeded. Perhaps Montgomery's friendship with the beautiful Frenchwoman was just a matter of "needs." That thought led back to an old perplexing subject for Caroline. For if men had needs, she could see why Montgomery would be drawn to the Countess. But what drew the Countess to Montgomery? What advantage was there to a woman? What did she get out of the whole procedure?

The Lady Annabelle had been accurate in her characterization of Almack's. The cake was indeed stale and the lemonade insipid. Without refreshment of sufficient interest to engage the attention, all present found the senses better occupied by intensive study of one another. For those of more libertine bent, this study progressed beyond the visual investigation of clothing and complexion, and resided chiefly in the indiscreet tactile probings made possible by the enforced proximity of the waltz.

More than a cattle market, the scene put Caroline in mind of a bad dream, in which everything becomes distorted and ordinary rules no longer apply. For among this select company, to which the cabal of ladies admitted only those who had proved themselves worthy in one way or another, danced ladies who had apparently dressed so hurriedly they had quite forgotten their petticoats. In this, and in their low-cut gowns, they proved the maxim that full dress is undress. And on some faces, there was more than a suspect trace of paint. This society, for which she had been prepared with such painstaking care and inconvenience, seemed to delight in its own contradictions.

Caroline accepted the looks of hate which the plain and proper girls directed toward her, urged on less by real malice and more by the prodding of their mamas. She accepted the appraising and dismissing looks of the bolder dancers—Countess Hélène among them, who seemed to think her a chit of no consequence, a young thing with good looks but insufficient sophistication to pose a threat to their pleasures.

She danced awkwardly with the young Marquess, holding herself stiff in his arms. And if she relaxed just a little with Warwick when he asked her to stand up with him, it was only out of relief to be away from the Marquess.

"You are different from all the others," said Warwick, unable to contain his impressions, as they rested after a whirl across the floor that had seemed to Caroline like being tumbled down the street in a barrel.

"You exaggerate, sir," she answered demurely, yet a combination of pride and shame within her made her tell herself she was even more different than the young man imagined. And that she was happy to be so.

There were others who asked her to dance, and some of them took liberties and some did not, and Caroline found it impossible to remember their faces or their names. How she wished some of the other girls would sit with her and talk to her. She missed having a friend, and she resented the high-born ladies who went *sans* petticoats and wore alarmingly low-cut gowns, but at the same time could decree that Emma was not fit to associate with a lady of quality. It seemed that if she were to be a lady, Caroline could have no feminine companionship beside the Lady Annabelle. With this realization, Caroline also acknowledged that she was appreciative for her sponsor's eccentricities. It made the Dragon a much more interesting companion.

However sharp-tongued the Dragon might seem at times, she was definitely an ally, as she proved once again by interrupting a tête-à-tête between Caroline and the Marquess. Ostrich feathers shot from her head instead of flames from her mouth, and Caroline looked with affection at this unlikely person who could be both ludicrous and imposing at the same time.

Caroline didn't even feign disappointment when the Dragon apologized but insisted on taking the girl away. "After all he's done, I think your guardian deserves a whirl with the most beautiful dancer here tonight," announced Lady Annabelle. "Ah, there he is!"

Montgomery and the Countess were sitting together on a plush velvet sofa, partly screened by potted plants. She seemed to be whispering something in his ear. Whispering, in itself, was not so shocking or surprising. Over the sound of the musicians, the din of conversation, and the rhythm of feet on the dance floor, it was hard to make oneself understood without speaking directly into the ear of the person for whom the words were intended. But the way the Countess leaned forward in conversation and touched the side of Montgomery's face, directing his gaze toward an unimpeded view of her cleavage and brushing through his hair with her long soft fingers even while she directed her words into his ear, she was clearly taking advantage of the situation.

The Dragon interrupted this private party as forcefully as she had the other tête-à-tête. Caroline wondered for a moment if Lady Annabelle did not really care a button whether Caroline was bored and miserable. It might be her much-vaunted distrust of foreigners, and no other reason, that made her anxious to separate Montgomery from the Countess.

"It was a struggle," reported Lady Annabelle to the Captain, "but I insisted that Caroline reward her guardian by saving him a waltz. You must take her onto the floor the moment the music begins again, or I fear we shall lose her again to her admirers."

The Captain's acquiescence was gracious rather than warm, but when the music began and he led her onto the floor, Caroline suddenly discovered how magical the waltz could be. Without holding back, she let him lead her, was actually unaware of following, so perfectly did their bodies flow together in the dance. A strange and sweet transition was taking place within her. For the arms around her were strong and comforting, just as they had been when she was a child in need of help, and they inspired in her the same warm feeling of loving trustfulness. But now, a new and startling, though delicious, dimension was added to the communication between their bodies, held together so near and close. The Captain was having a devastating effect on Caroline, and as she looked into his guarded eyes, she felt a twinge of disappointment that she saw no sentiment there. But as they dipped and swayed, the disappointment was lost and forgotten. All time was lost and forgotten. Montgomery's arms wiped out the pain of the past as if it had never happened at all. The new pleasure of being held close by him also banished, for a moment, thoughts and fears of the future still to come.

Caroline knew suddenly and without doubt that she loved him. There was nothing left to fight and she had no reserves of strength or pride to fight it with. She expected nothing good could come of this violent feeling that was raging and swelling in her heart, but she was happy enough for the moment she'd been granted. Distant and cold though he seemed, Caroline knew while he held her that there was still vitality and depth of emotion locked inside the man, and she wished fervently—more for his sake than for her own—that she could do something to help him banish the demons that had possessed his better nature. Though, she could never have him for herself, she longed to see him happy, to hear him laugh easily.

For the moment she was entirely his, but then she broke out of her dream with an abrupt, startled movement that interrupted the rhythm of the dance. She had almost allowed herself to lay her head on his shoulder, and abandon herself shamelessly and publicly to these new feelings.

The music stopped, and they silently left the floor. Caroline was horrified by her near misstep. Had she done anything else during the waltz and not been aware of it? It was one thing to harbor these terrifying sentiments within the depths of her heart and soul. It would be another thing, and quite unforgivable, to let her feelings show. After all Montgomery had done for her, after owing him so much, how could she stoop so low as to throw herself at him like some brass-faced lightskirt?

Lady Annabelle was watching her face keenly with those blue eyes that seemed to probe the depths of her soul. Caroline tried to think of the Marquess, or of the Duke of Enbridge, of any neutral person who had no hold on her heart. Because Lady Annabelle's penetrating gaze had convinced her that her inner thoughts were clearly reflected on her countenance. Much as Caroline inwardly criticized the hypocrisy and lack of candor in society circles, she agreed to herself that some things are better left unsaid and unknown.

It would be easy to tell herself that she had fallen in love with her guardian simply out of gratitude. But it wasn't gratitude that had made her thrill to his touch, made every inch of her skin seem suddenly alive and glowingly eager. But feelings like Caroline's were, alas, out of Montgomery's realm, beyond the limits he himself had set for his life.

Have I made a terrible spectacle of myself? worried Caroline as Lady Annabelle decided firmly it was time to leave. She cut a way through the social throng, steadfastly refusing to be swayed by the young male supplicants who hoped to win an extension of Caroline's stay.

"Roderick!" she called sharply, for the Captain had been standing beside her, but now was detained briefly by the Countess.

Caroline distinctly saw a folded piece of paper exchange hands before Montgomery left the beautiful French woman and rejoined the two ladies who were intent on going home.

Outside it seemed for a moment that Montgomery would ask the coachman to sit aside so that he himself could take the ribbons. Inside the carriage, Caroline held her breath. Then Montgomery climbed in. The three of them passed the ride home to Chelton House in silence. Montgomery and Caroline sat side by side, but he leaned against the side of the coach and never for a moment did their shoulders so much as touch. Still, Caroline was aware of a magnetic feeling between them, in spite of the cold look, almost of anger, on his face.

Later, alone in her room, Caroline thought of that pitiless look on Montgomery's handsome face, and a wave of anguish swept over her. She had no hopes of gaining his love, but she hated herself to think her willfulness had contributed to his mood of disillusion.

Instead of thanking him, I've said and done one unforgivable thing after another, she confessed to herself. She wondered if a buried realization of love had made her behave in so unbecoming a fashion. Had some instinct been making her heart fight and rebel against a hopeless attachment? she wondered.

She removed the emeralds Montgomery had given her, and let the precious stones balance a moment in her hand. She had taken from him time, help, money. She had given nothing in return. She had railed against the fusty society persons among whom she lived, but she'd treated them all politely. It was the one person to whom she could have talked, the one she could have laughed with—it was only Montgomery that she had treated shamefully.

I can't let it go on this way another minute! cried Caroline's heart.

Leaning forward so that her black curls came part undone and fell over her face casting beautiful shadows, she refastened the necklace. The clasp gave her a moment's work, especially since her hands shook briefly when she recalled Montgomery putting the jewels on her the first time.

Caroline knew how irregular it would be to visit the Captain in his bedroom, but he and she were both irregular people, she reasoned. Anyway, it was the only place where they could be alone to talk. Montgomery was rarely home, and when he did appear, Lady Annabelle was always present.

Caroline had no intention of confessing the new passion that burned away inside her. She tiptoed down the hallways, toward Montgomery's room, with a lamp in her hand.

She knocked lightly on the mahogany door. No, she wouldn't say a word of love. But she did have a confession to make. She had waited much too long to say thank you, to confess her bad behavior, to try to explain. There was no way to explain or justify, she told herself, and knocked again. She had to promise him to try harder and do better in the future. She had to let him know how cognizant she was of the tremendous burden he had accepted when he decided to help her. Knocking on the door, she felt she would burst if she couldn't unburden her guilty heart directly, if they couldn't talk and if she couldn't know she had his forgiveness and friendship. Knocking again, and receiving no answer, Caroline tried the doorknob. The room was unlocked. Her heart stopped a moment as she opened the door. This was surely a bold and brazen act, but she didn't dare knock any louder for fear of waking Lady Annabelle. Anyway, she'd gone so far in impropriety already, what was another mistake?

"Captain Montgomery?" she whispered, slipping inside.

The room was empty.

Caroline's eyes stung with tears. She remembered a note that had passed hands hours earlier as they left Almack's and the knowing smile of a pair of sensual French lips.

Montgomery's bed was still made up and unslept in. After depositing the ladies at home, he had slipped out of the house to pursue his own pleasures. After steeling herself, and taking her desperate steps down the hall, Caroline would more easily have faced a violent confrontation than an empty room.

The lamplight flickered even more as the girl's hand began to shake uncontrollably. Caroline fought to keep her tears silent.

Her contrition was utterly wasted. Yes, she had been cruel and wrong, but it made no difference to Captain Roderick Montgomery. He had his own life to live. And why not? He'd probably never given a thought to her rag-mannered willfulness. And why should he have done so?

He had taken Caroline Bramwell under his roof, but as the girl tiptoed back to her own chamber, she realized with a deadening certainty that she meant nothing to the man at all.

CHAPTER TWELVE

The days passed but Caroline's despondency did not pass with them. Each minute was a struggle against showing her feelings, for she had resolved that if she could not be happy, at least she would be mature and dignified. At the darkest times, she looked back almost with nostalgic longing to the days in Wales. Wretched though her life had been then, Caroline had awakened each morning sustained by her hope that the Captain would come. Surviving through each ugly day at Pemberton Hall, she had continued to believe that greater happiness lay in her future, and this belief had given her the strength to tolerate her daily existence.

The worst was over now, but suddenly Caroline could be happy no longer. For the future was now something to dread. She could not envision any circumstances of happiness anymore. There was no longer anything worth looking forward to. There was no longer any wish she could pray be fulfilled. To make Montgomery love her was as easy as stopping the sun in its tracks, she thought. It wasn't even within her realm to dream of it.

The Lady Annabelle soon remarked upon Caroline's listlessness, and on her new ability to spend half the day napping in her four-poster bed. The girl had been so full of life and so eager not many weeks before. She could rush about town all day and dance all night and never tire. Aloud, Lady Annabelle expressed the opinion that the child was exhausted from the dizzying social rounds and that the dances and parties and visits to which she was not accustomed had at last taken their toll. But sometimes, when the Dragon came to visit Caroline while she rested, the girl could tell from the searching look in those blue eyes that Lady Annabelle was not satisfied with the explanation she espoused to others.

If only, just once, Montgomery would look at her with as much probing concern as the old lady did.

You little fool, Caroline chided herself. *You didn't fall in love with a real man. You are still in love with the image of the gallant officer who stopped by Pemberton with bad news and promised to return. You were a child then. You created a Captain in your own unhappy mind, and the personage you dreamed about day after day never really existed. You haven't lost your love, you beggared chit. You fell in love with a phantom, a specter you conjured up out of fever and hunger and cold.*

The tub would be filled with hot water, and Caroline would lie for hours in a languorous state, leaning the damp tendrils of her hair against the back of the tub. At first, Mary was careful to return every now and again with fresh hot water so that her mistress would not take a chill, but Lady Annabelle soon put a stop to that. For it was only when the water grew cold and the discomfort finally penetrated Caroline's revery, that the girl would force herself to climb out of the tub. If Mary was present, she would see to it that Caroline dressed and joined Lady Annabelle downstairs. But only too often, Mary would enter the chamber to find the tub empty, and Caroline back in bed.

There were three constant callers to Chelton House during this time.

The Marquess of Holtsford, Robert Warwick, and Lord St. Clair paid frequent visits, and when they learned that Caroline was indisposed, rather than dampen their ardor, it seemed her unavailability only increased their interest. And they never knew, as they approached the house, if this particular morning Caroline might be receiving visitors, wearing a simple morning dress that accentuated her fragile beauty, her eyes dreamy, and her movements so slow and graceful they seemed to come from some vision of the Orient.

"You are like salt, my dear," said St. Clair one morning. "You were an exotic luxury when you first came to London, and you quickly became a necessity."

Lady Annabelle often left Caroline alone with her other suitors, but when St. Clair was present, she remained in the drawing room although always withdrawing discreetly to the far end. This way she gave the two an illusion of privacy, but her occasional interruptions into the conversation seemed intended to assure St. Clair that his behavior and language did not go unremarked. On this occasion, she broke in with a cackle: "I should think you could have made the same comparison with fine tea," she said, "and a lot more flattering it would have been. The very idea of comparing a young lady to a saltcellar!"

"I would much rather see you encourage young Warwick," commented Lady Annabelle after St. Clair was gone.

"But I'm not encouraging anyone," said Caroline evenly. Her emotions, once so near the surface, were now buried and held in restraint so that one phrase was very like in tone to any other.

Lady Annabelle considered this a polite and maidenly disclaimer that could not, for a moment, be accepted as the truth. "I've heard of men suddenly changing their way of life, but I still think once a rake-hell and a scoundrel, it's hard to change. Understand me, girl," she added, patting Caroline's hand, "every man abandons himself at some point to some form of excess, but a period of rakish behavior does not make a man a rake. Your Lord St. Clair . . ."

"He is not 'my' Lord St. Clair," corrected Caroline. There was no outrage in her tone, just precision. Caroline fully believed that she had managed to conceal her inner turmoil for days, but in fact, the truth was revealed by the very distance and aloofness she employed to keep her feelings from showing. Her calm and even tone worried Lady Annabelle who accepted the correction without dispute.

At least, thought Lady Annabelle, Caroline's rebuff was evidence that she was listening, even though her eyes remained fixed on some distant object. "He is a rascal through to his soul," continued the dowager. "It's not a matter of a few escapades. It's his character, Caroline. His first wife was driven to an untimely grave, and I pity with all my heart any woman who casts in her lot with such as he . . . And I fear there's more. He and Roderick used to be very much in charity—that's why I invited St. Clair to dinner—only to learn that now, for some reason, my cousin can no longer bear the sight of the man. He must have done him some grievous injury. So I warn you, Lord St. Clair is not such as a young girl can trust."

Caroline was aware that Lady Annabelle was talking out of concern and affection. For a moment, she considered confiding in the Dragon. She was certain that she would feel better directly she had unburdened herself of the crushing weight of her secret pain. But upon reflection, she decided that Lady Annabelle was simply the last person in the world who could be told. The Dragon would surely see her as a beggared chit trying to marry her way into a prominent family by taking advantage of the circumstances which had brought her under the Montgomery roof. And if Lady Annabelle became angry with her, Caroline felt she would have lost the only person alive who was anything like a disinterested friend. She would be cut totally adrift.

"The Lord St. Clair is a pattern-card," replied Caroline at last. "By studying him, I am better able to appreciate the virtues of other gentlemen."

"I am glad to see you have not lost your wits altogether." In fact, although she disapproved of St. Clair, Lady Annabelle had noted that his presence seemed to make Caroline more alert and alive. St. Clair was a fine one, after all, for bandying wits. Lady Annabelle suspected that the fatigue was of a nervous nature and that the distractions of social life were beneficial, and so she was inclined to tolerate St. Clair's visits and to ignore the advice of the doctor who'd prescribed a drop of laudanum in a glass of water each night. Surely, she thought, the doctor's cure would serve only to induce more lethargy. What the girl needed was distraction.

"I'm beginning to find life in London rather tedious myself." Lady Annabelle picked up the conversation again. "Dinners and Almack's are fine, I suppose, but I'd much rather a night at the theater." To her pleasure, she saw Caroline's eyes light up at the words.

"I'd love it!" cried Caroline, her unusual enthusiasm startling both Lady Annabelle and Caroline herself.

Rather than pluming herself on a shrewd guess, Lady Annabelle regretted her words. "Unfortunately, fire in its destructive aspect, " she remembered, "has rendered an evening at the theater quite impossible."

Caroline's look of despair caused the Dragon to add unwisely, "But cheer up, girl. It's no real tragedy for you. Think of those who must make their living in the theater."

Now Caroline's countenance expressed sheer fright—both for Emma's plight and for the possibility that Lady Annabelle knew all.

"Ah, you're too sensitive and kindhearted," chided the Dragon querulously now. "They won't starve to death."

Caroline was cheered both by the latter reassurance and this indication that her secret remained safe.

Without Drury Lane and Covent Garden, Almack's remained the one destination for pleasure-seeking members of the *ton*. For the ladies, that is. The men could repair, as always, to the delights of White's, Brooks's, or Watier's.

The next Wednesday, Caroline and Lady Annabelle dressed to go out but Montgomery brusquely said he would remain behind. At Caroline's look of dismay he said, "My cousin is an adequate chaperone. There's no need for me to be bothered protecting you from the rakes you persist in encouraging."

Lady Annabelle's retort came quickly enough to cover Caroline's speechlessness. "It's not a matter of protecting the girl, Roderick," she shrilled, clearly out of curl. "I hardly expect you to be cheerful and pleasant to a dreadful old creature like myself. But you show a scowling face to the entire world. You should accompany us for your own good. I think you are in need of some pleasure yourself to lighten your outlook on the world."

"You needn't trouble yourself on my behalf, Cousin," he answered, his gray eyes cold as ice.

Caroline was furious to see her ally spoken to so coldly and she recovered her voice. "Indeed, Lady Annabelle, your cousin pursues his own pleasures at night when decent people are abed."

Unlike some men who color with anger, Montgomery turned white with rage, making his scar stand out in livid relief. "And you, Miss," he cried, "must be determined to remain the curse of my existence. How am I to get you married off and gone till you learn to keep a chaste tongue in your head?"

"A chaste tongue?" exclaimed Caroline, affronted. "You could talk to me about chastity once, but I've seen your fine society now. Everyone knows there's a different father for each child of the Countess of Oxford. And your dear Countess de Lescaux is no pattern-card of maidenly behavior." The words once started could not be held back. "I may have a brazen tongue, sir, but your friends haven't a chaste spot in all their bodies."

"Enough!" cried Lady Annabelle.

Caroline blushed scarlet. She had no compunctions about speaking freely and frankly to Montgomery, but she had always maintained all propriety with Lady Annabelle.

"I'm sorry, Lady Annabelle," she murmured, aghast, but the confusion between the ladies did not put an end to the discussion as far as Montgomery was concerned.

"Mind your own conduct," he said in a threatening voice, "and as far as others are concerned, in future, I pray you will keep your observations to yourself."

"I *do* mind my own conduct," was Caroline's retort. "And you needn't worry I shall copy what I see among the ladies of your *haut ton*. The miners of Merthyr Tydfil don't eat well, but they show more respect one for the other than . . ."

Now Lady Annabelle took Caroline by the arm. "More than enough!" she declared. "This is the outside of enough. Roderick! If you are not accompanying us, be so good as to see the carriage is ready, and stay out of my sight."

Caroline fought back tears. "Why is it, Lady Annabelle," she managed to say, "that grateful though I am to that wretched man, when we speak it always ends in argument? What is the matter with me that I can behave so badly?"

"It's not your fault," said the Dragon softly, in a most undragonlike tone of voice. Caroline had long been convinced of the old woman's goodwill, but she had never spoken with such undisguised tenderness before. "I haven't seen much of my young cousin in the past few years, but enough to see the drastic change that has come over him. He was a cheerful loving child, forgiving and generous to a fault. Then, this disenchantment . . . I almost think it more of an enchantment than a disenchantment, as though some devilish spell has deprived him of the better part of his nature."

"Then I don't remember wrong," whispered Caroline.

"Remember what, dear?" asked Lady Annabelle.

"I met Captain Montgomery many years ago," said the girl hesitantly, "when I was a child. I always remembered him that way, with a warm and easy way. I didn't recognize him at first when he came for me."

"When he what?" asked the Dragon.

Remembering the lie she was living, Caroline stammered, "When he came for me . . . when he met my stagecoach at the Rose and Thistle."

"Yes, that's right." The lady shook her head knowingly. "It seemed a gesture that the Roderick of past years would have made. I was cheered, I'll allow, by his consideration for you, although it did make me nervous at first. I thought perhaps you would bring out the best in him again."

"Then what made you uneasy?" Caroline held her breath.

"I wanted to see Roderick in love. I wanted—I still would love—to see him married and with children. Our line is dying out, you know. But at the same time, I admit I was ready to find fault with any girl of his choice. When a man remains an eligible bachelor for so long, one naturally assumes he is waiting for perfection. But what usually happens is that he settles for someone of little consequence."

It was Jenkins who informed them of the readiness of their carriage. They walked outside in silence, but once seated, Lady Annabelle took Caroline by the hand.

"I thought he was in love with you, child, and I was quite prepared to dislike you heartily. I guess I was wrong on both counts. You are an exceptional young woman, but it seems my cousin will steadfastly refuse to let you—or anyone—make him happy."

In the dark of the carriage, Lady Annabelle could not have seen the blush suffuse Caroline's face. But somehow she felt in sudden communication with the girl's heart, and a suspicion of the reason for Caroline's recent apathy to life made itself known to the old woman.

"My dear," she said softly, "I would have encouraged a match if I thought it in your best interests. But I will not let you throw yourself away. I fear the Captain is an unfit companion for a woman of spirit and passion."

This last word made Caroline flush even more, and this time it would not have been uncanny had the Dragon perceived the reaction, so strong that heat from Caroline's cheeks radiated throughout the enclosed space. "Yes, passion, my dear. I'm not impugning your chastity, just remarking upon your character. If my cousin were a different man, I would happily give you both my blessing. But as things stand, even if you were in love with him," she said those last words carefully, as if to underline that she knew the true state of affairs with greater precision than she was ready to admit, "I should oppose your marriage with all my strength. Roderick is beyond redemption, I fear. But I shall not allow you to ruin your own life as well."

CHAPTER THIRTEEN

A woman's heart leads her in a dance in which her steps weave an intricate tapestry of desire and retreat. The rhythm is not so steady and easy to perceive as the three-quarter beat of the waltz. Memories of old dances and songs are shot through the texture like golden embroidery through silk. And in this world of images and sensations—which paradoxically is veiled and rendered mysterious by consciousness and by conscience—it is well nigh impossible to trace and follow the byways and to determine what drives a woman's will from one point to the next. So it would be futile to try and state with any certainty what made Caroline Bramwell begin to think on Lord St. Clair as a friend. She herself never stopped to reflect. She knew well she didn't love him, but she enjoyed his company in spite of—or maybe because of—the warnings she'd received from Lady Annabelle.

Of course she had no intention of being led astray or into any sort of dalliance with the man. Even had Caroline been a more brazen young thing, she thought his age and girth did little to inspire romantic sentiment. She did think of him as a friend, however irregular, and reflected that it was her fate to find herself always most happy with irregular people—a classification that embraced Montgomery, Emma, and even Lady Annabelle.

Perhaps she cared for him because his behavior broke though the ice of her grief and put up obstacles to her further withdrawal from the world. Or perhaps it was because of what he threatened. St. Clair was a rake and a scoundrel, the Dragon had said. St. Clair led women to ruin. But the old lady had also told Caroline that marriage to Montgomery would be throwing her life away. As she was unable to throw herself away on the man she loved, perhaps in the depths of her heart, she was tempted to throw herself away anyway with a man she didn't love. In this way she associated the dissolute St. Clair with the noble Captain. The men could not have been more dissimilar, yet each represented the possibility of destruction. And Caroline, who had lived through many dangers and no longer valued her life, was not afraid.

Caroline would have explained more simply why she felt such pleasure when St. Clair was announced at Chelton House: "He makes me laugh."

So she drew her brush quickly through her hair without bothering to call for Mary, and hurried downstairs one morning in early June.

Ordinarily, it was St. Clair's discourse that provoked her amusement and occasionally her anger. It was the parrying of wits that made his arrival a tonic to her spirits, though she sometimes thought how much more enjoyable it would be to engage in verbal battle with Montgomery instead. But on this particular morning, St. Clair's appearance left her gaping open-mouthed in astonishment before he'd even uttered a greeting.

Caroline was familiar with the phenomenon of gentlemen who enjoyed dressing as bruisers and coachmen. In fact, Montgomery's attire on the night he came to take her away from her uncle had been a relatively civilized variation on that theme. And considering the long, hard horseback journey Montgomery had undertaken in order to reach her, his common garb, his cloak, and riding whip had been practical accessories and not mere affectation. But nothing had prepared her for the sight of St. Clair.

"Whatever has happened to your teeth?" she asked, forgetting modesty for a moment.

"I've had them filed," he replied. "Easier to spit." No sooner said than done. St. Clair proceeded to demonstrate the ease of expectoration on the Turkey carpet of the drawing room. "Dust of the road," he explained rather than apologized. And then followed the spittle with a stream of oaths and curses that would have set Caroline blushing to the roots of her black hair had she understood the meaning of even the half of them.

"There will be circumstances when the most politic thing to do is to go on as though nothing were amiss," had been one of Emma's lessons. The advice had been in anticipation of the faux pas that Caroline herself was bound to make. But Caroline decided the wisdom might be well applied in this case. Besides, she knew not what else to do.

"Will you take tea, my Lord?" she asked agreeably as if the strange scene that had just passed were the most natural way in the world for a Corinthian to enter a drawing room.

"Tea?" thundered the man, covering up with noise and bluster his surprise at the calm way she treated his performance. "Tea! 'Twill not e'en serve to polish my boots. Noxious liquid, it is. 'Mme. Geneva' is my first love, and 'tis 'strip-me-naked' for me."

"Ah," she replied, still coolly. "If it's 'blue ruin' you seek, let me call upon Jenkins. Perhaps he can direct you to the nearest tavern. The city is a large and wondrous place, and I collect you have lost your way."

At that point, their eyes met and both Caroline and the Lord could restrain their laughter no longer.

The Dragon came scurrying into the room, attracted by the sound, and Caroline found herself glancing instinctively to the carpet and sighing with relief to see the moist spot quite lost in the overall pattern.

"Good morning, Lady Annabelle," said St. Clair in all formal politeness. He bent his head gracefully and took the Dragon's hand to his lips which curved slightly in a secret smile to Caroline. "I came around to invite Miss Bramwell for a drive." And without waiting for the permission he feared Lady Annabelle would withhold, he led Caroline from the room.

"Frenchified manners," muttered the Dragon, wiping the memory of the kiss off her hand and onto the old-fashioned bustle of her dowdy dress.

How could the servants have allowed St. Clair to be shown in and to be left alone with Caroline without first advising her? The Dragon was upset. And worse, she was angry at herself as well. Lady Annabelle knew that Caroline should not be out riding unchaperoned, but she had little enough power over the girl. And with Montgomery away from the house, she felt helpless.

Outside with St. Clair, Caroline was heedless of the worry she was causing Lady Annabelle. It was a beautiful day, with blue sky and fluffy clouds that held no threat of rain.

"Wait till you see it," said St. Clair proudly. "The stableboy will bring it back around directly."

"It?" asked Caroline, intrigued.

She hadn't long to wait before the elegant black high perch phaeton was in front of the house with its team of greys. It was astounding to see a vehicle that could be so open and so sleek and yet rise as high as the first-storey windows.

"Captain Montgomery drives nothing like that, I'll wager," continued St. Clair. "I may be the old man, but by Jove, he acts like one."

Caroline smiled at the portly, file-toothed gentleman fondly. One thing about St. Clair, she thought, he might dress up or be involved in stunts and misdeeds, but he was open and honest about himself. He might play a role for fun, but he never really pretended to be anything he was not.

"Can your reputation withstand a ride with me?" he asked, assisting her up to the high seat.

"Drive on, Methusaleh," she replied lightly.

"Your guardian threatens to develop into a fusty Tulip before too many years pass," commented St. Clair, and Caroline stiffened.

"I tolerate a great many liberties of speech because I find them harmless," she answered carefully as they trotted through Mayfair, "but I will not accept the company of one who speaks ill of Captain Montgomery."

St. Clair demonstrated his new ability by spitting over the side and onto the street. "I paid fifty guineas to be taught to do that properly," he added with a grin.

"I should have thought it a natural ability in man that required no cultivation," she said in a mockingly prim voice.

"All natural abilities can be improved with training and practice," he replied, feigning pomposity. "Especially in the hands of an experienced teacher," he added in a lower voice. "Don't you think?"

What a child he was! thought Caroline, laughing rather than taking offense at the implied suggestion. How could anyone be angry with him for long? She saw no manly virtues in the affected old gentleman, but surely Lady Annabelle was wrong to think he presented any danger.

"Don't set your bristles up, dear lady," said St. Clair, returning the conversation to the theme of her guardian. "Montgomery and I were friends of a sort once, but lately he's quite cut me off. Yes, I was invited to your little dinner, but he hardly directs a word to me. In fact, many of my old friends no longer recognize or receive me, and I'm quite at a loss to discover the cause for this sudden reversal of my notorious popularity."

This unexpected and frank account tallied with what Lady Annabelle had said. Caroline laughed to hide her prior knowledge. "And so that's why you devote so many hours to a poor provincial like myself. No one else will see you! I'm grateful that you've told me. Your attentions are now not half so flattering."

St. Clair's eyes strayed from the road as he regarded her face. "Dear child, I wonder that Montgomery hasn't pulled in your reins. You go your own way, girl, and I bless you for it. You lack the brazen audacity of our licentious titled ladies, but neither are you dull-witted and silent like the other blushing maidens one must dance and converse with, so tediously, all season long."

This speech, kind though it was, embarrassed Caroline and she was glad to cut it short: "I see, my Lord, why you lose your friends. You are so engrossed in this flattering exposition, you have failed to return the greetings of at least five people we have passed."

He shook his head. "Does nothing ruffle your feathers?" he asked, and urged the horses to greater speed, at the same time putting a restraining arm around the girl as they were momentarily thrown forward as the horses lurched, then regained a smooth, fast pace.

"Do you enjoy a fast pace?" asked St. Clair, growing exhilarated as he controlled the high-strung beasts under the blazing sun of a glorious day, ignoring the people whose attention had been fixed at the queer sight of him, in low garb, with Caroline laughing by his side.

Caroline's stomach fluttered almost unbearably with the speed and jouncing of the carriage, but she would not admit such a thing to St. Clair. Besides, the sunlight, the excitement, the wind whipping her hair in her face, were all bringing her back to life. She hated and loved the ride all at once.

"Yes, I do," she answered with deceptive self-control. "So urge them on, do. I didn't expect so sedate a ride beside so rough a coachman."

The horses broke into a canter, and other carriages pulled over to let them pass, unwilling to risk an incident.

"Faster! Faster!" cried Caroline, almost against her will. Her heart was pounding in such terror, she felt with the next turn it might lurch out through her mouth.

"Faster?" whispered St. Clair, in shocked admiration.

Servants jumped back to curbside and children were pointing and screaming as they careened on their way. The morning ride had suddenly turned into a deadly contest and neither side could have explained how or why or at what moment the game had begun in earnest.

"Faster!" demanded Caroline, thrilled by the man's hesitation and by the momentary look of fear that passed over his face before he managed to hide it. She leaned forward, laughing and hoped her laughter sounded relaxed when, in truth, it sprang from a terrified need to discharge the tension and fear.

"Surely you are happy now," said St. Clair, almost hoarsely as they whipped around a bend and the phaeton almost lost the road.

"Faster," she replied.

Caroline was determined to win the war of nerves with the old man. He was an experienced horseman and driver. She trusted him completely. When the way became too dangerous, he would ignore her challenge. But she would see to it that it would be Lord St. Clair who would have to back down and pull in the reins. Caroline Bramwell would go on calling for greater speed, for greater danger. Perhaps it was because she had so little control over her own destiny that she felt such a compelling need to emerge victorious over St. Clair.

"This is a most unfashionable hour to be seen in Hyde Park," she managed to gasp as he directed the phaeton into the secluded green.

"Then no one fashionable will be around to see us," he answered.

Lord St. Clair was not to be outdone by a mere girl. Many unflattering epithets had been applied to him, but coward had never been one of them. If Caroline wished the horses to run free, well, they would run free and wild. But St. Clair had not completely lost his wits or sense of responsibility. On the Mayfair streets, a tragedy could easily occur, and innocent people could be hurt. In the Park, there was little chance of a disturbance that could send the greys bolting out of control. And if any necks were to be risked, it would be his neck and the girl's, both willing participants.

Caroline was disappointed that St. Clair was so unwilling to admit defeat. Why did he have to make it so hard? Why couldn't he be gracious? She thought she'd surely be sick if the ride continued another minute, but Caroline was as stubborn as she was beautiful, and so when St. Clair, breathing huffily, asked, "Are you satisfied, my dear?" she held her seat and replied, "Can't your greys go faster, my Lord?"

St. Clair hesitated, discretion fighting a losing battle with pride.

The horses broke into a full gallop. The game was over and the real struggle had just begun.

St. Clair grabbed Caroline as she began to slide from the perch. "Stop them, please," she whispered, in a cold sweat and terrified beyond belief.

But her surrender came too late. St. Clair was struggling just to keep the sickened girl from falling and the horses were completely out of control. "It would be dangerous to bring them to an immediate halt," he lied, knowing that if he told the truth, they would both panic and that could only make matters worse.

At least the horses kept the track and didn't try to lose the phaeton by plunging into the trees. The carriage swayed drunkenly from side to side, and St. Clair's new fear was that they would come unhitched at any moment and be sent flying.

Through her shock, Caroline was aware of one sensation fighting through the nausea and terror. She wanted to live! It was only now, in a situation which she feared she might not survive, that she knew for sure she wanted to go on living. The dances at Almack's were tedious, but she wanted to dance. She wanted her legs to be healthy and strong, and she could see them, in her nightmare vision, crushed and broken beneath the chariot.

Oh, to be in the parlor taking tea with the Dragon!

Oh, to be sitting upstairs while Mary dressed her hair!

To be bored by the Marquess of Holtsford, to be scolded by Montgomery, to be beaten by the Lord of Bedlam. Anything.

"Help," she wept quietly, clinging to St. Clair. Panic had rendered him incapable of doing anything to regain control of the team. Sensing their superiority, the horses shook themselves and whinnied.

Suddenly, there was a black stallion bearing down on them. In the confusion, all Caroline could see were the rider's eyes—two gray eyes, darkening almost to black as they flashed with a dangerous and angry light.

The off-leader reared at the sight of the strange horse and rider and for an earth-shattering moment it seemed the occupants of the phaeton would be thrown. But Montgomery had the team bridle in hand. She could see his lips moving, talking in a voice so firm yet fierce it brought even the wild greys into gradual submission.

The gallop slowed to a canter. The phaeton and the accompanying rider continued the near-fatal ride through the Park, gradually slowing, the world gradually, slowly, slowly, becoming safe and secure and stationary once more.

But to Caroline, everything was still spinning. Sky and earth, horse and man, angry blazing eyes, blazing hooves. By the time the phaeton had come to a complete stop, she had passed out, unconscious, on the high perch.

CHAPTER FOURTEEN

She was rising, floating, drifting amid a chorus of voices and cries of alarm.

"I can't find the words to apologize properly. But she'll be all right?" A broken voice ending in a hesitant question.

Two strong arms holding her closer.

"Sir," echoing through her head, "you are not welcome in this house."

Laid down somewhere soft and steady, comforting hands, a girl's voice, "Miss! Miss!" and a pungent scent forcing its way into her consciousness.

The two men, familiar voices. "And I demand to know why. You know it goes beyond this, Montgomery."

"I don't think I need explain."

"Miss! Miss!" wishing to push the helpful hands away, to make the girl leave, trying to hear the conversation of the men. The girl is in the way. "Miss, please get well!"

"It is my relationship with Hélène?" the man asks quietly.

"You are not ashamed to talk of it?" asks the one called Montgomery. Ah yes, Montgomery, now she remembers Montgomery.

"Your standards of loyalty are far more rigid than mine," says the other. "Yet if you see my action as a betrayal . . ."

"And what else can it be called?" Montgomery is angry.

Why won't the girl take the smelling-salts away? If I push them away, thought Caroline, now aware of her surroundings and the people in her room, *Mary will holler I'm revived, and they will not forget themselves so much as to continue talking.*

"Oh, come, Captain. What are these treacheries between men but minor personal matters?"

"A minor personal matter?" repeated Montgomery, almost without giving credence to the words. "Are you such a blackguard," he cried, "that you do not even see the question of principle?"

Even Mary stiffened and ceased her ministrations, cowed by the outburst.

Please go on, thought Caroline. *Don't stop talking.*

"At least comfort yourself," put in St. Clair, "with the consoling thought that the connection has ended. She wants no more to do with me."

"And why should she?" asked Montgomery coldly. "She's a predatory creature. She got what she wanted and you are of no use to her any longer."

"My dear fellow," objected St. Clair, "Hélène is a worldly woman and free with her charms, but in what sense predatory? She never accepted tuppence, not a single token of my affection. Are you suggesting that ladies of easy virtue now seek conquests and carve notches on their bedposts? I do not recall seeing any such when I was permitted access to the furniture. Anyway, my friend," St. Clair's voice was reasonable and calm now, "your problem is an excess of discretion. When I first became friends with Hélène, I was quite unaware of your liaison . . ."

"My what?" demanded Montgomery.

"You must believe me," insisted St. Clair, "that the betrayal you charge me with was made quiet unawares."

"Unawares, you say," mused the Captain. "There may be more truth to that than you realize." Then, as though he were realizing for the first time that he and St. Clair were not alone in the room, he spoke briskly. "This is no place for such a conversation, sir. We are in a sickroom."

Caroline heard the clatter of their boots in the hall, and Montgomery's voice from the door, "Mary, I shall want to see your mistress when she is revived."

The words should have gladdened Caroline's heart, but the voice was ominous. The Captain would not be paying her a friendly visit.

She pondered the words she had overheard. *What did it all mean?* Then dizzy again, she was falling. Hours passed.

The velvet curtains were drawn so that the sunlight which filtered into Caroline's bedroom was muted, soft, and thick. The soothing atmosphere was torn suddenly by cries of annoyance.

"Don't push me, cousin. I'm moving as fast as I can." The Dragon sounded truly agitated. "If I fall and break my hips, or whatever, I shall denounce you. Let me go, Roderick!"

Caroline's peace was thus disturbed as surely as if the curtains had been rent asunder and a glaring sun had entered to blind her eyes.

Lady Annabelle flounced into the room and shook

Montgomery's hands from her arm. She seated herself before Caroline's dressing table and elaborately arranged her full skirts while regaining her affronted dignity.

The Captain, in his blue-gray morning coat and tight breeches that clearly outlined his muscular legs, had never looked so handsome. The color had risen to his face and the tension in his whole form suggested an outpouring of energy from what had for too long seemed a shell of a man.

"I wanted you both here," he began without any pleasantries or inquiries as to Caroline's health, "because what I have to say touches upon you both. It is not my station in life to run a boardinghouse for the fair sex," he said. "Miss Bramwell is here due to an obligation I seek to fulfill. And Cousin Annabelle, you are here for the sole purpose of supervising her and acting as sponsor and chaperone. You are my kin, and as such have your claims on my love and duty, but you know very well that you've a home of your own, and that your presence here is an inconvenience to both of us. I trusted you with regard to this young person and hoped I would be free to attend to my own business."

Lady Annabelle regarded herself in the mirror instead of facing the Captain. Adjusting her wig, she spoke, "I think, dear boy, that we should all be giving thanks for Caroline's safety instead of assigning blame. You do run on, you know, like some top-lofty parson hiding behind false piety and begrudging any moment of laughter in his parish."

"When I want your opinion, I shall call for it," retorted Montgomery, "but I suggest that you do not stand and wait for my call. I pursued you this morning," he said, directing the words to Caroline, "to save your reputation. Little did I know I'd end up having to save your wretched neck. I have been sadly mistaken in you."

"That is no way to . . ." interrupted an angry Dragon, but Caroline felt she had forfeited all right to support.

"Captain Montgomery, please," she whispered, tears welling up in her eyes.

"You told me once you were not the sort of young thing to require smelling-salts, and I took you at your word. Yet you've had us terrified all day by your failure to revive. I credited you with a ready wit, but you have since showed your total lack of common sense. I expect talk of this incident will be all over in no time, and will serve to frighten your more respectable suitors away. St. Clair might marry you to make amends, and that's probably the fate you deserve, yet I should be the laughingstock of the *ton* if the girl presented by my family married such a one as he."

"So what am I to do now?" she asked, chastened. "I promise you, I shall do as you say."

"I don't believe that for a moment," returned Montgomery, "but at least you are learning the right lines. To start with, I am sending your regrets to Carlton House."

"My what?"

"We have all been invited to the Prince Regent's fête," he explained, "but you, dear, will not attend. You are not, in fact, going anywhere at all for a while. Because I am going to lock you in your room. Let the world believe you indisposed from your escapade in the Park. Let them think what they will. But you are not leaving this room."

"For another four months, kind sir?" asked Caroline. "You forget I have practice in drawing upon my own reserves for entertainment."

"Whatever are you talking about?" demanded the Dragon, and Montgomery whirled around almost furious. It was unclear, however, just which of the ladies had aroused this latest access of anger.

"As for you, I have a key to your room, too, Cousin. Remember that. I shall not deprive you of the fête, but neither your age nor your title exempts you from the duty of obedience while you are under my roof."

"Well, I never!" exclaimed the Dragon, standing to leave the room. "Hospitality the like of this cannot be met with anywhere else in England!"

"This is not mere punishment," was Montgomery's closing remark before he, too, left the room. "You are being afforded seclusion to encourage you to meditate upon your misdeeds and make resolutions for the future."

Then Caroline Bramwell was alone, and a prisoner, once more.

Montgomery unlocked the door to allow the servants into the room at mealtimes, and he examined the dishes to be sure no means of escape could be provided, and that no books were being smuggled in with the food. "I will not have your attention diverted by literature when you should be reflecting upon other matters of more pressing importance," he said. Aside from those words, he did not linger in conversation.

And so it was with special joy and relief that Caroline saw the door open one day. The Dragon stepped inside, a finger to her lips in an exaggerated plea for silence.

"You haven't been forgotten, my dear," she whispered, kissing Caroline's cheek with her dry lips. "Let us hope he does not miss the key. Caroline, dear," she continued, "I begin to suspect you are not quite what you seem, and I am eager to hear all."

Caroline's laughter was nervous. "You've all made much of me," she said carelessly. "It's no wonder that you should all be disappointed to see what a silly creature I really am. I never thought I deserved the good opinion you seemed to have of me . . . but please, Lady Annabelle, I want to hear all about the fête. Captain Montgomery did let you attend, didn't he? He wouldn't have dared to lock you in your room?"

"For four months?" asked the old lady, meaningfully.

"Even for a night." Caroline refused to be drawn. "Do tell me everything."

Lady Annabelle began cautiously, unwilling to relinquish the subject that had aroused her curiosity, but as she began to describe the splendors of the previous night, she quite forgot herself as she relived the excitement.

"There were two thousand guests," she began, "if you can imagine such a throng. Roderick is an important man, my dear, and it's no wonder he has no patience for the ladies. There were only four hundred places inside the State apartments, and we were included, right there, not far from the Prince himself. Although, Caroline, I would for the pure pleasure have preferred to be outside."

"Guests had to remain out of doors?" asked Caroline.

"Under canvas. Why, they had built a perfect maze of trees and shrubs and all festooned with flowers. Hung over with lights suspended from the boughs. Thousands of lights, dear, more than stars in the clearest skies, and of all colors, too. There were covers laid for sixteen hundred out there . . ."

"Covers? People, two thousand people, actually sat for supper?"

"Not till well after two in the morning, and by then, many had supped enough on liquor so the food no longer held any charm to the palate, but a real party it was, dear. But that's all the least of it—it was Carlton House that was so magnificent, and that is what I should be describing to you . . ."

"But the fête must have drained the entire Royal Treasury . . ."

"Some said fifteen thousand pounds, some said as much as thirty thousand. Who knows? But such an occasion, my dear. I even let Roderick talk me into wearing a gown more suited to the era. Though I felt rather foolish wearing epaulettes on my shoulders like a soldier, still, he says it is the fashion for ladies today, and the epaulettes, I admit, were of embossed Spanish silver which did make them rather dear and not at all common." The excitement seemed to have pushed Lady Annabelle the last step into her second childhood, although some would have said the shock had restored her to her senses. She babbled on like a girl, quite forgetting the "original" role she preferred to play. "I had a silver tunic brought from Ireland, and I took out all my diamonds. My chains, my stomacher, my armlets and brooches—Dear, I'd quite forgotten what a dreadfully rich old woman I am. And, of course, my feathers. I feel naked in public without ostrich feathers. But this is hardly what you want to hear." The Dragon interrupted herself.

"Oh, but it is!" exclaimed Caroline, delighted as long as the subject stayed clear of dangerous waters.

"There were six tons of gold and silver plate to dine from, and the band of Guards, all in State, played the music. Caroline, you could not believe how beautiful it was. More colored lights than stars, and more diamonds than lights. The Prince was in scarlet, with gold lace, if you can picture anything more brilliant . . . And I do think he had heard of your presentation ball, my ball, for his decorators quite copied my own little idea . . . We had a bridge, New Bridge, do you recall? Well, the Prince had a river."

"A river?" Caroline laughed. "The Prince Regent had the river Taff running through the Throne Room?"

"No, not the Throne Room," admitted Lady Annabelle, "the Conservatory. And I doubt it was the river Taff. More a meandering stream. It started from a basin near his own seat at table—and wait, there were bridges—and not at all as fine as the one we had built for you—mere toys, and one with a small silly tower rising from it—to cross the stream, but of course, not strong enough to bear the weight of a proper person. Not a proper bridge like we built for you. And he stocked his puddle with gold and silver fishes. Ah, you cannot imagine the effect, that touch of rusticity amid the uniforms and gowns!"

"I wish I could have seen it," said Caroline, "because you are right. My imagination quite fails faced with the task of recreating the scene you've tried to paint in words."

"You can still see it," said Lady Annabelle. "The Conservatory and the Throne Room, too—you'll see the portraits and alabaster tables and you will not believe their perfection. We've an alabaster ornament here and there, of course, but not the alabaster the poets write about. That's what you'll see at Carlton House. As for the canopy—my dear, there are four helmets mounted upon it, and each one is of solid gold. But, of course, you know I've such a weakness for plumes—"

"The plumes are made of solid gold?" laughed Caroline.

"No, no, of course not. They are set in the gold, and must have been two feet in height, if you can see them, pure white, rising and waving lightly in the air before our eyes and above our heads. And the ballroom, when you see . . ."

"But really, Lady Annabelle. You've told me enough to make me regret my mischief most grievously. I don't want to know any more of what I missed through my own fault."

"But you will not miss it all . . ."

"What then? Have you brought me a private invitation to visit the Prince? Really, Lady Annabelle, what's done is done and an opportunity lost does not return."

Now Lady Annabelle brightened even more, and smiled like the bearer of good tidings. "The royal apartments are to be open to the public for days, until June twenty-sixth. Which gives us a week to have Roderick forgive you. You've been punished enough, and I don't think he'll want you to miss this. It's a vision of beauty you can see once in a lifetime."

"If it's up to Montgomery," said Caroline, "I suspect I shall live without the vision of beauty."

"Then we shall concoct a way to smuggle you from this gaol," replied Lady Annabelle promptly. "I won't see you deprived."

Caroline clasped the woman's hands with joy. "How can I possibly thank you?" she asked. "For everything."

Lady Annabelle held the soft hand in hers a moment before giving her reply. "By telling me the truth, child. About everything."

Montgomery had called the Lady Annabelle "the last person in the world in whom I would confide," but Caroline suspected he had never seen past his cousin's exterior. She trusted Lady Annabelle, and yet, she knew her story was so strange, and so improper, it was with some trepidation, though with infinite relief, that she began to speak.

Even when the story was told, Caroline still dared not raise her face and look at Lady Annabelle directly.

"My cousin surprises me," said the Dragon at last, lifting Caroline's face up and out of the shadows. "He surprises me by his goodness to you, and makes me love him. And he surprises me that after all you have suffered he could treat you so cruelly and with so little consideration. I could hate him for it."

"I don't hate him,' said Caroline vehemently. "I rather think he is uncertain how to go about bringing a young lady into society. He has my best interests at heart, it seems, but I tend to disagree with the way he promotes those interests."

"Don't be so understanding!" exclaimed the Dragon. "Think of yourself for a moment, my dear. You have allowed people to make your plans for you long enough. You are young and beautiful. You are healthy and you are here in London under my sponsorship. You can have anything you set your mind and heart to . . . You have only to determine what you want out of life, and then go after it . . ."

Lady Annabelle noticed with concern the change that had come over the girl. Caroline had been relieved and overjoyed when she first realized that Lady Annabelle was her ally, and that the woman was in fact moved and enchanted by her strange and romantic tale. But the old lady's words of encouragement and inspiration seemed to have had an effect opposite to that intended. The more assurance Lady Annabelle gave, the more listless and distracted Caroline became.

"Come, child, it isn't all bad," whispered the old woman. "Tell me, child. Remember, you were to tell me everything and to hold nothing back."

Caroline bit her lip, longing to speak and longing at the same time to remain silent.

"What is the trouble, child?"

Catching her breath and screwing up her resolve, Caroline spoke: "The trouble, Lady Annabelle, is that I do know what I want out of life . . . and you have already told me you would oppose such an outcome with all your strength."

"Roderick!" The old woman broke into mirthless laughter. "So that's the way it is," she said softly, and threw her old thin arms around the weeping girl.

CHAPTER FIFTEEN

When Montgomery entered the house later that day, Jenkins informed him that Lady Annabelle was waiting in the drawing room and wished to see him on a matter of great importance.

Sighing, Montgomery went to join his aged relation. Women, it was true, added color and life to a house. But what they mostly brought into one's life were wearisome complications.

"Cousin," she said, rising to accept a kiss upon her withered cheek. From somewhere in her memory, the Lady Annabelle had dredged up a recollection of seductive coyness. Her attempt to duplicate the manner she had practiced almost seventy years earlier had at least the happy result of placing her voice in a more moderate register, but the overall effect remained eccentric as ever.

"I know all," she breathed in a despondent tone, as soon as Montgomery had taken a seat in the well-padded armchair. "And I shall tell all."

The Captain looked up at her and his gray eyes

seemed to smoke and flash briefly. Then he quickly turned away.

Strange, thought the old woman. *Is he upset to see all his inconvenience and trouble go for naught? Or could that have been actual concern for the chit?*

"You didn't let me finish my thought," she added querulously, forgetting the role of blushing, soft-spoken youth. "I intend to tell all, unless Caroline is released immediately from the undignified confinement you have imposed."

"I'm surprised to hear you take her part," he said uncertainly. "What scheme is this?"

"It is no scheme. I'm fond of the girl, and since you have obligated yourself to assisting her in her distress, I intend to see that you do so."

Now Montgomery looked at her and the years seemed to fall away, until he was a little boy again, standing abashed before his elders, expecting a punishment and being surprised, instead, with a sweet.

"Cousin Annabelle, forgive me for misjudging you," he said at last, an adult once more. "I didn't expect you would take so kindly to this endeavor."

"You were quite right," agreed Lady Annabelle. "Had I heard the story first, I should have had grave reservations about the young lady before I even met her. But having first known and developed an affection for the young lady, her sad and romantic past only increases the fondness she inspires. She refers to herself as an irregular sort of person. I should say rather *unusual*, and her unusually good qualities merit an unusual story in the background. Anyway, I must compliment you both on how successfully you have managed. I should never have guessed that anything was amiss without the conversational indiscretions that resulted from your locking the poor girl in her room."

"You win," said Montgomery. "Here, let me give you the key and then you may release her with my compliments."

"I have the key, Cousin," said Lady Annabelle, holding it before his surprised, but amused, eyes. "But," she said, handing it to him, "don't you think you should release her yourself?"

If Lady Annabelle had expected Montgomery to offer a pretty speech as he unlocked the door, her expectations were disappointed.

We can't have everything we want in this world, she reminded herself.

But when she imagined how Caroline would search the man's face for some trace of feeling, and finding none, would settle at least for her freedom, Lady Annabelle found herself growing uncharitable toward her cousin.

And why can't we have what we want? she demanded angrily. *And why not? What is the matter with that man? Just tell me that,* she thought. *Why not?*

If Caroline was equally annoyed and disappointed, she did not show it, but reemerged brightly into the world like a young bird eager to fly.

And so it was that Caroline and Mary were seated together in Montgomery's carriage one afternoon, at a standstill, hoping for a breeze, and wondering when they would be permitted to move. Carriages in front of them, behind them, and to either side likewise waited, and the vehicles extended the entire length of Pall Mall.

"I don't understand," said Mary. Her voice was complaining but her eyes were alive with excitement and delight. "How came they to serve supper to two thousand when now the guards cannot even magage to admit the people who merely wish to take a look?"

"I think the entire population of London is here," replied Caroline, "and that's a good million."

"And is a million so much more than two thousand?" persisted Mary.

"Why, yes, it is. I fancy your eyes could not take in the sight of a million persons all at once."

"But if two thousand have already been, shouldn't there be one million less two thousand now?"

"Perhaps the lucky ones wish to take another look . . . besides their numbers would hardly swell or decrease this crush in any noticeable way."

"Gracious, but it's 'ot," continued Mary. "And I can't see 'ow the 'orses will ever get through."

Indeed, Mary was quite right in her doubts. "We'll do much better afoot," said Caroline. "Come, let's go."

Mary grabbed her arm. "Oh, no, Miss. 'Twould be one thing if I went, but 'tis not fit for a lady."

"Oh, come now, Mary, you know better than that. Ladies have legs the same as you and can use them."

"Yes, Miss, I do know that, but Cap'n Montgomery do not. I mean, most likely 'e knows you 'ave legs—oh, Miss!" Mary blushed in confusion. "—but you know 'e won't like your climbing out and through the crowd. 'E's a one that's like to lock you up again if 'e 'ear of it."

"But Mary, if I'm not to get to Carlton House, he might just as well have left me locked up to begin with. The Prince Regent has opened his doors to us, and think what disloyal subjects we must be if we do not make every possible effort to get past those doors." So saying, she jumped first from the carriage, and then assisted her embarrassed abigail down to the street.

"Everyone is staring at you, Miss," worried Mary.

"Let them," replied Caroline lightly. "If they've any sense, they'll join us, though I rather hope they do not.

If we're the only ones afoot, we shan't have difficulty in reaching the gates."

Holding hands to avoid being separated in the crowd, Caroline and Mary wended their way among carriages and horses, and coachmen who had jumped to the ground and were trying to soothe their unhappy, whinnying beasts. Caroline was in a hurry to leave the horses behind, reminding her as they did of her near disaster in Hyde Park.

At first Caroline and Mary were the only ladies on the street, but suddenly, as if she had given a signal or opened a door, ladies were following her example and alighting from their carriages all over Pall Mall.

"Shocking," muttered Caroline in irritation as the crowd swelled. "Have they no shame? No consideration for their fair reputations?"

"I'm so glad you set out, Miss Bramwell," cried a plain young woman whose name Caroline could not recall. "I've been begging Mama to let me go on foot, but until she saw you alight, her answer was no, no, and again no."

"I'm sure this is a gayer sight than the night of the fête," exclaimed Mary, cheering a bit as they continued to fight their way forward, and the little abigail was again correct. For Caroline had unintentionally started a veritable parade of London's most beautiful ladies, all dressed in their most elegant attire, and wearing jewels that would ordinarily be frowned upon for display during the daytime. While the fête had taken place beneath artificial lights, these ladies sparkled beneath the summer sun, which picked up all the facets of their jewels, and made the gold and silver embroidery and trim in their gowns sparkle and shimmer.

The parade began to disperse as the fine ladies overtook the crowds of common people who thronged by the gates, discussing the sights they waited to behold. Now, an occasional jewel was set here and there on the surface of the common throng. Silks and satins mingled with cotton, and an occasional hand sheathed in white kid could be seen gesturing above a sea of workmen's caps. Deprived of the sight of Carlton House, the members of the crowd were sharing the tidbits they had gleaned from others.

"I hear he's got a river running through the room," recounted a bluff and genial man, "and the ladies and gentlemen had got to fish fer their own suppers."

"Don't be a fool," snapped his wife, trying to hush him. " 'Tis an *ornamental* pool is wot it be."

"Ornamental fool is wot he be, I should say," replied the man, still bluff, but somewhat less genial.

"Oh, do hush, or they won't let us in."

"They say," another woman was holding forth to her circle of friends, "that directly acrost from the throne, there be a mirror twice as tall as a man so when you walk into the Throne Room, 'less you be the right sort wot knows his way around, you be tricked not knowing which be the throne in the mirror and what throne be the real thing."

"Spawn of the devil," commented an old man, spitting. "Crazy King George may foam at the mouth for all I care, he's still a sight better than his sons, driving us to ruin while they eat off silver and gold, chase our daughters and dance while we starve."

Mary's hand on Caroline's arm suddenly grew tight.

"What is it?" Caroline asked. The girl's grip was hurting her.

"Miss, I've got to be gone from 'ere," Mary gasped.

"But we're almost inside."

They were so close to the front of the mob, that when she stood on tiptoes Caroline could even catch a glimpse of the guards at the gate. Other bodies were pushed up close against them, and at one point, when Caroline got up on her toes for a better look, she was momentarily unable to get her feet back on the ground, but was carried just above the earth's surface by the crowd. "They will open the gates soon, and then we'll be inside," she assured the girl.

But Mary was sobbing. "Miss, there's too many people. I'm sorry. I'm so sorry."

People turned to look at the servant whose distress had mounted until she was wailing with anguish.

"Miss, it's too close. It's like being back in the mines. I can't leave you 'ere, Miss, alone, but I got to get out. I got to get away. It's the mines and we'll be buried. You can't breathe, Miss, and then the tunnel never ends. You never see the light. They push you on the trolley and the ceiling comes a tumblin' down on you, Miss. Please."

"Calm down," ordered Caroline. She felt sorry for her abigail but reasoned that a stern tone would restore the girl most effectively to her senses. All the same, Mary was right that the crush was near intolerable. Much as she longed to see the Royal apartments, Caroline would have considered leaving except that the two of them were trapped inside the mob and it was as impossible to retreat as to go forward. It would be easier to gain access to Carlton House than to work their way back to the carriage. *As soon as they open the gates,* she told herself, *we'll be through.*

"Open the gates!" shouted a man. "Will you see the people die?" And his shout was taken up by the crowd. "Open the gates!"

Indeed, the situation was becoming more drastic, as about them women were fainting away under the blazing sun. There was no room to carry them away or seek secluded spots to revive them, so the limp bodies were held propped up by the worried friends and companions.

"Open the gates!"

Caroline joined in the cry. She saw no other means to calm poor Mary whose nerves had quite given way. She got Mary to chanting as well, and at least while they hollered and clamored for an opening in the gates, they felt some release and became less mindful of their immediate discomfiture.

"Let us in!" cried Caroline. She didn't care what the interior looked like. She longed to reach Carlton House only as a sanctuary. Her bonnet had fallen from her head, and when Mary tried to retrieve it, she was almost trampled in the same crowd that trod the bonnet underfoot. Caroline grew more uneasy as she became aware of a tear through the fabric of her gown that had left one sleeve hanging and one plump arm completely exposed.

This is a nightmare, she thought, trying still to appear calm for Mary's sake if not her own.

"Down with the Prince!" came a thundering cry that was picked up in various parts of the mob. "Twenty thousand pounds for pleasure and naught for the workingman!"

No, thought Caroline. *With talk like that, they'll see to it that the guards never admit us. Shall we be trapped here days on end?*

Then a murmur ran through the crowd like a tide. The guards were opening the gates.

"It's all right now, Mary," Caroline said reassuringly. "Here we go."

Next, it was not a tide but a tidal wave, as the throng surged forward suddenly in a terrible and desperate rush. The mob tried to narrow and squeeze through the opening provided by the gates, compressing itself beyond the possible endurance of human flesh and bone, and then exploding out the other end. Caroline and Mary were lifted off their feet and carried away amid women's screams and a sea of wildly flailing arms.

Clinging together for safety, the two women almost succeeded in pulling one another to the ground to almost certain death. For before their horrified eyes, other ladies had indeed fallen to the ground and been tramped upon by hundreds of feet that were unable to stay their desperate course.

Even staying upright on foot did not necessarily save a person from brutal death, for the guards on horseback could no longer control their beasts, which reared in panic and bore down upon the crowd, crushing skulls beneath their sparking hooves.

All around there was the stench of blood and sickness and animal fear.

"Mary!" cried Caroline, for she had become separated from her companion. She called the girl's name again, but her voice could not have carried over the shattering noises of agony and terror. She would be better served to save her breath, she knew, rather than hasten her own suffocation by fruitlessly crying Mary's name.

At last she was still caught in a vast throng, but though the numbers seemed just as great as moments before, Caroline realized she was in the garden and breathing a little more freely, and had gone a few seconds without the rude and helpless jab of a knee or an elbow into her body. Her hair had come loose and was falling all over her face, and for the first time in what seemed like hours, she had enough room to move her hands and push the black curls out of her blinded eyes.

A lady stood not many yards away from her, completely stripped of clothing, trying to cover her body as best she could, and wailing piteously. Caroline pushed her way toward the poor thing, thinking only of helping her, when she realized that her own clothing, though not completely gone, was also in tatters and the state of her shredded bodice posed a great threat to her own modesty.

"I'm so shamed, I shall die!" cried the naked lady, hiding herself as best she could behind Caroline. "I shall die."

"No!" cried Caroline, suddenly sickened at a still more awful sight. For a surging crowd was approaching, kicking ahead of it a bundle that tumbled helplessly before the stumbling feet. Caroline determined the bundle was a body, a young woman's body, beaten beyond recognition. The flesh was torn and bruised, and lack of air had turned the face quite purple.

"Don't even talk about dying," said Caroline, deciding it more important to shield the naked lady's eyes from witnessing so gruesome a sight than it could be to shield the lady herself from view.

"Here, give her this," said a familiar voice, handing Caroline an apron. "Some poor ladies' maid is without it now, but at least it should be put to some use."

"Roderick!" cried Caroline, not noticing that in her shock and relief she had called him by his given name.

"Must I make it a full-time practice of saving you from danger?" he asked, it seemed with good humor, as he took Caroline by the hand. She grabbed the apron-wrapped gentlewoman with her other hand, and followed Montgomery into the house.

"A good captain always has alternate routes for retreat," he explained as he led them through corridors. At last they left the major part of the crowd behind.

"Mary?" asked Caroline weakly.

"I don't know," he admitted. "But I can't go after all of you at a time."

The ladies, who had risked their lives for a glimpse of Carlton House, now passed through it gaining only the briefest impression of tassels, drapes, pilasters, and girandoles.

"There was a temporary staircase built for the Prince Regent's entrance into the Conservatory . . . If that is generally known, the staircase will be the worst route to choose, but if it is unknown, we should be able to put the mob behind us and find our way to one of the private exits," he whispered to Caroline.

She followed him happily. It was a miracle he had come to save her just in time, and a further miracle that he was not angry with her. He seemed to be merely relieved and happy to have found her. They emerged into the ballroom with its arabesque ornamentations, and where Caroline saw their images reflected over and over in the niched French mirrors. Then down another staircase. Montgomery seemed to know the residence of the Prince as well as he knew the rooms of his own house. They groped for a moment in the windowless dark of the back stairs.

"Slowly and carefully, ladies," interrupted Montgomery. "You're both safe now, so you needn't press your pace."

But this counsel came too late. The apron-clad lady stepped lightly and quickly on the curved steps. Her dainty and unshod feet reached for where she thought the broad part of the step would be, and encountered nothing but air. She fell forward trippingly, pulling Caroline with her, while Caroline pulled her back against the wall, trying to break her fall.

Montgomery reached in the dark for his ward. Only

her torn sleeve came off in his hand. He could barely see her in the dark, but he heard her low cry and the quiet thud of her body against stone as Caroline went tumbling down the long dark stairs.

CHAPTER SIXTEEN

"I declare, this ward of yours spends more time in bed than Harriette Wilson!"

"Cousin Annabelle, you never cease to amaze me! Take care what you say now. She is awakening."

A radiant smile suffused Caroline's face as she opened her eyes to see Montgomery and Lady Annabelle both bending over her with tender concern. Time was suspended for a moment, and then memory returned and Caroline began to feel the insistent and painful throbbing in her ankle.

"You sprained it," explained Montgomery. "If you can't walk, maybe it will keep you out of trouble at last, and without my being compelled to behave like a brute in locking your door."

"I'm sorry," began Caroline.

"No, no, don't be," he stopped her apology. "I'm just grateful and happy that you're still alive . . . I've been thinking, Caroline, and though my intentions have been good, I assure you, I realize now I haven't been very understanding."

It was like a dream, Caroline thought. Had the doctor come? Had he given her laudanum to make her sleep, and was that why Montgomery looked like the man in her memory? Is that why he was suddenly kind and gentle? Because she was dreaming?

"The fault has been mine," he said. "I had quite forgotten what is was to love life, and to be hungry for sights and sounds and experience. I expected you to conform to a way of life . . ."

But as the events of the afternoon now came flooding back into Caroline's mind, a matter of urgency presented itself. As much as she was moved by Montgomery's words and wanted to hear more, she interrupted his welcome speech. "Mary?" she asked, with some trepidation.

"She found her way home bruised and shaken," said Lady Annabelle, "but her fear was mostly for your safety. I reassured her and put her to bed myself."

I'm such a wateringpot, thought Caroline, as silent tears began to leave tracks down her face. *For all my protestations to the contrary, whenever I'm moved by sadness or joy, the rains pour down with a will all their own.*

"Do you know what is strange to me?" she said, hoping by her conversation to distract the friendly eyes from her tears. "It seems my accidents always occur just when I think I've escaped a great danger."

"What do you mean?" asked Montgomery.

And looking at him and at Lady Annabelle, she was happy to answer. With these two friends there were no forbidden topics now and no secrets. The release from silence was the true meaning of freedom to Caroline.

"In the crowd," she began, "when I saw the horses rear and people fall, it reminded me of the night you came for me, when we were set upon on the road by those men. And do you remember? We escaped from them unharmed, and it was then, when it seemed everything was well with us, that Jupiter stumbled and I took that bad fall. It was the same today. I truly thought I would die, trapped in the panicked throng. Then you appeared, and led us . . ." She remembered the other lady.

"She has been restored to her family." Montgomery read her thoughts. "And when you next meet her, fully clothed, most likely you'll not even recognize one another."

Caroline smiled. "But what I mean is, only then, the same thing happened. We were safe, and then like a fool, I went tumbling down the stairs. Do you think there is a warning in all this from Providence?"

"What sort of talk is this?" Lady Annabelle was made uneasy by Caroline's words.

"That I should never count myself safe and secure? Or anyone for that matter. That danger may lurk where it is not expected . . ."

"You, my dear," said Montgomery, "have faced too many dangers for a beautiful young lady. Starting today, you are to be safe and happy. And that's an order."

"I shall gladly obey you in all, Captain," said Caroline, trying to hide the smile that wanted to break over her face.

Could it really be possible? Was everything going to work out right like in a perfect dream? Was it possible the Lady Annabelle had told him?

"Did the doctor give me laudanum?" she asked abruptly.

"No, dear. Why do you ask?" Lady Annabelle was perturbed anew by the question.

"Because I feel as though nothing can trouble me. I

wanted to be sure it's the effect of having you both here with me, and not a mere dream induced by medication."

Lary Annabelle cackled. "I'm relieved to see your accident has not made your mind any the less irregular," she said. "Now, if my cousin will leave us, I shall help you dress for supper."

"Why do I need to change my frock?" asked Caroline, longing to keep the Captain awhile longer by her side. "I shall be eating up here alone anyway."

"Is that what you'd prefer?" asked Montgomery.

"Of course not!" she exclaimed. "But until this ankle gets well, I suppose I must resign myself to another gaol term."

"I tried to apologize before," he began, "and you forced me to break off my words. Let me finish, now, Caroline. I've been rude and inconsiderate and left you too much to your own devices. No wonder you acted as you did—I refer to Berry's scales, and to that ill-advised ride with St. Clair. I am going to spend more time with you," he said, and she tingled to hear the words. "I'll carry you downstairs myself when you wish to be free of this room."

It was hard to believe. Caroline breathed deeply and looked around her. Everything seemed fresh and new. It was remarkable how everything could change overnight, how people could suddenly be what she had wished them to be.

"I must enjoy your company now while I can," Montgomery concluded, "before you leave us."

"Before I leave you?" Had she heard correctly?

"I thought your young Robert Warwick would be scared off by the incident in Hyde Park. His family is a great one for running from the slightest hint of scandal-broth. But apparently the lad is made of stronger stuff.

He's been inquiring after you for hours, and most concerned about your health."

"Is he waiting for me now below?" she asked in a voice that had become almost inaudible.

"Yes," said Montgomery, smiling fondly.

As though, thought Caroline, *he imagines he is giving me good news. Is this the explanation for his sudden courtesy, then?* she asked herself. *Just because he assumes I'll soon be taken off his hands?*

"I think I shall sup here after all," Caroline murmured. "I don't feel ready to face anyone just yet . . ."

"Nonsense," Montgomery assured her. "You look lovely."

Say it again, her heart urged him silently, and with some bitterness.

"Please send him away." She sent a look of supplication to the Lady Annabelle who seemed to hesitate and then to agree.

"Very well, dear. I shall send him packing, but I promise he'll be back tomorrow. He's quite determined to win you."

"I shall see to it myself that he departs," said Montgomery. Was it just Caroline's fancy, or did he really seem put out of the good humor he had displayed only moments earlier? "I take it you will sup with us, however? Let me know," he added shortly, "when you wish me to help you downstairs."

Caroline sighed, but decided to say nothing of her feelings when the Captain left the room. Lady Annabelle, who must have had a pretty clear idea of what was passing in the girl's heart, also refrained from any direct comment.

The two women soon had to enlist the aid of Lily, because Caroline found she couldn't support herself steadily on one leg, even leaning against the bedpost, and Lady Annabelle found herself too feeble to support the girl's weight and dress her at the same time.

"If your theory is correct, my dear," fussed the Dragon, "the worst is still to befall you. Now that you are safe from your accident, you are about to break your precious neck while attempting to dress for supper."

Lily was so alarmed at this ominous prediction, she made a quick and sudden movement that could have caused it to come true. At least her hands were quick and sure as she helped pin the floral patterned skirt to the flaps of the bodice. "It's like to invite bad fortune to talk suchlike is what my mother would 'ave said," she mumbled.

"I can manage brushing my own hair," said Caroline, dismissing the girl gently and allowing Lady Annabelle to help her to the seat before the looking-glass.

"I warn't trained fer a lady's maid," Lily pointed out loudly to herself as she headed down the stairs, still frightened by the near disaster.

"You'll be glad to have Mary to attend you again," laughed the Dragon.

"Poor Mary!" cried Caroline. "If she's awake, I'd like to see her right away. I never told you," she continued to Lady Annabelle, "that girl is as much a fraud as I am myself. She was no abigail when Montgomery took her in to serve me, but rather, he saved her from my uncle's mines. And when the crush started at Carlton House, poor thing, she felt she was back there, with the walls closing in around her and all the air gone. She wanted to leave, and she warned me. I didn't want to listen to her, but even if I had, there was no way out, nowhere to go . . ."

At this very moment, Mary appeared in the doorway, looking like a ghost. She was pale and barefoot in her nightgown, her red hair undone and standing out from her head.

"Oh, Miss!" She ran forward and embraced Caroline where she sat before the mirror. "They did tell me you was all right, but I had to see fer meself."

Caroline was embarrassed lest it appear she had been less than concerned about Mary's fate. "They told me you were asleep, but promised I should see you directly you were awake. I'm sorry for dragging you into so terrible a place," she added shyly.

"Yes, it was terrible," said Mary, "but it's over now." However, it appeared that it was not entirely over for the poor girl, because she still carried the horror of what she had undergone. "I was on the bottom awhile, Miss," and she began to cry. "It seemed like forever I was down there, and I thought they'd snap me neck with their boots, I did. But that kind of dying didn't 'ave me afeared. It was the air, Miss. With all the skirts around me face and all the people crushing down upon me, I thought I'd strangulate fer sure. I thought I'd never get to me feet again, and not knowing where you was, that's what made me fight me way to stand again."

"It's all right now," Caroline assured her. "I should have stayed in the carriage just the way you told me. Don't cry now, Mary. I should promise both you and Captain Montgomery to be more obedient in the future. I've learned my lesson."

"Forgive me if I sound incredulous," said a male voice from the doorway, and Caroline thrilled to have Montgomery again in her room. "But I fear it's no more in your nature to be obedient than it is the nature of a cow to live underwater. But stop crying, anyway, Mary. We'll just have to keep close watch over our girl since there's nothing we can do to convince her to be more careful for herself."

Mary's hands flew to her uncombed hair, and with blushes, bobs, and curtseys, she hugged Caroline once more and then fled from the room.

"Ready to go downstairs?" he asked, and before she could answer, he had swept her up in his arms. "No sudden sneezes now," he cautioned. "If I fall on the stairs this time we'll both be killed."

Caroline started to respond with a joking reply, but her mind went almost blank. All she could think of or feel or know was the reality of the arms that held her. She could feel the draught of air hitting her legs where her skirts had ridden up. There was the sudden dizziness of being raised into the air and carried down the hall. But over and above and most of all and penetrating all her senses, there were Montgomery's arms and the heart she could hear pounding in her ear. She fought an overpowering impulse to press her lips against his neck in which a single throbbing vein was the only contraindication to the impression that he lifted her with as much ease as a feather. She loved the smell of him—leather and horses and soap.

And though the aromas of Mrs. Gregory's supper rose to her, delicious and tantalizing, Caroline was sorely disappointed when Montgomery disengaged her arms from his neck and set her down at the table for the evening meal. She ate in a daze, wanting on one hand to prolong the meal forever so that she could go on seeing him near her, and on the other hand, wanting it to be over so that he would lift her again in his arms and carry her back up the long, curving stairs.

There was something new happening in her heart. Caroline had confessed to herself for some time now that she was in love. But it was only now that she associated loving this man with her wish to have him touching her and holding her and feeling his body close to hers. There was a sudden fascination with the roughness of his cheek and how it would feel rubbing against the softness of her own. And the terrible scar down his face! Once, she recalled, she had given his face a bloody symmetry by tearing her nails down the other cheek. Her scratches had left no trace. The other scar would never heal completely, but maybe she thought, maybe, if she touched it gently enough, running her fingers, white and cool . . .

"Is everything all right?" he broke into her thoughts, only aware of how she sat staring at him, her fork poised in midair, and not understanding why.

"Yes," a soft syllable rising from her throat.

Even matters that had previously repelled her no longer seemed so frightening or ugly. At least not with *him*. She shuddered at the thought of being that way with any other man, of letting anyone else touch her like that.

"You're shivering." He stood and was quickly right behind her chair. His voice was full of question and concern. His hand was on her forehead, then slipped down a moment to her shoulders and lingered there.

When he carried her to her room and placed her gently on the bed, it was only natural for both of them to have sudden disturbing memories of what had passed between them in the inn. To Caroline, the memory came with a rush of revelation. Her new emotions explained and fit into place the aspects of that episode she had never been able to comprehend. For now, although she still had not experienced even the most chaste and timid of lovers' kisses, her heart and her instincts were suddenly mature.

To Montgomery, however, the recollection passed through him bringing shame and unease. He quickly excused himself and hurried from the room.

Lady Annabelle met him in the corridor. She had been following up the stairs, a kindly and discreet distance behind, and had thought to help Caroline prepare for bed.

"Cousin, I must have a few words with you," he told her hoarsely.

In the meantime, Caroline was swaying to the song she played over in her head, and tried to stand unaided. She loved to be carried by Montgomery, but basically, she was an independent girl and chafed under the constant attentions of well-meaning people who would treat her as an invalid.

She would show Lady Annabelle how well she could manage on her own, and edged her way along, holding onto the bed, reaching for the wall, and then along to the wardrobe which held her nightgown.

Quietly, now, she told herself. If she hopped, she would reach her goal more quickly, but would certainly be overheard. She almost laughed aloud to think how everyone would come running to prevent her from doing anything for herself. As she slowly moved along, ignoring the pain in her ankle, she heard her name. Caroline abandoned her original goal, and leaned against the wall, close to the door, listening.

"This Warwick fellow, will she marry him?" asked Montgomery.

She felt her heart stop. So he was concerned that she might actually take such a definitive step! What would Lady Annabelle say in answer?

She didn't answer at all, and this perturbed the Captain.

"Come on, come on! You're a woman, cousin, try

though you do to hide it. You must know the signs, how to tell when a young girl is in love. Will she have him?"

Caroline could imagine Lady Annabelle's confusion, caught between affection for Caroline and Montgomery, between confidences, trust, and truth, between what she thought best and what she knew Caroline wished for.

"He hasn't asked for her hand as far as I know," she answered cautiously.

"But he will," insisted Montgomery. "That seems to be the direction he chooses to follow. He's not a bad fellow, is he?" he asked, almost as an afterthought.

"No," said the old woman at last, "he isn't. And I suppose you are right. He'll ask her."

"Will she have him?"

Caroline strained and heard only silence. Not a sound out in the hall. Surely they would hear her breathing and know she was eavesdropping. Finally Lady Annabelle spoke again.

"No," she said, "she doesn't care for him. There will be no marriage to Robert Warwick."

Caroline held her breath. What was Roderick thinking? Was he relieved to know she was still free? And if he asked why she wouldn't accept Warwick? What would Lady Annabelle tell him?

But Montgomery didn't ask. Instead, Caroline felt the vibration of the wall as his fist slammed against it with a frustrated thud.

"Will she be here forever?" he demanded angrily. "Cousin, I can stand no more of this."

Caroline gripped the wall to keep from falling. Everything was spinning again, sickening and dizzy. Montgomery spoke words better suited to the Lord of Bedlam. Did he really hate her so much? Had she interfered so very badly with his life? The kindness, the comfort

. . . were these gestures really so distasteful for him to make?

She groped her way back to the bed. Lady Annabelle would doubtless open the door in a minute, and Caroline did not want that lady to know the conversation had been overheard.

"You're a fool, a young fool," she heard Lady Annabelle say.

And then Montgomery's voice, crueler than ever before, raised in anger. "I want her out of the house," he said. "If she had no offer, there would be no help for it. But if she has an offer, she will accept it. I will not have her staying under this roof."

CHAPTER SEVENTEEN

I can't be indisposed for the rest of my life, thought Caroline when she woke up in the morning.

Ordinarily, Caroline woke slowly and languorously as the daylight infiltrated her eyelids one sunbeam at a time. She would stretch and yawn luxuriously, and let her dreams recede, drifting back and away until her consciousness was firmly and entirely centered in the real world of day.

But this morning, she was awake instantly, poised and alert as a cat.

Or like a soldier, she thought bitterly. One of Montgomery's soldiers, attuned to any sound or movement that could affect his life.

I have to make some decisions, she thought.

Her life was being twisted in the coils of circumstance, leaving her little room to maneuver. But she recognized that events were rapidly approaching some sort of conclusion, and unless she looked to her own interests, she would have no influence whatsoever on her fate. Of one thing she was certain: She might waver in her resolutions, but her emotions would remain steadfast. She loved Montgomery, deeply and with all her being, and that love was not about to change. The difficulty lay in the way to express what she felt, how to give it life.

Ideally, she would have loved to hold him in her arms as he had held her in his. She wanted to restore his happiness and the enjoyment of life's pleasures she was sure he had once known. But he seemed to protect the scars on his soul the way another person would protect the soft vulnerable parts of his body. It was hard to believe Montgomery could be afraid of anything. It wasn't fear that made him fight back any attempt to heal him, she thought. It was some kind of bitter pride, as though Montgomery believed an honorable man had no choice in this world but to brood and scowl. *He's afraid that without his anger, he will cease to be himself,* she thought. But why is he so angry? And why must he direct it against everyone? Is he afraid love will make him soft and tender and unable to go on fighting whatever it is that he fights?

Oh, I could sit and think about him for days on end, she thought sadly, *but that does nothing to advance my understanding of what I must do.*

The terrible fact remained: The one thing she could do to make Montgomery happy was to marry Robert Warwick and be gone.

Though she recoiled against the very thought, she tried to steel her nerves and calm her heart. Warwick was a gentle and earnest young man. She would never have thought to marry him just for his money and position, both of which were considerable. But Caroline knew that life with Robert—though it would be devoid of great passions and joys—would nevertheless be painless. He was considerate and kind. As for his appearance, he was unassuming rather than unattractive.

Marrying Warwick would not be a tragedy, she reasoned. The only tragedy lay in loving the other.

He hasn't asked me yet, she remembered, grasping at the last hope of safety.

But Caroline was as sure as Lady Annabelle had been. The young man had a *tendre* for her and wanted to make her his wife. His timidity had stood in his way.

I shan't encourage him to speak, Caroline thought. *But if he does, I suppose I shall accept. At least it will be a pretty change to move to a home where I am welcome.*

She wondered if she would have to go on living a lie with Warwick once they were man and wife. Would she ever feel comfortable enough with him to talk about days and experiences that had done much to shape her character? Or would she have to hide those parts of herself, forever, beneath fine clothes and mannered speech?

What a spoiled thing I am! she thought critically. *My life has turned into a fairytale, but I must be the greediest creature on earth. No sooner do I begin to have a few pleasures, than I want the whole world. One year ago, lying in my kitchen, had I imagined that I would be sitting here in a bedchamber fit for a queen, grumbling and feeling sorry for myself . . . what a shocking wretch I am!*

This thought cheered her, leading her to believe that if she was indeed so shocking a wretch, she was probably too scandalous a character to prove acceptable to Warwick's puritanical family.

Then Mary was knocking at the door, offering to

bring hot water to fill the tub. Montgomery had pronounced that a good soaking in hot water was the best remedy for a sprained and swollen ankle.

Caroline lay back in the water, letting it run over her entire body in a soft caress.

Very considerate of Montgomery, she thought. Like brushing the ponies and checking their teeth and hiding the saddle sores before they go to market. Yes, life with Montgomery was odious and intolerable, even if somewhat exciting in its unpredictability. It would be easier to live with Warwick, without a doubt. Yet she couldn't get over the idea that if she linked her life to Robert's, she herself would be somehow diminished.

Mary helped her out of the tub and into a morning dress with long creamy white sleeves and a pale fragile floral pattern on the skirts. No sooner was Caroline dressed, and her hair arranged suitably for daytime, when she was faced with a most surprising visit: Robert Warwick himself entered her bedroom.

The fairness of his youthful face was emphasized by the pink blush that announced his embarrassment. He refused to take a seat, but rather paced nervously as he explained himself.

Caroline felt a sudden envy, that he could pace, while her injured ankle precluded her finding so easy a way to relieve the unbearable tension of her nerves.

"I hope you will forgive me," Warwick was saying, hardly daring to glance in her direction.

All in all, his state of confused shock made her mind hearken back to an image of Montgomery, stammering and abashed in the inn when he'd felt compelled to explain to her about country matters. The memory would have made her burst into affectionate laughter had the present situation not been so devoid of true humor.

"I realize this might seem very forward of me, to enter your room this way."

Make your point, dear sir, thought Caroline impatiently. No, on second thought, it would be immensely preferable were he never to reach the point of his discourse at all.

"Your guardian gave me his permission to approach you this way," he explained. "Rather, it was Captain Montgomery who suggested that a certain dispensation was in order, due to your injury, and as such that it renders you unable to join me more properly in the drawing room, so that he at least felt, under the circumstances, and bearing in mind that I've left the door to the hallway entirely open lest there be any misunderstanding that could give rise to the sort of, well, you know, what we would both wish to avoid . . ."

This ponderous discourse was made yet more lengthy by the long pauses in between phrases, as Warwick groped for words, and added pomposity upon pomposity in order to inject some measure of respectability into what he himself apparently considered a shocking violation of convention.

Caroline scarcely listened to his words. All she had gained from them was the wrenching knowledge that Montgomery had sent the man to her bedchamber. Montgomery was strongly promoting this match, almost forcing Warwick's company upon her.

It is his wish, she thought. *And must I obey*?

She knew well that any obedience on her part in accepting this match would be obedience born not of duty but of love.

She made no move to speak, and poor Warwick was thereby left no choice but to continue.

"I will make the admission that I was not always so convinced of your own attachment to propriety," he said, "but please, do not take offense at what is meant not as gentle criticism, but rather is in the way of a prelude to my explanation and apology."

The part of the speech which followed was delivered with somewhat more assurance and with an obvious improvement in grammar, syntax, and thought structure. It had apparently been rehearsed.

"I found it difficult, Caroline—if I may call you Caroline—I confess, to countenance or understand some of your, shall we say, escapades? Yours was not the behavior I had previously observed in the young ladies with whom I have lived in close contact. By that, of course, I mean my sisters. When I learned of your ride with . . . with that person . . . in Hyde Park, much as I gave thanks that you had escaped unscathed, the incident convinced me that you were not . . . of the sort of sensibility and upbringing as to make for a lasting companionship.

"But when I reflected longer upon your behavior, I suddenly realized the cause of your behavior. And once I understood the sentiments that had inspired your little rebellion, I could no longer hold back in the feeling that had been growing within me day by day."

Caroline looked at him a moment in horror. What could he possibly know about her innermost thoughts? Were her feelings toward Montgomery common knowledge? Even to the Captain himself?

"Forgive me," he continued. "My shyness, in the face of your beauty, made me neglect you. It wasn't neglect, Caroline, but fear. You were right to provoke me, to try and rouse my jealousy and my fear for your honor and your safety. The fault is not yours, but rather mine, that you had to risk dishonor in order to force me to gather my courage. I accept the full blame and responsibility. I trust your gentle instincts and maidenly honesty enough to know that you would never have left here alone in that man's company if only I had declared myself sooner."

This was all beyond belief. She had been ready to hear a proposal. It was going to be unwelcome, but at least predictable. Now she was vexed and amused that her actions could have been so completely misinterpreted. Warwick's character now took on an unpleasant, and hitherto unremarked, dimension. Yes, he was timid and earnest. But if he really believed for a moment what he was saying, the young man was also a terrible egotist.

A real Narcissus, she thought, *to imagine I am motivated solely by regards for him.*

"I have told my intentions to my family, and upon hearing my reasons, my parents have indicated they will look upon what I am about to say with smiling eyes."

She steeled herself for the coming emotional ordeal.

But Warwick was still preparing the way, unable to come right out and say what he had been trying to say for almost an hour.

"Of course, I do not expect any response from you now, in these indelicate surroundings, and following the terrible strain you have been under, and of course, realizing you will require time and quiet in order for your injury to heal, and due to the serious nature of the subject which will require you to give it sober and careful thought and the benefit of reflection over a period of time which I nevertheless hope and pray will not be too long in duration, yet long enough to assure you that your decision has been taken in accordance with a thorough understanding of the obligations to be contracted."

He looked at her hopefully. Then the leather of his new Hessians creaked a little as he awkwardly knelt on one knee, not exactly at her feet, but rather still from a discreet distance.

As she fought tears, Caroline almost broke into nervous laughter as she realized the poor boy was balancing himself awkwardly, his knee a hair's breadth from the floor. He was apparently unwilling to risk soiling his boots or his light-colored breeches.

I'm glad no one else is present to witness this implicit distrust of our housecleaning, thought Caroline tartly. She had not said a word to the young man since he had begun to press his wordy suit.

"I'm asking you to link your destiny to mine," he said at last, "as my wife, in this world and the hereafter. It is my understanding that your guardian will not oppose our match, but I shall not speak to him of it unless I have your clear and unequivocal consent."

At least he does not beseech my joyous consent, she noted.

"And to prove I do not wish to press you or bullock you into giving a premature answer, I'll be gone, but I shall not rest easy," he assured her, rising stiffly to his feet, "until I have your word, your hand, and your . . ." Now the difficulties almost silenced him altogether, but he managed to croak out the final word—"love"—before he turned and fled.

Minutes after his departure, Lady Annabelle knocked tentatively on the door, and Caroline called "Come in" to a very nervous and guilty-looking Dragon.

Lady Annabelle took a seat and waited for Caroline herself to broach the subject. And Caroline, who had maintained absolute silence in front of her verbose suitor, could not bear to give her ally the same treatment. So rather than prolong Lady Annabelle's discomfiture, she volunteered the information.

"Warwick spoke for at least an hour, but if you boil

it down and extract the essence, yes, he has asked me to marry him," she said, trying to make light of the event.

"I'm sorry, dear," said Lady Annabelle, shocking the girl with her honesty. "What have you told him?"

"I never said a word," laughed Caroline, in spite of herself, "but I suppose I shall have to answer him shortly."

"He's not a bad young fellow," commented Lady Annabelle, "a bit of a dandy, but not a real fop."

"Earnest, honest, rich, and true," added Caroline in exasperation.

"And altogether too good-natured for a hornet like you," grumbled the old woman.

"No, I'm not too much of a hornet," reflected Caroline sadly. "I should think my behavior would have driven him away, but he reads meanings where none exist, and has pardoned my trespasses against common decency in devious ways that do us both credit. . . . Well, have you been sent up here to convince me to accept?" she asked pointblank.

Lady Annabelle colored. "I haven't spoken to young Warwick."

"No, he's a sight too straightforward to press his suit through you, I think. I mean, you are here at my guardian's expressed wish, are you not?"

"Yes," said Lady Annabelle, unwilling to expand on the unfortunate answer.

"Well then, you shall tell Montgomery that I have resolved," she paused, and caught her breath with dramatic effect, "that Warwick shall be," another hesitation, "the first to know my decision. I should hate to repay his delicacy by communicating my thoughts on this matter to anyone other than the man most directly concerned."

The Dragon lowered her eyes. Both women knew that the man most directly concerned was in fact Montgomery.

"Caroline," said the old lady at last, "I think Robert Warwick would make a good husband and provide well for you. But I should not be one to force you to marry a man . . ." The word 'love' was unthinkable. ". . . with whom you would not wish to share your life. I am not used to spending long periods of time in London. I'm much more at home and at ease on my estate in the Lake Country. I live a quiet, retired life there, and shall probably soon die there, and I meet with few people. Certainly, there are very few young men in the area and of those, few come to call. I know if you were in residence, there would be somewhat more flurry and activity. What I'm trying to say, dear," and she took Caroline's hand in her own, "is that I'm fond of you. I don't want to see you bullocked into a distasteful alliance. I cannot promise you gaiety at my home, or give you much hope for a future, but if it becomes intolerable here, if you cannot remain here and have no other place to go, you are welcome to take shelter with me for as long as you want or need."

Caroline embraced her aged friend and kissed her cheek. She had known the Dragon was her ally, but this display of affection and offer of assistance was more than she could have expected. Although she was quite sure that she would not accept the offered sanctuary, her heart swelled at such thoughtfulness and concern for her well-being.

"By your leave, I have matters to discuss with Mrs. Gregory," said the Dragon, making an excuse so that she could escape before the girl could see her dragon-sized tears.

* * *

Caroline chatted pleasantly at dinner, inquiring after the naked lady of Carlton House, and comparing the newspaper account of the tragic happenings with her own personal experience. She made no reference to her visit of the morning, knowing full well that Montgomery had joined the ladies only because he hoped to obtain some clue as to her inclinations.

Let him hope in vain, she thought. *His doubts will be resolved soon enough.*

All day and throughout the evening she played her carefree role. A casual observer would never have guessed that any matter of import lay heavy on her mind. In fact, it would seem that this young lady had been born and bred to leisure, that she was used to having her every whim catered to, and that she had never experienced the sensation of thinking, let alone making a painful and difficult decision.

She maintained her pose even when shocked by a surprise even greater than the one provoked by Warwick's unexpected morning appearance. For Caroline was sitting alone on her bed, brushing her hair, when Montgomery strode into the chamber.

"One would think I'd taken lodgings at an inn," she commented dryly, "and that the keeper, forgetful that this room is already occupied, persists in sending visitors upstairs."

But as she turned to look into his eyes, she realized the humor was misplaced. She recognized desperation in his face, a tension so terrible it seemed he would be defeated by it. She almost expected to see him begin to tremble and shake.

"You are not usually so merry, Miss Bramwell." He forced out the words in an ordinary voice, but she was quick to note the "Miss Bramwell." She had been "Caroline" to him for months. Once more, apparently, she had incurred his displeasure.

But it's no fault of my own, she thought, *if he took on unwelcome responsibilities. He could have left me in Wales if this ridiculous guardianship was really so poisonous to his spirits.* It was his choice she argued, while thinking that, as in her own case, people are sometimes compelled to make choices which they expect will bring them unhappiness.

"You are hiding your true feelings, I'll wager," he said.

She didn't doubt that her face reflected the accuracy of his guess.

"In fact, you are terrified. I know what has happened," he said. "Warwick asks for your hand, but there is an obstacle that makes it impossible for you to accept."

She looked at him closely now, and saw that Montgomery, himself, was so frightened and agitated he could hardly go on.

"And it's not only Warwick who is repugnant to you . . ." he added.

The space between them seemed to be charged with magnetism, with warring forces that tended to throw them together, or tear them apart, in either case violently and in either case against their wills. Time seemed to stand still, and in this total suspension, Caroline suddenly knew what he was going to say. Was it possible? Had all her tears and worries been unnecessary after all? Could it really be true? She looked at him beseechingly. What if he didn't speak?

"It's because of me, isn't it?" he asked. "That's why you can't tell him yes."

Caroline was speechless. She felt weightless as well, as though she were flying into space, floating above the earth, released from the tired body of a frightened young girl in a London room.

She returned to reality to find Montgomery beside her, holding her gently against his chest. An excess of emotion made her sob.

"Shhh. I know how you feel," he whispered hoarsely. "This is wrong, Caroline, very wrong. It's irregular and wrong, but the problem began with improprieties, and that is the only way, I fear, for it to be resolved."

Suddenly, his lips were on hers, soft at first, slightly open, pressing against her skin with warm, moist, and gentle pressure. He ran his fingers through her loosened hair, and she was dazzled by the splendor of his kiss, by the radiance that seemed to glow around them as they sat clasped together. He loved her! Everything was right. He said it was irregular and wrong, but it was perfect and right. She found her mouth taking on a life of its own, opening without the operation of her conscious mind, aching to drink from him all the love he could give.

At last, when he realized she was responding with pleasure to his tender ministrations, Montgomery moaned and pulled his lips away. He held her against him one brief and fleeting moment more.

"I should hate to remind you of what happened back in that inn," he said quietly, "except that it is only too clear to me that you have not been able to forget. You remember I told you then that what passes between a man and a woman is not always so ugly . . ."

He loves me, she thought, her heart beating and singing and flying. Could such incredible beauty be real?

"Many people would think it wrong for a maiden's lips to have been kissed by any lips other than those of her bridegroom."

Now he disengaged himself gently and stood above

her, his hands resting lightly on her trembling shoulders. Though her head was upturned toward him, now he didn't look directly into her luminous eyes.

"But you wouldn't accept my word," he said. "I had to show you myself, so that you would believe the truth. You don't have to be afraid, Caroline. It will not be frightening or brutal or bad when Warwick takes you to his bed."

Caroline was so stunned, she sat frozen, as if icy water had been poured into her veins, or as though she had been turned to stone.

Such disappointment, such treachery! Her senses had been reeling with joy. Now she was flung into a dark, spinning, and bottomless pit. How could this nightmare be real?

CHAPTER EIGHTEEN

Caroline had hidden and lied and played a part for months. But it was only when she began preparing for her wedding that she truly felt like a fraud.

She would be married as soon as the banns were posted and her ankle had healed. She considered forcing herself to walk, hoping to aggravate the injury, but there was nothing to be gained that way. After all, she had accepted the man of her own free will, and sooner or later, the wedding would have to be.

Dressmakers, milliners, glovemakers, and jewelers visited the Green Room of Chelton House and worked feverishly to have the trousseau ready in time.

And everyone, friends, tradespeople, members of his family—everyone, in short, who saw her during those days—thought Caroline the very image of a maiden deeply in love. She regarded everything through a daze. Nothing was solid or real. Nothing really mattered. And only too often her errant thoughts returned to the night that Montgomery had entered her chamber. The eyes that seemed unaware of what was happening around her were occupied, looking inward, and looking back into the past, and seeing again and again Montgomery's face and form so very close.

His touch, his lips . . . yes, he had taught her desire, and left her yearning feverishly for a more total union, but how little he really understood. How like a man he was! Couldn't he have foreseen what would have befallen? He hadn't succeeded at all in allaying her fears about the marriage bed. The proceedings remained as distasteful as ever as long as she contemplated them in that strictly objective way. She didn't want "proceedings." She wanted Montgomery. And in wanting him totally, with all the depth of her soul and with every inch of her skin and with every drop of her blood, the "proceedings" were no longer a strange detached ritual. She would happily submit to him, to lie locked together, to let him slake his thirst and her own. She would sit and imagine it, until some word, reaching her from the outside real world would bring her to her senses and she would turn scarlet, hoping no one could guess what had been on her mind.

And everyone—friends, tradespeople, members of the groom's family—all realized exactly what was on her mind, why she seemed so distant, and why she blushed so ardently and violently when called to her senses. Their only mistake was in assuming, as was only natural, that young Warwick was the object of her passion.

Only Lady Annabelle was at all aware of the true state of affairs. "You could have come with me to the Lake Country," she said one day. "You still can come. It's not too late."

But Caroline didn't even seem to hear the words, and turning, made some vague reply that had nothing to do with the offer.

The more she tried to suppress her wanton thoughts, the greater the part they came to play in her reveries.

Montgomery opened his coffers and spent lavishly. Her trousseau would have no equal, he vowed.

Yes, he's happy, she thought while she let still another dressmaker take her measure.

"What have you done now?" demanded Montgomery in a rage at supper.

Caroline looked at him in shock. He had been so happy and good-natured ever since she had accepted Warwick's offer. What had gone wrong now? What had she done to anger him this time?

"I don't know," she answered in a timid voice.

"You're in the Betting Book again," he accused.

"Believe me, sir, I haven't any notion how or why . . ."

"An anonymous wager. Placed there more to spread gossip than to gain a few guineas—that much is clear."

"But what does it say?" asked Lady Annabelle.

"One hundred to one that the wedding will not take place."

Even Montgomery's obvious anger and disappointment could not stop Caroline from thrilling to these words. Was she to be saved after all? Her feeling of relief was so intense that Caroline realized for the first time just how terrible a disaster it would be if she did indeed have to go through with the marriage. Montgomery could rave and scream. He could storm around like the Lord of Bedlam, but in that moment, Caroline knew that the wedding had to be stopped.

All the same, Caroline hadn't the foggiest notion what to do next. As it turned out, she didn't have to do anything, for two days later, a letter came on paper bearing Warwick's monogram.

She opened it with the feverish excitement appropriate to an eighteen-year-old beauty receiving word from her lover. It was the first time she had been so eager to hear from her intended, and her flushed haste did not pass unremarked.

"Miss Bramwell," she read, "I do not hold you accountable for your conduct. It is clear that you have but been used as a pawn in a game plotted by your betters. Their motives I fail to understand. But you will surely understand why our union will not, and cannot ever, be sanctified. I shall try to forgive you your deception practiced against me, and shall pray that Divine Guidance lead you into a path of repentance and regeneration."

It's wonderful! she thought gratefully. But what does it mean? Apparently the conspiracy had been revealed. But how? By whom?

Montgomery returned scowling from the streets. He had fared unsuccessfully in discovering the cause of the broken engagement. Everywhere, his friends and acquaintances turned from him and refused even to acknowledge him, let alone enlighten him.

It was finally Mary who brought home the story, besieged as she had been by other London servants who were eager for a first-hand account of what it was to serve *The Miners' Nightingale*, for this was the name the *ton* had now assigned Caroline in her disgrace.

"I've told them as talk to me who you be, Miss," said the girl, tears streaming freely down her red face. "But none as wants to believe it. 'Tis said all over town that you were a lightskirt wot found 'er employment sellin' 'er charms to the miners of Glamorgan when you chanced ter meet the Cap'n. They say there's a innkeeper will swear you and the Cap'n was locked together in a room for days, Miss, not even leavin' the bed to take your meals."

Glad though she was to be freed of Warwick, Caroline's heart railed against the injustice that was done her. Yes, she was caught in the toils of the deception she herself had perpetrated, and Caroline had grown up knowing it was wrong to lie, but she felt the *ton* had forced her to be less than truthful. The rules of society had forced an honest girl to live a lie, and now that lie had overtaken her. The result was ruin. And worst of all, it seemed Montgomery was ruined, too.

"They say 'e dangled you in front of yer young man," continued Mary, "when I knows you didn't even care a feather fer that boy."

"And you told them that?" asked Caroline.

"Yes, Miss, I certainly did."

Caroline sighed. "I know you meant well. But if it wasn't to be a love-match, what other cause had I to marry him?"

Mary's hand flew to her mouth.

"Whether they think it was to steal the Warwick family fortune or to blacken their good name, or simply to play a nasty joke . . . the gossips will have to figure that one out for themselves . . . But did you tell them who I really am? And about my uncle?"

"Yes, Miss, I did. And it seems yer uncle be the one wot tells about you and the miners, Miss. I did tell them 'e is, beggin' yer pardon, crazy from his mind half-time and crazy from the jug t'other half. But they won't mind wot I say, Miss, since it be only nat'ral they say fer me to take yer part."

"But Montgomery? What do they say about his part in this affair?"

Mary now gave up all attempts at delicacy. She realized she had already done much harm, and now might as well simply tell the story as she had heard it.

"They say there be nothin' wrong with a gentleman

seekin' 'is pleasure with a doxy, even one that's knowed the embrace of common workin' folk as we be back 'ome, provided she be beautiful, of course, as 'is excuse. But to present you as 'is ward, they say, was a insult t'all the decent people in the Kingdom. They say 'is influence with the Prince and the Prime Minister be lost fer good now."

Caroline considered this in silence. Montgomery hadn't loved her, and yet he had sacrificed everything on her behalf. Montgomery had lost the gamble in which he had stood to gain nothing. That she should be the cause of his ruin cast Caroline into a despair deeper than she had ever known.

Only a single ray of light broke into the gloom that had suddenly transformed Chelton House into as forbidding and loveless an edifice as Pemberton Hall. A young couple, dressed smartly but not richly, entered the entranceway in a state of subdued and tentative spirits and nervous anticipation.

"Do you really think she will see us?" asked the young man.

Before his companion could answer, Caroline herself appeared, running down the stairs in reckless disregard of her barely healed ankle, and flung herself, laughing and crying, into Emma's arms.

The two women exchanged kisses, words of sympathy, grief, and delight.

"No one else has come near me," confessed Caroline. "I'm surprised you dared. But I think I could bear disgrace many times over if it would remove the barriers between myself and my friends. And if only Montgomery could have been spared implication . . . Oh, Emma, what am I to do?" she cried. "Will you let me run off and be an actress with you now after all?"

Once they were seated, and Mary had come in to

join the tender reunion, Caroline first took note of the young man. He was extraordinarily attractive, and his brown eyes had an expressive range of emotion. At times they were liquid and tender, the eyes of an actor. But at times she could see a keen and thoughtful intelligence in their depths.

"Forgive me," she said, "we have not been introduced . . ."

"But you know about him," Emma said softly. "This is Edward."

Caroline smiled and her eyes lit up for the first time in ever so long to realize that this was the young man on whom Emma had set her heart.

"Caroline, dear," Emma began slowly, "I didn't come to flaunt my own happiness in the midst of your suffering. But I hoped my story might bring you some cheer."

Edward took up the thread. "Until this terrible thing happened, Emma preserved your secret as carefully as another woman would preserve her own life. I had admired her from a distance for years, but felt I dared not approach her while all I could offer were the insecurities of an actor's life. By the time my own position began to improve—I have written and sold three plays now, and have a part-ownership in a Manchester theater—Emma had accepted—at least, so I thought—a position which made me lose my respect for her. Until yesterday, I believed she was Montgomery's paid mistress. It was only yesterday that she revealed the part she had played in this drama, and I have asked her to be my wife."

Caroline was sincerely delighted and embraced the loving couple with joy.

"And remember," added Emma, "not long ago, I

told you such an outcome was quite impossible. So please don't despair. Things may still take a turn for the better."

"I don't see how," she sighed. "Both Montgomery and I are utterly ruined."

"Montgomery!" exclaimed Edward, and he and Emma exchanged a quick look. "Caroline," he said, "a great deal of time and money and effort went into this affair."

"I know. Montgomery has spent a fortune on me. And look how he has been repaid," Caroline replied brokenly.

"No, no, no," insisted Edward. "I mean the affair of exposing you. Neither Emma nor I could imagine how you could have given rise to such terrible enmity . . ."

"There are many families, I'm sure, that hoped to marry a daughter off to Warwick," said Caroline. "There must be many people who would have wanted to prevent this alliance from taking place."

Emma took her hand. "No, Caroline, it seems to be more complicated than that. It hadn't even occurred to us until you spoke. But this was done—this had to have been done—for the sole purpose of discrediting Montgomery."

"If that's true," said Caroline, "his enemies have certainly succeeded. But how can you be sure?"

"From what I hear in town," replied Emma slowly and carefully, "a very exalted personage whom no one will name concerned himself most actively in bringing this information to light."

Caroline's heart skipped a beat, but then the moment of optimism passed. "What difference does it make?" Her voice admitted total defeat. "So we know a clandestine effort was made to find something to use to discredit my guardian. Unfortunately, that does nothing to change the facts—that Montgomery and I were indeed compelled by circumstances to share a room in the lowest sort of inn, and that I entered society and made my debut in a tangle of lies and deception . . . No, the worst of what they say is false and odious. But no one will believe us now, and I don't blame people. I doubt I should accept the word of one such as I."

Then Caroline, the guests, and Mary, froze in their seats as they heard a commotion at the front door, Montgomery hollering, the clatter of his boots. Minutes passed, and then he entered the drawing room.

"What are you doing here?" he demanded of Emma. "I was told we had visitors and scarcely credited my ears."

He's drunk, Caroline realized. She wanted to tell Emma, in order to excuse Montgomery's rude behavior, but the man's intoxication was apparent and required no explanation.

"They've come to tell us," said Caroline, controlling her voice, trying to impart the news in the light social voice of any proper lady in a proper drawing room, "that they are to be married."

Montgomery showed no surprise nor even much interest. "And so are we," he replied.

The tears that stung Caroline's eyes were angry tears now. It was one thing that he didn't love her. That couldn't be helped. She couldn't force him to care for her any more than she could have been forced to love Warwick. But how could he make a joke of marriage? Yes, he was ruined, but so was she. With the whole world against them, by all rights they should have turned to one another as friends. But instead, Montgomery had to be cold and insulting, making a mockery of her ruined life.

"And we're to be married directly," he added.

It was Emma who had the nerve to demand an explanation for his words.

"There are grave doings afoot," he replied, "and it's no time for me to lose the trust of my friends in the government. They must be convinced that these vicious rumors are lies. The story must be scotched."

When the party remained silent and uncomprehending, he lost his temper and cried, "Well, I wouldn't marry a miner's doxy myself, would I now? If I marry the girl, it's because she is what I say she is. They'll have to believe me then."

"No," murmured Caroline. She would have given anything to become his wife, but not like this.

"What about you two?" he demanded, ignoring Caroline entirely.

"What about us?" asked Edward, almost belligerently.

"Are you ready to be married, too? We can have the vicar kill two birds with a single stone."

"We have not posted the banns," said Emma quietly. "And neither have you."

"This is an emergency, my dear," said Montgomery with a sneer. "The license is there for the asking when the vicar is both underpaid and understanding."

"No," repeated Caroline, a little louder.

Montgomery turned upon her in a rage. "There is too much at stake," he cried, "to worry about your maidenly feelings. I shan't bother you, girl. This is a marriage for the eyes of the world outside these doors. That is all it is."

She had been willing to marry Warwick to please this strange and violent man. Now, like a wish granted in reverse so that nothing could ever come out right, she would have to make him happy by becoming his own bride—but only in name.

"Now, go wash your face," he told her, as though he were giving an order to a recalcitrant child. "The carriage is waiting and the vicar expects us directly."

CHAPTER NINETEEN

"I forbid you to go through with this," shrieked the Dragon, looking away from the pale and trembling girl and turning infuriated upon her cousin.

"Hold your tongue and prepare for a ride," replied Montgomery coldly. "Your dignity will add countenance to the proceedings."

He did not notice Caroline's blush at the word "proceedings" which had a most definite meaning for her, although she realized she might now never know the experience the word was intended to convey.

Emma and Edward ceased their protesting and consented to accompany the unhappy couple. Montgomery adamantly insisted that they be wed, too; Emma, after all, could bear witness to Caroline's good character and so she should play a role in the farce. Emma, for her part, agreed to cooperate not for Montgomery's sake, but so that Caroline should not have to face so unfortunate a situation alone. Emma was also well aware that Caroline had had a *tendre* for Montgomery for some time. She fervently hoped that this rough and brutal shove into matrimony would not fully poison what might, under better circumstances, have been a fairly happy match. And shocked as she was at Montgomery's inexcusable behavior, Emma still entertained a great fondness and respect for him as well as for Caroline. Perhaps this lunatic union would end by growing into love, she tried to convince herself. Perhaps by making it a double wedding, some of what she and Edward felt for one another would infect Caroline and her surly bridegroom.

This hope seemed misplaced, however, as they stood in the private chapel and went through the ceremony most unceremoniously. Montgomery's mind was elsewhere, and Caroline, too, seemed to be in another world.

"Wed but not wanted, joined without joy." These words ran through Caroline's head like a childish rhyme, muting the cleric's voice and adding to the unreal atmosphere around her. She did have enough sense of place, however, to sorrow that Emma's wedding should have been tainted by the unspeakable horror of her own.

"This was a very somber wedding," Caroline ventured to say afterward, "for one brought about by an exalted personage."

"What are you talking about?" asked Montgomery irritably.

"Why, our downfall, of course. It was engineered by someone so august, Emma could not even determine his name."

The sun was setting as they left the chapel, and Caroline could see its warm rays reflected equally in the eyes of Emma and Edward. Montgomery's eyes, however, were glinting and cold.

The return trip to Chelton House passed in silence,

but Caroline was not quite as dazed as she seemed. At the door, they found a messenger waiting, and as Montgomery took the cream-colored note from the boy, she was aware enough to realize she had seen that style of paper before, and alert enough to remember when and where: it had been her first night at Almack's, and it had been the Countess de Lescaux who had pressed the note into Montgomery's hand.

"I shall not be able to sup with you," he said, calling to the groom to saddle Jupiter.

He could at least have tried to sound apologetic, thought Caroline, fuming with rage but containing her feelings, unwilling for her anger to show on her face.

"But perhaps the happy couple will stay and share the wedding feast."

The happy couple, thought Caroline. *He says it as if to point out the contrast. They are the happy couple in opposition to us. We are the unhappy one.*

"I shall speak with you later," he concluded, "as we have much to discuss as far as making our accommodation, one with the other."

When Montgomery was gone, Caroline tried to dismiss her friends as well. Emma was reluctant to leave her at such a trying time, but at last bowed to Caroline's desire to be left quite alone. Even the Dragon, whose eyes flashed with the rage that Caroline dared not express, had to agree at last that the bride's nerves were not being steadied by company, no matter how well-intentioned.

Caroline's ankle was swollen and aching again as she hobbled awkwardly up the stairs to the familiar room where she would spend her wedding night. Mary, who was aware of the reason for the marriage, but uncertain as to all the arrangements, did not know whether Caroline's mood was one of joy, fear, or resignation, and so she dared not say a word as she helped prepare her mistress for bed.

Alone at last, and overcome with the strain of the long and wearing day, Caroline prepared her emotions for the promised encounter with Montgomery. And so, hour after hour, she waited for him to return from his visit to the Countess. Her ears strained for the sounds of his approach. He wouldn't be coming as a husband or a lover. He was coming to discuss their "accommodation" for the future.

"Wed but not wanted," the childish chant continued in her head. "Married but not marred, tied but not taken." He couldn't stay with that woman much longer. Any moment she would hear his footsteps and he would be pushing open the door. "Joined without joy, hitched but not had, espoused but not despoiled," the words came unbidden to her mind. Bid Montgomery though she might, she could not make him appear so easily. Hypnotic, rhythmic, the chant continued, "married but not marred, wed not wanted." Her head ached from unshed tears. "Tied but not taken, hitched but not had," and the long night passed and no one came to Caroline's door, "married but not marred, wed but not wanted," and at last she fell into a restless sleep.

She was awake again before dawn, thoroughly alert and her mind racing in spite of her strain and lack of sleep. Caroline's eyes glowed with fever and her mind was made up. She had seized upon a desperate plan. But nothing could be worse, she thought, than to go on living with Montgomery under the circumstances. She would do anything to extricate herself from the nightmare she found herself living. She had told Emma many times she would be happy to seek her own way in the world. Well, the time had come. She would be a burden to Montgomery no longer. Why, he despised her so, he would not even spend the night under his own roof!

As for his reputation and standing in London, she had no illusion that their marriage, in unseemly haste, would have improved matters. Only if she disappeared altogether might he begin to regain what he had lost. And, the marriage being unconsummated, he should have no trouble gaining an annulment and being freed of any and all responsibility toward her.

Her resolution taken, Caroline could wait no longer, but hurried from her room in a state of great excitement. Carrying her oil lamp, she set out quietly in the sleeping house as she had done once before. This time, would she pass Montgomery again on the stairs? She hoped not. She had waited for him all night long, but she didn't wish to meet with him now. She moved cautiously down the stairs, gripping the handrail and favoring the bad foot. At last she had gained the servants' hall. If only she remembered correctly which room was Mary's.

She gave thanks for Montgomery's cynical gesture of the evening before. He had given the servants the morning off, "because we shan't be needing you early," he'd said. The man was hateful, but at least it meant even Mrs. Gregory would sleep late and give her the freedom she needed to further her attempt.

She opened the door and gave thanks again when it gave way silently. She started back a moment, but then realized she was in the wrong room. The girl in the bed before her was Lily, and Lily was not alone. The lovers held each other, even in sleep. For a few seconds, Caroline's eyes were riveted in shock, curiosity, and then even envy. Their sleep was so deep and untroubled, she thought. And, she concluded, it was really not her business to supervise the morality of servants. She was in the wrong by opening strange doors.

Caroline hesitated outside the next door. What if she was wrong again? What if she were to find Mrs. Gregory in bed with Jenkins? Did everyone in the world sleep coupled except for herself? What if even Mary had a man? At last, she found the courage to turn the handle. She peered inside and sighed with relief to see Mary's form, in bed alone.

Mary almost screamed, so frightened was she to be awakened by someone standing by her bed and shaking her gently. The sight of Caroline with her hair swinging loose and her eyes alight with a strange fire did nothing to allay her fears

"Your brother's letter," whispered Caroline. "You still have got it, haven't you?"

"Yes, Miss." Mary jumped from the bed and, turning frequently to look at Caroline as though she expected her eyes had deceived her, she went through her effects and delivered the letter into Caroline's hands.

"What is it, Miss?" asked Mary, now on the verge of tears.

"Ah, here it is," murmured Caroline, "a one-legged Captain named John Cox. Mary, I'm off to America," she whispered, not with real delight.

"Miss, you are not feeling ill, are you? Let me 'elp you upstairs." Caroline's words had thrown the abigail into a real panic. " 'Ave you the fever . . . ?" She paused. " 'E didn't frighten you last night, did 'e?" she asked.

"Frighten me! I didn't even see him." Then, not failing to note the very real concern with which Mary heard her words, Caroline calmed herself and explained her thinking to the girl.

Mary listened carefully. "Well, Miss, if that's as it's

to be, I'm comin' with you." As Caroline started to protest, she continued with her own line of reasoning. "I've a brother there, and won't mind the journey. And you are not fer goin' off alone. It's no trip fer a lady. Besides, 'ow can I keep stayin' on 'ere with Cap'n Montgomery after 'elpin' you to run away?"

"He'll thank you for it, Mary. I'm just a burden to him," insisted Caroline.

"Well, if *you* be a burden, wot use 'as 'e fer me? No, if you be goin', then me along with you, Miss."

Caroline was surprised, but not unpleasantly, by Mary's decision. In truth, she had faced the prospect of taking such a step entirely alone with a great deal of fear.

"But, Miss, I 'ear as there be not so much use for labor now as there was. We can go to me brother, but I don't know that there's bonds to be 'ad fer work . . ."

"We shall pay the way with my jewels," Caroline answered, "Not all of them. I should feel a thief to take everything Montgomery has given me. But I shall not hesitate to take what we need for the journey. Montgomery would surely agree his money couldn't be better spent. And we shall travel as sisters. You must lend me clothes, Mary."

"But, Miss, anyone can see that you be a lady!" objected Mary.

Caroline shook her head, torn between irritation and amusement. "So I've learned my lessons well. I spent four months learning to appear a lady of quality, and now I must in one morning undo all that and become what I was before."

"You was always a lady to me," sobbed Mary.

"Hush now, I shall await you upstairs. Dress quickly and pack up what things you wish to take. Now give me my attire." Caroline went hastily through Mary's wardrobe. "May I have these?" and receiving the girl's assent, she added, "and do make haste. We must be gone before the house wakes to the day."

"Mr. Cap'n Cox sure took you fer a lady," commented Mary as she and Caroline were given inside seats in the Bristol mail coach. "We could be aridin' on the outside 'angin' on by our toes with the rest."

Caroline hushed the girl. She didn't wish their fellow travelers or the mail guards, ostlers, or coachmen to know anything of their provenance. Silently, she doubted whether the one-legged seaman knew that such a thing as a lady existed. She hadn't liked the appraising looks he'd given her or Mary, and had been almost relieved when Mary took upon herself the task of discussing business with the immensely fat and grizzled cripple whose own pungent smell could be unmistakably remarked over the competing scents of the murky water and tar.

It had been a horrid journey through early morning London! They'd found two chairs to carry them to the wharves where in spite of the hour they saw men drinking and fighting, and where Caroline had to close her eyes in pity at the sight of ragged mothers and their dirty squalling babies, and the urchins who poked about in reeking piles of refuse and fought each other over the prizes they found within.

So unsavory did the waterfront appear that Caroline could not for the life of her imagine that great men of history had embarked from the Thames in their glorious vessels. There was not a single ship in the estuary that did not present an evil, brooding aspect to her impressionable eyes. And so she was pleased when Cox told them they must go to Bristol for the voyage they had in mind.

Spitting with considerably greater volume, force, and pleasure than St. Clair had been able to achieve even following his lessons, Cox had directed the runaways to a "fellow wot knows wot's wot in all relatin' to ridin' the water to America."

That businessman looked no less unsavory, but he assured the young ladies that he would receive his commission from Mr. Cruikshank "at the other end" and would not accept any payment. "The fare is paid for a willing worker," he explained, "and you've both got the look of them that's willing to do a fine job . . . You're not really sisters now . . . ?" he asked, a glint in his eyes.

For all that the two girls were dressed in almost identical clothes, their features and build were of such distinct natures that it stretched credibility to ask observers to think them sprung of common stock.

Nevertheless, Caroline had answered firmly, "Warn't our mother's way to tell a lie," and the man pursued the point no further.

"When you get to Bristol, you just say you be from Cruikshank," he told them, "and someone will be waiting to take you to the ship."

It was almost too easy to be real. Caroline was left wondering why more girls didn't simply run from home and seek their fortunes. *I could have left my uncle and done this years ago*, she thought.

In spite of such easy progress, panic assailed both Caroline and Mary briefly but intensely as two more people climbed into the confined space of the coach.

"We are all to ride together?" asked Mary in alarm. Her journey to London had been effected on the outside of a stagecoach, and though she had been rudely exposed to cold and the elements, at least she had felt free beneath the open skies. She had expected riding inside, in the vastly more expensive mail coach the way fine people did, would be a much more luxurious experience.

But now the passengers were crushed so tightly together, arms and legs were locked in place and could barely be moved.

"Hold your breath, girl," commented the tradesman who had taken the seat opposite Mary. "You'll take less space."

" 'Tis like Carlton House again," murmured the abigail, and began to tremble. Caroline would have tried to comfort her, but didn't wish to speak before strangers, and when she tried to put her arm around Mary's quaking shoulders, she found her limbs were pinned close to her sides.

"It's not the crowding will kill you," continued their fellow traveler cheerfully. "It's the breakdowns, the overturns, and the drunken coachmen who will race each other on a wager. You ladies traveling for pleasure?" he asked.

"We aren't the sort wot discuss our matters," replied Mary in a firm but polite setdown. The threat to her virtue and propriety had been enough to restore her to her wits and drive away fears of suffocation.

Caroline, meanwhile, was thinking back contentedly on the events of her life. She felt comfortable to be wearing lowly clothing again, as though she had slipped back into her own skin after a strange absence. Now that they were past, her painful trials seemed like so many fascinating episodes from a book.

She could imagine herself growing old, years hence, in America, telling stories of where she had been and what she had done. Image after image crowded her mind—of an idyllic childhood, she and Percy gazing out at the yews by moonlight or racing their horses over the meadows. The way the sun flashed on her father's buttons as he rode away for the last time. She had danced with titled nobility. She had been whipped with a riding crop. A handsome hero had rescued her, and together they had ridden through a forest and been attacked by robbers and had escaped. She knew the secret passageways of the home of the Prince Regent, and she had wandered the evil wharves in the hours around dawn. She had almost been killed in a scandalous escapade in Hyde Park.

I've never seen France, she thought. *But I shall see America. And perhaps even meet an Indian. Then, surely, my life will be complete.*

But the word "complete" disturbed her revery, for it reminded her too roughly that, in truth, she would always remain empty. She could run away from the lies that others told about her. But there was no escape from the truth she told herself. Deep inside she was hollow. Because she knew for all her adventures, for all the tales she could weave to hang like ornaments over her emptiness, she would go on wanting Montgomery. Deep inside, she needed him to make her complete.

CHAPTER TWENTY

The *Atalanta* lay at anchor in Bristol harbor, bobbing gently, her sails down, and her decks unmarked by activity associated with the sea. For rather than seamen swabbing the decks and pulling tarred rope, rather than the laying in of barrels and provisions through hoists and sweat labor, as Caroline and Mary approached the ship in a small boat, accompanied by Cruikshank's associate and two oarsmen, all they could see aboard were clusters of young women, their hair blowing free in the breeze.

"It looks like a schoolroom outing," laughed Caroline. "I am set at ease in my mind to know we shall travel among congenial companions."

"More than congenial," their guide assured the girls. "Twixt one of you and t'other, there's scant difference to be found."

Caroline regarded the man curiously. His words were spoken in good humor, but seemed to lack in courtesy in a way she could not quite determine.

A sailor let down the gangway and as they crossed to

the deckboards their guide bade them farewell. "You two make it full load," he said good-naturedly. "You'll be sailing, I reckon with the tide."

"And are there no other sailors, kind sir," inquired Caroline, still perplexed to see only young ladies aboard the vessel.

"Only the most trusted men be aboard her now," he replied. "The others will be let on her when it's time to sail. The cap'n don't like his men to mingle overmuch at the start with this type of cargo. But it's a long voyage to America, and you'll be making the acquaintance of them all before long."

The swaying of the ship on the water sent funny sensations through Caroline's stomach. It seemed much harder to adjust oneself to the motion of the sea than to the rhythm of a good horse, she thought. But she plumed herself on her adaptability and her freedom from missish disabilities.

"She's a fine ship and it's a glorious day," she remarked to show her ease, and she thanked the man for his assistance in furthering the journey.

He smiled in return, showing his broken yellow teeth. "Enjoy your voyage," he wished her, "and never fear but soon you'll be singing to the men of the western frontier."

"Miss? What think you 'e meant by that singing?" asked Mary, echoing Caroline's own silent question.

Caroline's horrid suspicion was confirmed almost immediately when two of the young women aboard rushed to greet them, wide-eyed and laughing. Close up, Caroline could see the schoolgirls were not young after all, and were not ladies either.

"An' you be the Miners' Nightingale, be ye not?" cried one painted creature. "I seen yer picture in the shops, I did, an' recognized ye even from afar. Ask

Meggie here—dinna I say that one be like the picture I seen of the one wot's been causin' all the fuss among the fine folk of London?"

"A good job you did of it, gel," said the one named Meggie. "We all had a bit of a laugh at it, you know. No harm intended to yerself, you know, but you see wot comes of liftin' yer skirts to the fine dandies. Oh, they think them so fine, but the miners, now dinna they give you a thank you along with a shilling? Unlike these fine gents wot takes their pleasure and then turns you out in the street. That's wot I said, I did. No, I wouldna be goin' but I've had a touch of the pox meself, and they say in America the market on the frontier be so open, none is like to worry over a little thing like that."

An excited crowd had gathered, but as Caroline stood motionless and horror-stricken, and as Mary burst into tears and wails, the mood of the traveling women turned from curiosity to anger.

"I sees they ain't takin' so kindly like to bein' wi' us," came a voice from the crowd. "A doxy be a doxy, but there be some as thinks they be good as ladies."

"This yer best gown?" asked a cruel voice, and a hand reached out and tore at Caroline's humble dress.

"An' wot that one be cryin' 'bout?"

"She needs air," Caroline gasped at last. "It's the crowd. She worked in the mines herself, you see, before she secured . . . better employment. It's the crush, the crowd. It brings it all back to her."

"You talk a pretty voice, you do," said another hostile woman, but Caroline's account of Mary's tears won much sympathy, and the crowd slowly dispersed, leaving the two runaways alone on deck. They were both shocked and frightened, and Caroline refused an offer to be shown to her cabin. Somehow she felt safer out in the open.

"Can you swim?" she asked Mary urgently. There was no time to waste in bewailing their situation. The only thing to do was to plan a way to escape.

"No," cried Mary.

It had been a foolish question, for Caroline had never tried to swim either.

"I still have the jewels," she whispered. "Perhaps we can buy our way back to shore."

"But if they know ye've got the jewels, they'll just take them," answered Mary. " 'Tis plain to see we're among folk with no honor. They'll take the jewels, but we'll not get back to the land. Oh, 'ow could me brother 'ave truck with such as these?"

That was the least of their worries, Caroline reasoned, but she still took time to reassure the girl that her brother had probably no idea that Captain Cox and his friends dealt also with such enterprises as the one in which they found themselves hopelessly enmeshed.

"But it's not 'opeless, Miss," insisted Mary suddenly. "For, please don't be angry with me, but I left word fer the Cap'n."

"For Captain Cox?" asked Caroline, puzzled.

"No, not fer 'e. For the Cap'n, for Cap'n Montgomery."

"You did what?"

"Miss, I know it were a secret, but I was afeared, and I left a note to tell the Cap'n where we'd gone," Mary confessed.

"But Mary, how could you?"

"I was afeared."

"No, I don't mean how you could have disobeyed. I mean how could you leave a note. You don't know how to write." Caroline was now totally confused.

"I don't write much, 'tis true," admitted Mary, "but after me brother's letter come, I 'ad Jenkins start to teach me. You bade me 'urry, Miss, so it warn't a good note, but I left it just the same, that fer bein' a burden you fled to America and went to John Cox with one leg. The Cap'n will be lookin' fer us, Miss."

"No," said Caroline bitterly. "If you'd left the note for Emma, or Lady Annabelle, perhaps we'd still be saved. But Captain Montgomery is well rid of us. He'll never chase us to Bristol. Once the tide is in, we're lost."

Mary began her sobbing again. "Miss, I said I wouldna leave you. But once we sail, if the Cap'n be not 'ere, I will throw meself to the sea, Miss. That's wot I'll do."

Strange how everything happened, thought Caroline. The escape had seemed so easy, but as always, the easy escape was followed by disaster. Once, she remembered, I told myself that at all the worst times, a guardian angel appeared . . .

She thought of how she had pictured herself growing old in quiet peace and dignity in America, telling stories to people gathered around her. Her arms drew around Mary's heaving shoulders.

Sailors had appeared on deck at last and were hoisting canvas. She tried to block out the creaking of ropes and sails and the seamen's shouts. Was there one among them, by chance, who might take pity at such distress?

"Can you see?" asked Caroline, telling a tale. "Somewhere in the distance, there's a horse and rider. He's a gallant Captain astride a brave black stallion. Jupiter's nostrils flare and he shoots sparks with his hooves."

Mary lifted her head and gazed at the shoreline as if the horse and rider were actually about to appear.

"There 'e be!" she shrieked, as a man and beast came into view. " 'Tis the Cap'n, sure as I be alive!"

"No," said Caroline sadly, for the horse was a bay. Even as they watched, they saw the beast collapse and fall, while the man sprang off, barely escaping injury.

"The horse be dead!" cried Mary, " 'E rode it to death!"

"It's a bay," said Caroline quietly.

"Jupiter couldn't go this far away so fast by 'isself," insisted Mary. "The Cap'n been changin' 'orses at each postinghouse, Miss."

"Gracious heavens," murmured Caroline, her voice trembling with emotion. "I think you are right."

For it was Montgomery, it had to be Captain Roderick Montgomery. No one else stood so tall and strode with that graceful yet manly gait. No other figure would have towered so against the shoreline, his face to the wind.

"Just the way I imagined him," she whispered, thinking of the man she had dreamed of through the long years at Pemberton Hall. "I'm not imagining things, am I, Mary?" she asked.

They both sat transfixed, too filled with astounded hope to wave or call to the man on the shore. They saw him pull a pouch from under his cloak and then two small men hastened toward him. They watched as the Captain climbed aboard a dinghy, and dissatisfied with the boat's progress, soon took the oars himself.

The dinghy pulled up alongside the *Atalanta*.

"Where's the captain of this ship?" cried that dear, familiar voice.

Caroline didn't dare move to the rail to see him. She was almost afraid to be seen by him. But other members of the cargo were swarming all over the deck, screaming with delight at the sight of the handsome man who demanded to be admitted aboard.

A threatening sailor warned him to stay back, but

Meggie threw down a rope, and Montgomery climbed his way to the deck.

Yes, it was he. Montgomery had come to save them, but Montgomery was the same man as ever. He regarded Caroline with a cold eye, and addressed not a word to her.

"Take me to the captain," he ordered Meggie, and was soon lost to view.

When he returned, he was accompanied by a burly ginger-whiskered man of about forty years.

"There they are," said Montgomery, gesturing toward Mary and Caroline. "Name your price for them, Captain, and I'll pay. But as I explained, I will not tolerate runaway servants from my home. It puts ideas into the heads of the others."

"I'll be honest with ye, Guv'nor," said the ship's captain. "I get two hundred fifty guineas for each one delivered, but only a portion of that be my share. There are associates to consider, and expenses . . ."

Montgomery's offer of one thousand guineas for the two young women was quickly accepted. The pouch changed hands, and soon Caroline and Mary were lowered to the dinghy where Montgomery joined them.

It was Mary who first broke the silence with effusive words of thanks.

Montgomery didn't respond, simply went on staring at the shore.

"You struck a fine bargain this time," said Caroline. "Two for the price of one." But he did not rise to her words with either anger or laughter.

How could he be so good and yet so cold? How could it be that he had appeared once again, just in time to save her, when he didn't really seem to care a feather for her? She almost wondered if her nerves were better equipped to face real dangers than they were to face Montgomery's moods.

He had a private coach hired and waiting. After assisting Caroline to the seat, Montgomery asked Mary if she would mind riding outside with the coachman, and the abigail was only too happy to comply with the request.

Ah, thought Caroline, *he's saved his angry words for me alone. How discreet of him to spare poor Mary the vision of his wrath.*

"Caroline," he began when they were alone, "when I first found you were gone, my first impulse was not to follow."

She had known him well enough to guess that. "I am grateful, sir, for what you've done," she said timidly, ashamed of the caustic words she had previously uttered. "You had no obligation to protect me as you have done. Or to incur such expenses on my behalf."

"I would pay the thousand guineas ten times over . . ." he began violently, but then caught himself, "and probably would have been required to part with that amount," he added lightly, "if the scoundrel had known I was ransoming back not my servingmaid but my wife . . ." Then, with a deep breath that seemed to struggle in his chest and compete with a mounting sigh, he asked, "but I need to know why you ran."

"Surely you know that, sir," she said.

"I'm not 'sir,' " he corrected. "I am your husband. And I *don't* know. I thought at first you fled in horror of me, because you could not bear to live as wife to a monster like myself, unfit for the company of human beings."

"How can you say such things of yourself?" she demanded, suddenly springing to his defense as though the critical words were being spoken by an enemy. Her hand flew up in exasperation, and he caught it and held it.

"Mary's scrawl led me to think perhaps I was wrong. That you fled out of consideration for me."

"Yes," she confessed. "I saw no way for you to regain your position while I remained in London."

His fingers were now lightly brushing the back of the hand he still kept prisoner within his own. "My position, Caroline, has been vastly improved due to what you once referred to as our downfall . . . I'll explain in a moment, but I bring good tidings for you, too. Your uncle is dead."

She gasped. "There was no love between us, but pray, do not call good tidings those that speak of death."

"Very well," he agreed, solemn for a moment until his gray eyes seemed to light with laughter. "I bring you the very bad news that you are his sole heir and now in possession of Pemberton, the mines, the rolling mills, the forges . . . You can make the miners happy now in ways the gossips never dreamed of . . ."

"Decent wages," she said at once, caught up in the sudden excitement of being in control. "And no more children in the tunnels. No more Marys with their nightmares of no air left to breathe. . . . Oh, Montgomery, it *is* good news!" And she spoke now with her natural cheer, forgetful of all the barriers that still stood between them. Her joy was followed swiftly by a sobering thought: Montgomery had followed her to prevent her flight because he knew she now had the means to live independently and would need him no longer. Otherwise, surely he would have merely let her go. Well, she concluded, if that's how it is, so be it. Independent she would be!

"But your situation?" she recalled.

"That's a longer story, but we have a long ride . . . It begins, actually, with Percy's death. You know, you never did ask me the details, and I never told you."

"I don't think I could bear to hear it," she said quickly. "I'm sure he died a hero, and that's all I need know . . ."

"Very well," he agreed, "I won't give you the details. But one thing you must know. Your brother was in command of a small detachment that had gone to fortify a village. Their position was totally secret. And they were massacred. Someone among us had sent word to the enemy. . . . Caroline, I don't know what happened to me after that. I could trust no one. And was ashamed to wear my uniform because there were traitors among us who wore one like it. When I returned to London as military advisor, I soon learned the problem was greater than anyone had realized. Loyalty began to seem like the exception rather than the rule.

"I saw the worst in everyone. You remember how I treated you, then. Sometimes I thought I wasn't fit to live, but other times I knew I had to go on until I'd found the source of corruption. Because it had become apparent that very secret and confidential information, prepared on the highest levels of His Majesty's Government, was finding its way to Napoleon's camp."

"Emma would have called this talk a lot of flummery," commented Caroline, not certain whether she could believe in so much intrigue.

"Emma, you, and I agree on many matters," Montgomery conceded, "although I have chosen not to make such remarks publicly. I, too, believe in reform, and know that treachery within the government is the main obstacle to reform. When all are under suspicion, none dare criticize or ask for changes. . . . Early on, we found the French in possession of certain names that could only have come from your friend St. Clair."

"St. Clair a spy?" exclaimed Caroline. "I don't believe it for a moment!"

"I didn't at first either," he said. "But St. Clair was gradually eased from his responsibilities. And because of him, less information was shared with the Lords, and those who suspected why let him bear the brunt of their anger. I hated him then. But when we brought you back from Hyde Park that day, we had a talk and something he said made me think. It turned out that St. Clair thought I was out of sorts with him because he'd taken up with Hélène. He said he'd betrayed me unawares—insisting that he hadn't known me to be involved with the lady.

" 'Unawares.' That's the word that I caught on, Caroline. Because, you see, I was never involved in any liaison with Hélène. I suspected her of being a French agent. There she was, admitted to the highest circles, talking about how she'd barely escaped France with her life and taking a most avid interest in all of our military planning. I became convinced she was in league with our enemies, and St. Clair's frequent attendance upon her made me believe he might be one of her sources.

"I am quite certain now that he was. But as he said, unawares. I am convinced that in moments of intimacy, when people share thoughts and secrets, she persuaded him to tell her things of which he should not have spoken. I can believe him a fool, then, but not a traitor."

Caroline could not help but smile. She was fond of St. Clair, but did consider him a weak and silly man. It was not hard to imagine him being led into error.

"I had suspected from the start," Montgomery explained, "that the reason she tried again and again to tempt me into amorous adventures was so that she might try to gain information from me. But the problem still remained," he went on, "how did Hélène pass her information to the French? And you, my dear, gave me that answer yourself."

"I did?" But her tone of surprise sprang less from the credit and more from the fact that he had called her "my dear." *It's simply a form of speech*, she told herself, but felt the pulse begin to throb in her fingers which were entwined with his.

"I was on their trail," he said, his eyes glowing still more with excitement. "I was so close, they tried to ruin me. You were the one who said we had been undone by a personage too august to mention. Then we returned from the chapel and there was an urgent summons from Hélène, asking me to meet her at an address in Kensington. I suspected immediately she was trying to lure me out of town. I spent so much time at her house, observing all those who called, it was clear that her most secret rendezvous had to be held at a time when I would be conveniently out of the way. The summons I received on our wedding day wasn't the first time she had urged my presence at a location where I would wait and wait and find no one there. So as soon as I received her message, I was certain she was expecting the traitor at her house. That's why I dashed off without a word. And I was right.

"It all fit together. With her, I found the exalted personage who I later confirmed was the very one who disclosed our past."

"But who was it?" cried Caroline.

He smiled and shook his head. "I handled this matter privately with the Prince Regent, and he asked that, at least for now, I make the person's name known to no one. Confidence in the government and in the throne could be shaken too badly. You know, our Prince is not popular among the people, and word of a traitor who enjoyed so high a level of trust and esteem could only make matters desperate."

"But now it seems you're a hero again," she said proudly.

"Both of us, it seems," he said. "The Prince has asked us to dinner, Caroline. He very much wants to meet you. And Emma and Edward for that matter. The *ton* will not dare to snub you when you meet with the Prince's approval."

"My life certainly doesn't take an even course," she laughed. "I misjudged you many times," she added on a more sober note. "Those times you went running off without an explanation. And I never knew why you were so moody and angry all the time. I think I'm beginning to understand."

"I am beginning to understand, too," said Montgomery, bringing her hand to his fervent lips. "I stormed into Lady Annabelle's room, you know, to see if she knew anything of your whereabouts when I found you gone. She didn't, but she told me something I didn't know. Caroline, I loved you from the time you sat beneath the blankets and talked to me like a comrade. I loved your courage, your spirit, and wit. I loved your beauty and your straightforward nature. But after my behavior, and considering the sorry sort of man I thought I'd become, I never thought for a moment that you could feel anything good toward me. I thought you deserved much better a companion than I could ever be."

Her throat was so dry she had to struggle to speak. "All the time, I thought you wanted me gone."

"I did want you gone. Do you know what torture it was to be living with you beneath the same roof? I feared I would not be able to control myself any longer.

But I loved you so much, I put your happiness first. I desperately wanted you to marry Warwick as quickly as possible. You see, I thought that would be best for you. I valued your happiness so highly, I almost threw happiness for both of us away forever."

"Roderick," she began shyly, but then her voice grew vibrant and strong with her own rising passion. "I have loved you since the day you first rode up to Pemberton, appearing like a miracle in the snow. Even when I didn't understand you, even when I hated you, I loved you."

She would have said more, but their mouths met, and she found her tongue could express her feelings more eloquently without words. His hands ran over her body which thrilled to his touch as though it were new, just created, only coming into being with his awakening touch.

"London is so far away," whispered Caroline, her lips lightly touching his ear. "How I wish we were home!"

"I have a summer house in Bath," he said smiling. "We shall be there directly. Do you think we can control ourselves one hour more?"

"Roderick?" she asked. "Is it wrong for a wife to want her husband as much as I want you?"

"Wrong? I thought you had all your lessons from me," he replied, in mock indignation, "and I never told you anything like that. Caroline, we've made enough mistakes about each other to last a lifetime. From this moment forth, everything between us is going to be absolutely right. Do you believe me?"

"Yes," she breathed, while the coach continued on its way and Roderick clasped her in his loving arms.